A Season for Killing Blondes

by

Joanne Guidoccio

A Season for Killing Blondes

Cover Art by *Kim Mendoza*

The Wild Rose Press, Inc.
PO Box 708
Adams Basin, NY 14410-0708
Visit us at www.thewildrosepress.com

Publishing History
First Mainstream Mystery Edition, 2015
Print ISBN 978-1-5092-0173-0
Digital ISBN 978-1-5092-0174-7

Published in the United States of America

I noticed a man making his way through the crowd that had gathered outside the front window. Tall and lean with salt-and-pepper hair, the man sported a black leather coat and a light gray suit. When he stopped to talk with Uncle Paolo, he flashed a badge. As I approached the two men, my heart started beating faster. Carlo Fantin. How could I have forgotten my old high school crush? If anything, he looked even better now than he did back then. He hadn't bulked up or lost his hair. He was still hunk material.

He stared, his blue eyes widening in surprise and something else I couldn't quite define. Amusement. Anticipation. Maybe even lust. He stopped talking to Uncle Paolo and gave me his full attention.

He flashed the beautiful smile that had once captivated me and every other female student at Sudbury Secondary. "Hello, Gilda. It's good to see you again. Uh, in spite of these circumstances."

"Hi, Carlo, I'm—"

"Detective Fantin," my uncle shouted in my ear.

Before I could say anything, Aunt Amelia piped up. "We're so glad you came, Detective. We'll sleep better tonight knowing that you're in charge."

My mother and Sofia appeared at my side. All those years ago when I had fantasized about connecting with Carlo, I had envisioned many wonderful scenarios where we would bump into each other and fall in love—on the beach, dance floor, even at a bar. Never in a million years, did I think we would reconnect in these circumstances with my family in tow.

Dedication

To the five angels
(Carla Barnes, Karen Beasley, Fil Derewianko,
Judy Guidoccio, Magda Viehover)
who helped me survive and thrive
during the most challenging season of my life.

~*~

A portion of proceeds will be donated
to the Canadian Cancer Society.

Acknowledgements

To my family—Tony, Augy, Ernie, Judy, Lilly, Joan, Christina, Deanna, Olivia, and Ava. I appreciate your ongoing support.

~*~

To my wonderful teachers and mentors—Karen Cafarella, Susan Fish, Brian Henry, Jen McBride, and Deb Quaile.

~*~

To the members of Guelph Write Now and Guelph Writers Ink, especially Patricia Anderson, Cindy Carroll, Judy Emery, Mike Fisher, Dennis Fitter, Linda Johnston, Bonnie Marshall, Sue Ricketts, and Monika Wright.

~*~

To my fellow toastmasters in Guelph. Thank you for inspiring and motivating me to continue with my creative endeavors.

~*~

To Johanna Melaragno, Rhonda Penders, Kim Mendoza, and the dedicated staff at The Wild Rose Press, Inc. Thank you for making this book possible.

Chapter 1

Thursday, October 20, 2011

Three thousand euros worth of pastries. *Can you believe it?*

When I agreed to import the pastries, I had no idea I would be subsidizing the failing Italian economy and helping Silvio Berlusconi stay in power for a few weeks longer. Left to my own devices, I would have gone down the street to Regency Bakery, picked up some pastries and just walked them over. But my mother and Aunt Amelia were adamant. The open house for my new career counseling office needed a proper launch, one that could only be achieved with pastries from a Sicilian bakery.

To be fair, both of them were horrified when they saw that final four-figure amount on the invoice and swore me to secrecy. While conspicuous consumption is valued in the Italian community, being taken for a ride is not, and we would never hear the end of it from Uncle Paolo who is still complaining about the ten cents he has to pay for a shopping bag at No Frills.

I watched my mother rearrange the amaretto cookies, stuffed figs, biscotti, and other delicacies that had arrived yesterday. She and Aunt Amelia had brought in their best silver trays and carts and spent hours—according to Uncle Paolo—creating a colorful

Italian corner.

"Everything is perfect. Maybe too perfect." My mother made the sign of the cross and mumbled a Hail Mary.

"Relax, Ma. I've got everything under control. Nothing bad will happen."

"Things have been going too well, Gilda. The lottery win. Your new career. This beautiful office. I've had one of my dreams, and you know what that means."

Not today. Please not today. For once, I wanted to get through an event without my mother's doom and gloom predictions. Was that even possible? I wondered. Any other day, I might have made more of an effort, but I couldn't risk any energy drains today. I plastered a smile on my face and hugged her. "Maybe we're in for a lucky streak. Don't you think we deserve it?"

"What's up?" Cousin Sofia caught the tail end of the conversation as she entered the room. "What's all this talk about lucky streaks?"

"Ma had one of her dreams," I explained.

Sofia glanced at her watch. "It's eleven thirty, and we're ready, way ahead of schedule. We could have an early lunch." She winked at me.

My mother's face brightened, and she licked her lips in anticipation of the luncheon feast that awaited her. Capicola, mortadella, prosciutto, and provolone from Giacomo's. Fresh buns from Regency. And, of course, the pastries. I saluted Sofia who smiled and shook her head.

As we headed toward the small kitchen in the back area, we heard a familiar scream coming from outside. My mother shook her head. Sofia rolled her eyes. Aunt Amelia again. A hypochondriac well known for exaggerating, over-reacting and fainting whenever she was on the sidelines of an event.

I shivered as we approached the back door, propped open with boxes and small garbage bags.

Sofia muttered, "Why the hell couldn't they have waited? I would have taken care of it."

Uncle Paolo appeared at the back entrance. His eyes were unfocused, and his lips trembled as he ran his fingers through a thick crop of white hair. "Come. Come quickly. There's a dead woman in one of the Dumpsters. And…and Amelia fainted."

We followed Uncle Paolo outside to the Dumpster. Halfway there, my mother stopped to help Aunt Amelia who struggled to get up. When I reached the Dumpster, I took several deep breaths and gripped the edges with my trembling hands. I stood on tippy toes and gasped with disbelief at the beautiful blonde draped over the refuse. I tried to swallow with a mouth that had suddenly gone dry. Blood roared in my ears as I took in the horrifying scene before me. I had expected to see a stranger, a homeless woman, not Carrie Ann Godfrey.

Wet tears streamed down my cheeks as I remembered the young woman who had been crowned Prom Queen and won local pageants. In high school, we had sat side by side in those classes where teachers insisted on seating everyone alphabetically. While I hadn't been part of her circle, I had enjoyed an easy camaraderie with her. I had just seen her yesterday when she dropped by and chatted about switching careers.

"She's looking good," Sofia muttered. "Once a golden girl, always a golden girl."

I turned away from Carrie Ann's body and focused

on Sofia. We were first cousins, daughters of two sisters who had married two brothers. With such tight, interwoven bloodlines, you would think I could predict Sofia's actions and reactions. But there were moments—like this one—when I didn't really know or want to know my cousin.

"The woman is dead. Show some respect." My eyes traveled back to Carrie Ann.

Her marble white skin and blue lips were framed by a sleek blonde pageboy. A printed scarf draped over a cream sweater and her right forearm hooked through the straps of a bronze tote. Her watch and jewelry were intact, and I had a sneaking suspicion that nothing had been removed from her bag. Picture perfect, even in death.

"Who could do…?" I stopped speaking when I heard the familiar moaning.

My mother and Uncle Paolo had revived Aunt Amelia. The two sisters hugged and comforted each other. Thankfully, neither one had seen Carrie Ann's body, up close.

"Do you want me to call nine-one-one?" Sofia asked.

My mother gasped, and her hand flew to her mouth as she trembled from head to foot. As her tear-filled eyes met mine, I caught glimpses of an old, but not forgotten, fear. She had traveled back in time to war-torn southern Italy and memories of German soldiers who had marched through her small town. To this day, she feared any man in uniform.

"What's your hurry?" Aunt Amelia asked. "The woman is dead. We can cover her up with some bags and call the police later. That way, we can still have the open house." Her voice rose. "I'm thinking about the stuffed figs. They're so moist today. Who knows how long they'll last."

Was Aunt Amelia trying to cover up her own fears, or was she thinking about the money that had been spent? You could never tell with her. Her reactions were always off; she never rejoiced during the good times and couldn't comfort anyone during the sad times.

Uncle Paolo sputtered, "I…I can't…a woman is dead and you're worried about figs…I don't know…I just don't know." He took several deep breaths and deliberately moved away from his wife. "I'll call nine-one-one." He headed inside.

Aunt Amelia grabbed my arm. "Gilda, stop him! He doesn't understand about the figs. They won't be the same tomorrow."

I swallowed hard as my pulse raced faster. I couldn't break down and cry in front of my mother and aunt. It would add to the drama and accomplish nothing. I managed a tight smile. "There won't be any open house. Not today. Not tomorrow. Not for a while."

Aunt Amelia started crying, and my mother joined in. Sofia and I watched as they headed inside toward the kitchen.

"They'll feel better after they've had their espressos and lunch," Sofia whispered. "You better call the radio and television stations and let them know the open house has been canceled. I'll call the Italian bakeries and meat markets."

Sofia headed toward the main reception area. I decided to make the calls from my office. I knew that Uncle Paolo would take charge and deal with the police when they came. After the last call, my eyes traveled around the room.

When I had found this large space, I couldn't believe my good fortune. The previous tenants had been three accountants, each with their own private offices. The space also included a large reception area with partitioned sections, a fully-equipped kitchen, two bathrooms and a utility closet. It had remained vacant for over a year after the accountants retired their practices. No one wanted to pay the exorbitant rent that such a space demanded. That is, no one until I came along with my nineteen-million-dollar lottery win and the dream of a career counseling practice that catered to boomers.

I got up and headed toward the reception area. I noticed a man making his way through the crowd that had gathered outside the front window. Tall and lean with salt-and-pepper hair, the man sported a black leather coat and a light gray suit. When he stopped to talk with Uncle Paolo, he flashed a badge. As I approached the two men, my heart started beating faster. Carlo Fantin. How could I have forgotten my old high school crush? If anything, he looked even better now than he did back then. He hadn't bulked up or lost his hair. He was still hunk material.

He stared, his blue eyes widening in surprise and something else I couldn't quite define. Amusement. Anticipation. Maybe even lust. He stopped talking to Uncle Paolo and gave me his full attention.

He flashed the beautiful smile that had once captivated me and every other female student at Sudbury Secondary. "Hello, Gilda. It's good to see you again. Uh, in spite of these circumstances."

"Hi, Carlo, I'm—"

"Detective Fantin," my uncle shouted in my ear.

Before I could say anything, Aunt Amelia piped up. "We're so glad you came, Detective. We'll sleep better tonight knowing that you're in charge."

My mother and Sofia appeared at my side. All those years ago when I had fantasized about connecting with Carlo, I had envisioned many wonderful scenarios where we would bump into each other and fall in love—on the beach, dance floor, even at a bar. Never in a million years did I think we would reconnect in these circumstances with my family in tow.

"I will need to talk with each of you," Carlo said. "I would like to do it now rather than have all of you report downtown. My officers are already in the back alley. They've set up a perimeter around the Dumpster, and they'd like to use a room in your office as a command post. I've also stationed an officer outside the front door. He'll stop any clients you have from entering."

I couldn't believe all of that had happened while I was cocooned in my office. I smiled at Uncle Paolo. Thank goodness he had taken charge.

Carlo spoke directly to me. "Paolo tells me there are three offices. I'd like to use one of them for the interviews."

"Of course," I replied. "Use the middle office."

Carlo nodded to Uncle Paolo. "We'll start with you first, Paolo." Both men headed toward the back area.

My mother clapped her hands. "He couldn't take his eyes off you."

Aunt Amelia winked. "And he's such a catch."

Sofia shook her finger. "You don't know anything

about him."

"Oh yes I do!" Aunt Amelia said. "His wife died of cancer two years ago, and he has been alone ever since. His children are married and living out west somewhere. Vancouver, Alberta, one of those places. I heard it all at Maria's Beauty Salon. I could give her a call—"

"There's no need. I know the rest." My mother's eyes sparkled as she spoke. "His parents are both dead, and he still lives in that big beautiful house in Moonglo, mortgage free." She raised her voice. "This could be your last chance."

Even with a dead body in a Dumpster, thousands of euros of pastries wasting away, and policemen swarming about, my mother and aunt could still indulge in their favorite hobby—trying to find me another husband.

Chapter 2

My mother and Aunt Amelia pulled up chairs and huddled around the Italian corner. Sofia had almost lost it this morning when she saw that colorful corner of red, white and green. The two-for-one Wal-Mart plastic centerpieces with fake flowers and strategically-placed Italian flags clashed with Sofia's upscale shabby chic decor. I couldn't bring myself to disappoint my mother and my aunt, and I had also persuaded Sofia to let it go. I didn't want any drama, and now I had a different kind of drama.

Uncle Paolo was still in the middle office with Carlo. Sofia fussed with the vertical blinds, and I sat at the reception desk taking incoming calls and watching as the plaza filled with spectators.

I had selected this south end location, minutes away from the Four Corners, because of its high customer traffic and proximity to the university, downtown Sudbury and the highway. The storefront was ideal with its large picture window and its location next door to a bank. I had just experienced the downside—probably the only downside—of making such a practical business decision.

The banging on the front window startled me. Sofia nearly fell off the step ladder, and my mother and aunt rushed over. We could hear the policeman shouting, "You can't go in. Ladies! Ladies! Get away from that window."

Rosa Geraldi and Maria Rossi ignored the officer and continued to bang on the window. Rosa yelled, "We've known Gilda all her life. We're practically family. We need to be here." I opened the door and spoke to the officer trying to restrain the two women who appeared to have the advantage with a combined weight of over four hundred pounds. "It's all right, officer. Maria is my godmother, and Rosa is her sister. They won't stay long."

The officer reluctantly let the two women pass. They hugged me close.

Maria shook her head. "What a disaster! We were driving by and saw all the commotion." She frowned. "Where's the dead woman? Have they taken her already? Where's Paolo?"

Maria and Rosa didn't waste any time on pleasantries.

"The police roped off the area, and a few officers are in the back alley attending to the body," I explained. "Carlo is taking Uncle Paolo's statement. He plans to talk with all of us."

Rosa's eyes widened. "Carlo Fantin? Is he handling all of this?" I nodded, and she continued. "I hear he's one of the best in that department. And he's available." She winked at me.

"It's too bad you had to meet him like this, but you look beautiful," Maria said. She waved her hand toward my mother, aunt, and Sofia. "All of you look beautiful today."

"Gilda insisted on suits," Sofia said.

I had only made the suggestion, but after a few initial protests they had relented. Sofia wore a pink tweed suit and dusty rose blouse that complimented her dark hair and light olive skin. My mother and Aunt Amelia had selected shifts in navy blue and purple with matching three-quarter length jackets. I had stuck to my zebra colors and topped my light wool black suit with a cream blouse.

"You look like Ginas," Maria said.

It was one of Maria's best compliments, and she did not give it too freely. Gina Lollobrigida was her favourite Italian actress, and Maria believed very few women could compete with the raven-haired, voluptuous beauty. We all laughed and felt the tension breaking.

"I wonder why Carlo is taking so long with Paolo?" Aunt Amelia asked.

"He's a good man, and he'll get to the bottom of this." Uncle Paolo walked toward us. He nodded to Aunt Amelia. "Detective Fantin wants to see you next. Keep it short and don't go on and on about the figs."

Aunt Amelia lowered her gaze and walked quickly toward the middle office.

"What's this about the figs? I thought they had arrived yesterday?" Rosa asked.

Maria jumped in. "Did someone take the figs?"

Both sisters shared the gossip gene and delighted in being the first to share news—good and bad—with the rest of the Italian community. And they didn't hesitate to add their own spin on the situation. While I didn't approve of Aunt Amelia's comments, I didn't want everyone in Sudbury knowing that her primary concern was the stuffed figs.

I walked over to the Italian corner, uncovered the first cart and wheeled it over. I motioned to Maria and

Rosa. "Please, help yourselves."

My mother flashed me a grateful smile and relaxed her tensed up shoulders. Sofia joined me, and we watched as Uncle Paolo and the women started eating the stuffed figs and pastries. The telephone continued to ring, but I let all the messages go to voicemail. No point repeating the same message over and over again. My open house was canceled, and I had no idea when I would be ready to take clients. I sighed. "I wonder how much longer this will take."

"I can't see Carlo spending too much time with any of us," Sofia said. "Except you, of course."

"Why would you think that?"

"You're the last person who saw Carrie Ann before—"

"You think she was actually killed here?" I struggled with the thought of Carrie Ann dying right after leaving my office. So many negative scenarios whirled through my mind. Was someone lurking in that back alley? Would I have to make sure my clients used only the front entrance? What about the evening workshops I hoped to facilitate?

Sofia shook her head. "Why would someone go to all the trouble of killing her someplace else and then depositing her in one of your Dumpsters? The murderer would have to drag her into a car, pull her out again, and then throw her into the Dumpster. I don't think he would have gone to all that trouble."

"You're so certain it was a man?"

Sophia narrowed her eyes in doubt. "You think a woman could have lifted Carrie Ann into the Dumpster? She's thin, but I'm sure she weighs at least one hundred pounds."

"You have a point, but I can't imagine any man killing Carrie Ann." I had a flash. "Wait a minute. A woman had to be involved. No man would have fussed with her hair and scarf."

Sofia lowered her voice. "I wouldn't be too keen about sharing that particular insight with anyone else, especially Carlo."

Did she think that I could be implicated?

Sofia started to speak, but stopped when Aunt Amelia emerged from the middle office. Sofia immediately went to her side. "Ma, are you okay? What happened in there?"

"Carlo was so nice, but I…I was so nervous. I hope I answered everything okay. I don't want to get into any trouble." Aunt Amelia closed her eyes and rubbed her temples.

"Don't worry. You're not a suspect in this case. What did Carlo say?"

"He wanted to know what Paolo did this morning…what I did…I don't know…" She moaned, "No more questions. My head hurts too much. Oh…and he wants to see you or Assunta next."

"I'll go." Sofia headed toward the office.

Maria and Rosa came to Aunt Amelia's side and persuaded her to sample the pastries. I smiled as she bit into a stuffed fig and exclaimed about it.

My mother left the group and joined me. "You're starting to fade away. You didn't have any lunch, and you're thinking too much again."

Bone tired and hungry, I considered helping myself to a pastry, but I didn't want any sugar in my system. I nodded toward Aunt Amelia. "Someone made a quick recovery."

Her lips tightened. "She's fine as long as she's the center of attention and doesn't have to deal with any unpleasant situations. It would be another story if this were Sofia's office."

"Is she sharing Aunt Matilda's secret recipe for amaretto cookies? I thought you had all been sworn to secrecy."

"She's like a runaway train when she gets started. What that woman will do for attention is beyond belief. Especially on a day like—" Her eyes filled with tears, and her right hand shook as she reached for a tissue.

I needed a distraction. Anything at all to take my mother's mind off the dead body. "I don't know what I'm going to do with all those pastries. I guess I'll have to freeze them tonight."

My mother perked up. "Don't worry about the pastries. Amelia and I have already discussed it. We'll put aside three platters for Paolo's birthday on Saturday and freeze the rest." She lowered her voice. "I'm so sorry we talked you into spending all that money. I had no idea it would cost so much."

"It's all right, Ma." The money had been spent, and while the pastries wouldn't be eaten today, I knew that my mother and aunt would make sure that they didn't go to waste.

Sofia appeared at my side. "Aunt Assunta, Carlo's ready for you now."

I waited until my mother had disappeared from sight before speaking with Sofia. "How did it go?"

Sofia shrugged. "Pretty tame. I gave him a quick rundown of what happened this morning. Oh, and Carlo wanted to know about my last encounter with Carrie Ann."

"When did you last see her?"

"Oh, I see…saw her all the time. I ran into her at the grocery store, the malls, Curves." Sofia tugged at her waistband. "I've been going for over a year, and I've barely lost an inch off my waist. Last week, Carrie Ann bragged about losing three inches off her waist."

"You've never mentioned any of this before." I wondered when Sofia found time for Curves. Her days were booked solid with decorating, planning church fundraisers, and at least one dinner party a week.

"It's been kind of hard to talk about normal, everyday stuff since you won the lottery."

I sensed an edge to her voice and decided not to say anything.

Sofia gestured toward her mother. "She's having the time of her life. No moaning or complaining about aches and pains or even dead bodies." She checked her watch. "I think my parents are about ready to go home. Rosa and Maria can take your mother home." Sofia moved toward the group. "It's time to go."

Uncle Paolo frowned. "Did Carlo say we could go? Who is he talking with now?"

Sofia pointed toward the side office. "He's talking with Aunt Assunta. He said everyone can leave except Gilda."

Maria gasped and pressed her hand against her chest. "Maybe you should have a lawyer with you."

Sofia snorted. "Gilda has nothing to worry about. This is her office. Carlo wants to ask her a few more questions, that's all." She nodded toward Rosa. "Could you and Maria take Aunt Assunta home?"

"Of course," Rosa said. "Ah, there she is now. Assunta, we'll take you home."

My mother turned toward me. I nodded and waved her away. “Don’t worry about me, Ma. Go ahead with Rosa and Maria. I won’t be long.”

Chapter 3

Carlo had removed his suit jacket and rolled up the sleeves of his light blue dress shirt. His tie lay on the desk. The rumpled look suited him to a tee. And his large black-rimmed glasses accentuated those unforgettable blue eyes. Bluer than blue. Sky blue. Cornflower blue. Robin's egg blue. Years ago, Adele Martino and I had come up with thirty-seven descriptions of Carlo Fantin's eyes when Mrs. Gillespie assigned one of her Monday morning English composition exercises. As I tried to recall the other thirty-three, I realized that Carlo was speaking to me.

"…he'll be taking notes as well."

Darn! Another officer in the room, and I had missed his name and more importantly, his title. Was he a detective or a constable? I'm sure Sofia would know. In the meantime, I better stop daydreaming and start listening. I nodded in the direction of the beefy officer. Dark hair. Dark eyes. Expertly trimmed moustache. A big bear of a man who reminded me of Magnum P.I.

Carlo cleared his throat. He was ready to get down to business. Police business. "It appears that Carrie Ann was your first client. You haven't opened this office for business yet. How did that happen?"

My heart raced as I spoke. "After Sofia and my mother left…I'm not certain about the time…um…I…I heard a knock at the front window. I looked up and saw

Carrie Ann. Hadn't seen her in ages." I paused and then added, "Still wearing the same pageboy hair style and that blonde color—"

Carlo waved his hand. "Stick to the facts, please."

I felt myself reddening as those piercing blue eyes bored right through me. "Oh, sorry. Um, I let Carrie Ann in."

"And?" Carlo said when I hesitated.

I shrugged. "We just talked for a while, then, uh…" I closed my eyes and tried to recall the conversation. But nothing concrete came to mind, only Carrie Ann's infectious laugh and bubbly compliments about the decorating scheme. When I opened my eyes, the other officer offered me a water bottle. I thanked him and gulped down half the contents.

"You scheduled her for a session tomorrow morning," Carlo said as he held up my appointment book. "Carrie Ann is…was considered one of the best interior designers in town. Why would she need counseling from you?" His dark brows drew together in a suspicious frown. "Were you planning to tell her to give it up?"

"For your information, Detective, career counselors don't tell people what to do with their lives. We provide a sympathetic ear and help them gather all the relevant facts before making their final decisions." I knew that I was using my teacher voice, but I didn't care one bit. I was passionate about my new business, and I didn't want people getting the wrong impression about career counseling. I caught a glimpse of the other officer wiggling his eyebrows and trying to suppress a laugh. If Magnum was anything like some of my former students, he would mimic me afterward and tease Carlo about being reprimanded.

Carlo grunted and waved his hand again.

Bits and pieces of yesterday's conversation started to come back. I took several deep breaths and continued, "I remember her glancing at her watch and mumbling about having to be somewhere before six. She then headed out the back door."

Carlo flipped through his notes. "You said she knocked on the front window and came in the front door. Why would she need to go out the back way? Did she park back there?"

What did it matter whether she came in the front entrance or back? "I assume she parked out front. She had just come from the bank so it wouldn't make much sense to park in the back alley."

"Did she give you any idea where she was going?" Carlo asked, moving closer to me, so close I could smell his aftershave.

"All I remember is that she needed to get there by six."

Carlo scribbled something and underlined it for emphasis. He spoke to the officer, "Get someone to check all the offices within walking distance first thing tomorrow morning." He fixed his eyes upon mine. "What did you do after Carrie Ann left?"

"I needed to get to the bank before six. So, I grabbed my purse and walked over."

"What about the doors?"

"I locked the front door after me. The back door locks automatically."

"Who served you?"

"Karen Anderson. We sat in her office for about ten minutes…no, it must have been longer than that because the bank was closed by the time I left." More details rushed through my mind. "Karen accompanied me to the door, unlocked it and let me out. When I got back here, I started to check my email messages. Sofia called and told me to leave the office."

Carlo raised one eyebrow. "Does she do that often?"

Warmth rushed up to my cheeks, and I knew that they had turned a deep shade of pink. I didn't want Carlo to know about my tendency to obsess over every detail, but again I had no choice. "Sofia wants me to lead a more normal life, so she calls or drops by before six. But it must have been later than that yesterday."

He pointed to the telephone.

"I erase all my calls before I leave each day." I saw him frowning, and I tensed up again.

"We need to account for every minute after Carrie Ann left." He mumbled, "I'll have to give Sofia a call."

"Do you think she was murdered yesterday afternoon…right after she left here?" My stomach churned at the thought of murderers lurking in the back alley. Would I ever feel safe again?

"Right now, I'm considering all possibilities." He sighed in exasperation. "Do you remember anything…anything at all…that could pinpoint the time?"

I racked my brain for details and came up with one morsel. "I didn't check the time when I returned from the bank, but I spent about fifteen minutes answering emails before I left the office." I perched on the edge of my chair and accessed my email account. I scrolled down through the list of sent messages. "There it is. My last message yesterday at six forty-seven."

Carlo continued to write in his black notebook. "Where did you go afterward?"

"Uh…I went…uh…home and then grabbed a quick supper…yoga." I couldn't believe how incoherent I sounded. Had I lost the ability to speak in complete sentences?

He gave me an appraising once-over but said nothing. Magnum smiled and wiggled those eyebrows again. Was he flirting or playing good cop? Either way, I decided not to make eye contact. I had enough problems recalling details and didn't need any more distractions. "The class ended at nine, and I joined a couple of the ladies for coffee at Tim Hortons."

"I will need to know the location of the yoga class and which Tim Hortons you visited."

"The yoga studio and the Tim Hortons are in the Canadian Tire plaza. Jean Taylor is my instructor, and I had coffee with Laura Jamieson and Adele Martino." My hands trembled as I reached for my purse. I didn't want to involve anyone else in this nightmare, but I didn't have much choice in the matter. A murder had been committed and, as Sofia had pointed out, I was probably the last person Carrie Ann spoke with before her tragic death.

"Don't worry about that now. I need to hear what happened this morning."

"I don't know what you mean—"

"Well, for one thing, you discovered a dead body. That bears some mention."

I must be turning every shade of red today, and I couldn't escape from those icy blue eyes. I wasn't at all comfortable with Carlo's detective persona, but I had to answer all his questions and somehow get through this inquisition. “I got here about nine. Sofia had just arrived. Our mothers and Uncle Paolo came earlier. I’m not sure what time they came.” I added, “They created an Italian corner out front.”

“Yeah, I saw that.” A hint of a smile crossed his face as he checked off a few items in his book. “Does anyone else have a key to this office?”

“Just Sofia. She’ll be helping out for the next month or so.”

His eyes widened. “Is Sofia a career counselor?”

“No, she’ll be helping with reception and general office duties. And she’s done all of the decorating.”

“Hmm.” Carlo raised his eyebrows as he glanced around the room.

Sofia had worked her magic and created the perfect backdrop for ReCareering. She had allowed only dusty roses, mint and sea foam greens, and varying shades of ivories. Mint and sea foam greens. Thanks to Sofia, I could now—at age fifty-one—differentiate between the two shades. For the furniture, she had insisted on light oak, antique oak to be more exact. But the Georgia O’Keeffe prints on the wall had been my idea. I loved the feisty artist and hoped her bold prints would inspire my boomer clients to shake up their lives.

“Gilda! Gilda! Are you with us?” His eyes darkened with annoyance. I had to stop daydreaming and focus.

“You had just arrived this morning,” Carlo prompted.

“Oh, yes. We divvied up the duties. I finished getting my desk in order. Sofia organized folders for the guests. Uncle Paolo unpacked and assembled some of the chairs and tables that had arrived yesterday.”

Carlo's head shot up. "Furniture arrived yesterday. You didn't mention that before."

"You asked about Carrie Ann," I said. "The furniture arrived yesterday afternoon around one. Two men from the Furniture Mart unloaded the boxes and left them in the back offices."

"Which entrance did they use?"

"The front entrance. They weren't here too long."

He gave an impatient wave of his hands.

"By eleven-thirty we were ready for lunch. My mother, Sofia, and I were in the front office and making our way back to the kitchen when we heard my aunt scream. Uncle Paolo came inside and told us about the dead body. Sofia offered to call 911, but Uncle Paolo placed the call."

"When did you move into this office?" he asked.

Was this a trick question? I hadn't watched too many police shows lately, but I knew they often tried to catch suspects in lies. My pulse raced a little faster as I answered Carlo's question. "Uh…Last month…right after Labor Day." It must have been Tuesday, but I couldn't be one hundred percent sure.

"Have you noticed anything out of the ordinary in the back alley?"

"Just a lot of cars—"

"That are illegally parked." He shook his head. "We get three or four calls each week from some of the other business owners. Today's an unlucky day for anyone who decided to park back there."

When they were pressed for time, Sofia and Uncle Paolo liked to park right next to the Dumpster. I decided not to volunteer that information.

Carlo finished writing and closed the black

notebook. He sighed deeply.

I wondered about Carrie Ann's injuries and cause of death, but I knew I couldn't ask him. Especially not today with Carlo in detective persona and the other officer observing me.

Carlo yawned. "It's getting late. Why don't you go home? Drop by tomorrow afternoon and sign the report. It should be ready by then." He got up and put on his jacket.

A knock at the door startled me. Carlo opened the door to one of the officers. "Sorry to interrupt, Carlo. We're tying up a few loose ends, and we'd like to leave soon."

Carlo nodded in my direction and followed the officer out the door.

Chapter 4

Friday, October 21, 2011

The perfect day to stay home and play hooky. Not a cloud in the sky and sixty-two balmy degrees. Practically Florida weather. When I moved back to Sudbury, I expected an early frost in September and snow in October. At least that's how I remember the autumns of my childhood.

I sat on my balcony and watched as couples and groups of women walked along Lake Nepahwin. Two young men were canoeing, and I could see a sailboat in the distance. I loved living on this lake, and it was one of the main reasons I had come back to Sudbury. With over three hundred lakes in the Greater Sudbury area, I was never more than a short drive away from any one of them. I had my choice of lakefront properties, and in the end, had selected this three-bedroom condo in one of the newer buildings.

I still hadn't made any plans for the day. The other officer—I still didn't know his name—had advised me to stay away from the office to give the police more time to complete their investigation. He warned me that reporters and overly curious friends would drop by if they knew the office remained open for business.

After that grueling session with Carlo, I grabbed a quick supper, took the telephone off the hook, and fell asleep as soon as my head hit the pillows. I didn't wake up until eight this morning. In two hours' time, I had managed to shower, get dressed, and eat breakfast. I didn't know how I would get through the rest of today, let alone two or three more days.

I went back inside the condo and replaced the telephone receiver. Within several minutes, it rang. I checked call display and saw Jean Taylor's name and number. Calm, thoughtful Jean, my yoga instructor.

As soon as I picked up the phone, Jean started speaking. "I tried to call you last night, but your line was busy." Anger and alarm rang in her voice. "Carlo Fantin called yesterday afternoon. That call threw me off for the rest of the day. My students suffered because of it. And my husband wasn't too happy. You could have warned us."

Was this the same Jean Taylor who lit candles and radiated kindness and goodness to everyone? One phone call and she falls apart? What kind of yogini is that? Tempted to make a sarcastic comment, I took several yoga breaths before responding. "I'm sorry to hear that you're so upset. When Carlo questioned me yesterday, I had to tell him where I had been when Carrie Ann was…um…died. He probably called to confirm that I was at the studio between eight and nine that night. I don't understand how that could upset you or your husband."

She hung up. I had been planning to go in for more yoga sessions this week, but I thought I'd give Jean some time to reconnect with her spiritual self.

The loud and persistent knocking at the door startled me. Someone had managed to get past the controlled entry of the building. After checking the peephole, I opened the door to an angry and frustrated Sofia. "I've been calling you all morning. I can understand you not wanting to talk to anyone last night, but are you planning to leave the telephone off the hook all day?"

"Sorry! I've been in a daze since I got up. I put the phone back a while ago and just had the most unpleasant conversation with Jean Taylor." I gave Sofia a recap.

Sofia raised her eyebrows. "What happened to all that peace and calm she preaches about?"

"I still can't figure out why her husband is upset."

"Taylor…Taylor…Do you know his first name?"

"I'm not sure, but her son's name is Michael. She calls him Junior sometimes so, maybe—"

"Michael Taylor…Michael Taylor…Omigod! He's Carrie Ann's ex." Sofia smiled knowingly. "I bet Carlo asked a few questions about *his* whereabouts that night. And maybe Mr. Taylor didn't have an alibi."

"Why would he even need one? Carrie Ann told me they parted amicably and still talked to each other."

"That's *her* version of the story," Sofia said. "I heard he had a nervous breakdown and took a long time to get his act together. He married someone much younger, sounds like your Jean." Sofia frowned. "Is she the one who gave you that ugly plant?

Trust Sofia to focus on the aesthetics. If I hadn't intervened yesterday, she would have thrown out the river rock lucky bamboo plant that Jean had ordered for the occasion. For weeks, Jean had gushed about the three symbols inherent in each plant—wealth, happiness, and longevity. I explained, "She went to a lot of trouble to get the plant and even made a special trip out to the office before…oh no…Jean was there the other night."

"What are you talking about?"

"I got to yoga class just before it started. Jean told me that she had dropped by the office before coming to the studio. She wanted to bless my office before the open house. She's into that kind of thing and—" My mind went into overdrive. "I left the office before seven, and she probably arrived at the studio about twenty minutes before class started at eight. So, she could have been at the plaza sometime between seven and seven-thirty. Maybe that's why she's so upset about Carlo calling her."

Sofia rolled her eyes in annoyance. "Carlo called her to confirm your story. He wouldn't be asking about her whereabouts that night. And I don't think she would have volunteered that information."

My eyes traveled to the telephone. "I should let Carlo know."

"You didn't see her at the office. It's her story to tell, not yours." Sofia fluffed the sofa pillows, adjusted one of the prints on the wall, and turned the television set to Channel 59. Sofia and all my relatives liked this particular feature of condo life which provides an excellent view of the entrance to the building and allows me to screen all my visitors.

"I'm glad to see more color in your cheeks today. You looked so washed out yesterday." Sofia did not hesitate to change the subject if the conversation got too intense or uncomfortable.

"I thought I held up well."

"Don't worry. Our mothers didn't notice. They were too caught up in all the drama and excitement."

She shook her head. "You should have seen your mother's house last night. She had a steady flow of visitors, and the last group didn't leave until after midnight."

"I hope it wasn't too much for her."

"My mother and I helped out with coffee and desserts. We made a serious dent in those boxes of Italian pastries."

I had forgotten all about the pastries. And I no longer cared what happened to them.

"Not to worry. Your mother wasn't alone last night," Sophia said. "She needs a lot of people around in a crisis situation."

"Maybe I should call her now. I wonder what—"

"I dropped our mothers off at the New Sudbury Shopping Centre. They're planning to spend the day shopping and eat in the food court. I'll pick them up later in the afternoon."

"I can't believe how well you handle these crises." After my father's death four years ago, Sofia added my mother's concerns to her ever-growing list of responsibilities. When I returned to Sudbury, I had hoped to take some of that pressure off Sofia. But it hadn't worked out that way. If anything, Sofia was even more pressed for time as she juggled her own household, decorating my office and condo, and her aging parents.

"I don't mind doing it. In the end, it's easier if I just take over and handle all the details." She gave me an appraising once-over, taking in my yoga pants and T-shirt. "I take it you aren't going into the office today."

"That officer who sat in on the interview thinks I

should wait until everything settles down."

"You mean Detective Luke Matthews?" Sofia raised an eyebrow. "Didn't Carlo introduce him to you?"

"I didn't catch the name."

"How was your session with Carlo?"

I decided not to share too much with Sofia. I still can't believe how frazzled and incoherent I was throughout most of the inquisition. "He wanted to know all the details from both days. And I gave them to him."

"Did he ask you out?" Her eyes sparkled with mischief.

"He can't do that during an investigation where I…I…guess I'm a person of interest." I thought back and realized that Carlo had behaved professionally in every way. Maybe too professionally. The only time he had shown some emotion was when I mentioned the Italian corner.

Sofia smiled confidently. "He'll call once all of this blows over. He has your number."

"He'll be giving you a call sometime today."

"Why would he need to do that? Is there some problem?" Sofia's pupils dilated in surprise. Or was it irritation?

"Relax. He just wants to know what time you called me the other day." There was a definite edge to her voice, one that I didn't hear too often.

Her eyes thinned suspiciously. "What are you talking about?"

I explained. "You know how you like to call or drop by around six each day just to make sure I go home at a decent hour."

"It must have been around ten to six or so." She

started fussing with the centerpiece on the table, trying to decide where it should be.

"No, you didn't call that early. I went to the bank right after Carrie Ann left, and I didn't get back to the office until after six."

Sofia shrugged. "I guess I don't remember then. Is it important?"

"It could be. They're trying to pinpoint the time of death."

"You mean she could have been killed while you were talking on the phone with me or checking your emails?" She shivered. "I wouldn't share that with your mother or anyone else."

"I'm so glad I have you to bounce things off. I don't know what I would do if I were alone." I leaned over and hugged her. The mood had passed, and she was warm, helpful Sofia again.

The telephone rang and startled us. Sofia glanced over at the television screen and groaned as she watched two blonde women standing in the lobby. "Great! Just who we need to see today."

I moved closer to the screen, but still couldn't recognize the two heavy-set women wearing black pantsuits. "Who are they?"

"Anna May and Jenny Marie Godfrey."

While I hate using clichés, I couldn't help thinking "How the mighty have fallen" as I observed the two middle-aged women on the screen. The years had not been kind to the former "it" girls who dominated every social event during their high school careers. Unlike Carrie Ann, Anna May and Jenny Marie had not maintained their spectacular looks and figures, but they were still using those double names. "An affectation," one of the grade nine teachers had commented when Carrie Ann corrected the teacher several times during the first week of classes. The usually pleasant and co-operative Carrie Ann persisted and the teacher stopped calling her Caroline.

I picked up the phone and spoke into the receiver, "Come on up. I'm on the fifth floor—507." I buzzed them up.

"You could have ignored the call," Sofia said. "That's what I would have done."

"I have nothing to hide. And I am curious. What happened to them?"

"They got old and fat," Sofia said. "And I don't think they'll be too thrilled to see you either."

"Do they think I had something to do with Carrie Ann's death?"

"I don't know about that," Sofia replied. "But I know three things for sure. You're thinner, richer, and better looking than both of them."

Before I could respond, I heard the knocks at the door. I opened the door and welcomed the two women. "Come on in. I'm so sorry we had to meet under these circumstances. My condolences to both of you."

I couldn't take my eyes off the sisters. Anna May wore a tight, black pantsuit which did little to diminish her girth. Her straight, blonde hair was styled in the same pageboy as Carrie Ann's, but the color and texture appeared less natural. Her complexion was still smooth, and her makeup was artfully applied. Jenny Marie was shorter and not as heavy. She sported the same hairstyle as her sisters, but her skin was splotchy and showed signs of sun damage. She also wore a black pantsuit, but hers was not as form fitting.

Their eyes were puffy and red-rimmed.

Anna May spoke, “It’s been a long time, Gilda.”

“It’s unfortunate we had to meet under these circumstances.” I already said that. Why was I repeating myself? And why was I on edge? I motioned toward the living room.

“Yes, very unfortunate. That’s one of the reasons we’re here.” Anna May sat on the sofa. Jenny Marie, Sofia and I joined her.

“You have a lovely condo,” Jenny Marie said softly as her eyes traveled around the room. “This is the first time I’ve been in this building and, I must say, I’m impressed. Did you decorate it yourself or hire someone?

“Thanks, but I can’t take any of the credit. I just told Sofia what I liked, and she did the rest.”

Anna May dropped her purse on the floor. “I’m going to cut to the chase here. We’ve spent most of this morning between the police station and the funeral home, and we have a million other details to attend to. We don’t need to spend any more time making small talk and discussing decorating schemes.”

Jenny Marie gasped. “We aren’t in that much of a rush.”

Anna May’s face darkened as she continued to glare at me. “We hear that Carrie Ann visited you and shared some of her career concerns. I don’t know how desperate you are for business, but I find it appalling that you would claim her to be your first client. If she wanted a career change, she would discuss it with us, not a total stranger. Tell the truth unless you have something to hide.”

“I’ve told Carlo everything that happened, and I

have no intention of taking any of it back. I don't owe you or anyone else an explanation." I forced myself to smile while rage surged through my blood. How dare this woman accuse me of lying?

Anna May stood. "My sister visits you, leaves, and is murdered in the back alley. Something fishy is going on here, Gilda Greco, and you're at the center of it."

Before I could speak, Sofia stood. Her eyes blazed with anger. "How dare you accuse Gilda? She didn't harm Carrie Ann in any way. As for being desperate for clients, she doesn't need the business."

"I had forgotten about the lottery win," Anna May smirked. "How kind of you to remind me, Sofia." She moved closer to me. "Why couldn't you just travel and live it up like all the other lottery winners?"

"Anna May!" Jenny Marie raised her voice. "You're out of line."

"I'm out of line?" Anna May threw up her hands. "If this new millionaire hadn't decided to play Lady Bountiful and open up that career shop, Carrie Ann would still be alive today." She sank into the sofa, shaking and sobbing uncontrollably. Jenny Marie leaned over to comfort her and mouthed "I'm sorry" to me.

My hands shook as I watched Anna May unravel before us. While I didn't want to add fuel to the fire, I knew I had to say something. I waited for her to stop crying and then said, "I'm sorry you feel that way, Anna May. I'm just as horrified as you by Carrie Ann's death. But I didn't have anything to do with her murder. You must understand that."

Anna May sat up straighter. "I don't need lessons in understanding from you, Gilda Greco. So spare me."

She breathed heavily. "I'll be watching your every step—"

"You have no right to come in here and threaten Gilda!" Sofia shouted.

"The loyal and devoted cousin." Anna May stood up again and moved closer to Sofia. "How well you play that role, Sofia."

"That's enough, Anna May. I will not be insulted in my home, and I won't allow you to insult Sofia either. Please leave." I rose and moved toward the door.

The telephone rang, and my eyes traveled to the screen. The other women followed my gaze. Maria and Rosa had arrived.

I picked up the phone. "Come on up." I entered my code and then hung up.

Jenny Marie continued to watch the screen as an elderly couple followed Maria and Rosa into the building. She sighed. "I wish my daughter had this setup in her apartment building."

"Jenny Marie, we need to get going." Anna May stood impatiently by the door.

Jenny Marie ignored her. She watched the screen as a young woman with a cartful of groceries punched in her code.

I heard the knock at the door and opened it. Anna May stood to the side as I welcomed Maria and Rosa into the condo. Maria carried a large, steaming casserole, and Rosa had a covered rectangular Pyrex dish.

Sofia sniffed the air. "Something smells wonderful. Could it be lasagna?"

"What a nose you have, Sofia!" Maria headed toward the kitchen and placed the casserole on the counter.

Rosa offered her plate to me. I peeked inside. “Pineapple cheesecake—my absolute favorite!” I hugged her and then went over and hugged Maria. “You shouldn’t have gone to all this trouble.”

“Calories and cholesterol. Ladies, you need to watch it,” Anna May smirked again.

How could Anna May even think of offering anyone diet advice? I decided to take the higher ground and say nothing. No point adding to the acrimony that already existed between us.

Rosa reddened and her eyes flickered with anger. Before she could speak, Maria reappeared and placed a restraining hand on her arm. Thankfully, the moment passed.

“Jenny Marie, let’s get out of this place.” Anna May pointed a finger in my direction. “Remember, I’m watching you, Gilda Greco.”

After the door closed, Maria and Rosa came over and hugged me again. I tried to smile, but found it difficult to let go of all the tension that had built up inside.

“What did she mean by that?” Rosa asked.

“She thinks I had something to do with Carrie Ann’s death,” I replied.

Maria made the sign of the cross. “Stay away from Anna May. She’s mean to the bone and likes to stir up trouble for everyone.”

“I don’t understand why they even came,” Rosa said. “You’re not that close, and if they think you did it, why didn’t they just tell the police?”

Rosa had a valid point. One I hadn’t considered while Anna May accused me of having something to do with Carrie Ann's death. She was grieving, but there was some other emotion beneath all that. Could it be fear? What on earth would Anna May Godfrey be afraid of? The Anna May I remember walked confidently and fearlessly through the halls of Sudbury Secondary.

"...and we heard it all over the news. They're asking for witnesses or anyone who has heard anything about the death," said Maria.

I gathered they were talking about a news release issued by the police. I hadn't listened to any news since yesterday morning. Maria and Rosa could pick at this all afternoon. We needed a diversion, so I plastered a smile on my face. "Let's have lunch and put all this unpleasantness behind us." I turned to Sofia. "Why don't you give Maria and Rosa the grand tour while I heat up the lasagna and make the salad?"

"That's a great idea." Sofia lowered her voice, but I could still hear what she said to Maria and Rosa. "Please don't mention anything about the Godfrey sisters to our mothers."

"I don't think you've heard the end of Anna May," Maria said. "Wouldn't it be better if you kept your mothers informed?"

"No, Maria." Sofia raised her voice. "It's better if we don't tell them. And I would hope that you wouldn't gossip about it either."

"How can you even suggest that? Gilda is my godchild, and I love her like a daughter." Maria sounded hurt.

As I chopped up the vegetables, I could hear the oohs and aahs coming from the other rooms. Sofia delighted in showing off her masterpiece to first-time guests. She had decorated the condo in whites and off-whites with subtle pink and pale-green undertones. Everything from the soft, Italian leather sofa in the living area to the Egyptian cotton sheets in the bedroom had been selected to create a calm, muted feeling. Sofia had attended to every detail, and the results were spectacular. I didn't mind letting her do the honors.

It didn't take long to get lunch on the table. We took our places and chatted about food and sidewalk sales. The earlier tension had dissipated. Was this the calm after the storm, or the calm before the next storm?

Chapter 5

Monday, October 24, 2011

Carlo wore a black tuxedo. He carried an enormous bouquet of white roses and offered them to me.

"They're so beautiful, Carlo." I started to count them. "And so many of them."

"Twenty-nine to be exact."

"Twenty-nine?"

"It's the number of years that we have been apart."

"How thoughtful and romantic of you—"

I woke up to the incessant ringing of the telephone. Darn! Only a dream. I picked up the phone.

"It's about time you answered," Sofia said. "Where were you?"

"Asleep in bed."

"It's past ten. Are you feeling all right?"

Since moving back to Sudbury, I had to explain every move or deviation from the Italian norm. "I'm fine. I just felt like sleeping in." The weekend had been a very busy and hectic one. We had celebrated Uncle Paolo's birthday on Saturday, and while it wasn't a milestone, twelve of his relatives had come up from Sault Ste. Marie and Thunder Bay.

"I'm sorry," Sofia said. "I didn't mean to disturb you. I could call back later. But then it might be too late, and I know you like to know things ahead of time."

"All right, you win. What's up?"

"I went to Curves this morning. Everyone was talking about Carrie Ann's death. A few of the ladies suggested that her death could be related to financial problems at Three Sisters Decorating. They also talked—"

"Whoa! What kind of financial problems?" I sat up in bed and gave my full attention to the conversation.

Sofia explained, "Some of the suppliers have complained about items and amounts on their invoices and never getting paid on time. And a few irate customers threatened to sue the sisters after they discovered that poor-quality paint and wallpaper were used."

"Hmm. So there are a few unhappy campers out there. I could see them wanting to kill Anna May, but what could they possibly accomplish by killing Carrie Ann?"

"I don't know," she replied.

"Where are all these women getting their information?"

"Two of the women are wives of police officers, and they hold nothing back."

"What about confidentiality?"

"Are you thinking of reporting them?"

"Of course not. I have no intention of stirring any more pots."

Sofia changed the subject. "But I called for another reason. I wanted to make sure you knew about the memorial service this afternoon."

I knew about the service and still wasn't sure if I wanted to go. I decided to focus on the murder investigation. "Did you find out how Carrie Ann died?"

"She hit her head on the edge of the Dumpster and died instantly," Sofia said. "They also found bruises on her upper body. They're not certain about the exact time, but they're pretty sure the crime took place Wednesday evening."

"Why would anyone want to harm Carrie Ann?" I still couldn't wrap my head around it. How could someone so kind and considerate die such a brutal death?

"The police are thinking it could be a robbery gone wrong. There was no money in her wallet."

"Anything else missing?"

"No one seems to know." Sofia said. "Back to the memorial service. Visitation is at two. At three, Father Cleary will conduct a prayer service."

"Father Cleary must be ancient."

"I don't know how old he is, but he is their uncle, and he is willing to do it. From what I hear, the prayer service will be short. Then, there will be refreshments in one of the meeting rooms."

"It's surprising how much you learn at Curves. Do you get any exercising done?"

"Very funny. I double-checked everything with the funeral home. So, do you want to go?"

"No…yes…I don't know what to do. Are you going?" While I didn't want to see Anna May again, I didn't want to spend another day cocooning.

"I'm going if you're going."

"Okay, I'll go." It sounded much tamer than the traditional Italian funeral with the receiving line. I didn't think I could handle anything like that. "What time do you want to go?"

"Around a quarter to three. That way, we wouldn't have to mingle too long, and we could stay for the prayer service. I can pick you up around a quarter after two."

"Sounds like a plan. See you later." I put the telephone down and forced myself to get out of bed. I had almost four hours to get ready for the service and nothing else planned for the day. I put on my track suit, grabbed several CDs, and took the elevator down to the exercise room. I spent the next ninety minutes exercising vigorously, and then I went for a swim in the pool. I often ran into a few other residents, but I welcomed the time alone today. I needed time to think and get re-energized before the service, and I didn't feel like talking with anyone.

I went back up to the condo and took a long, luxurious bath. Something else I hadn't done since I relocated to Sudbury. Setting up the office had taken up a lot of time and energy. I decided on a light black wool pantsuit with a lilac blouse. As I finished applying my makeup, I heard Sofia's distinctive knocks at the door.

I opened the door and greeted my cousin. Her eyes widened. "Wow! You'll be the belle at this funeral…oops…I mean memorial service."

She had also gone with a black pant suit, but she had chosen to wear a cream-colored blouse. "You're looking slim. Curves is paying off."

"Yeah, I guess. But I wish I could lose the inches faster." She glanced at her watch. "We should leave now if we want to get a good parking spot and arrive before the service starts. I don't want to walk in late on Father Cleary. You know what he's like."

"What he *was* like. I think he might have lost his

bark by now."

Sofia drove, and we arrived at the funeral home in less than ten minutes. The parking lot was filled, but Sofia managed to find a spot on one of the side roads. It always amazed me how she could maneuver her car, even in the tightest of spots.

We made our way across the street and joined a group of older ladies who were entering at the same time. There was a line-up at the donations desk.

Sofia said, "Let's pay our respects first and worry about donations later. It's the first room on the right."

Sofia glanced around the room crammed with wall-to-wall floral arrangements, plants, and people. "Jenny Marie is at the far right talking with an older gentleman. Why don't we chat with her for a while?"

We made our way through the crowd and found ourselves face-to-face with Jenny Marie. The older gentleman's voice trembled as he spoke. "Edith has become more housebound and hardly ever goes out now. We both appreciated everything that Carrie Ann did for us after Edith had her stroke." He took Jenny Marie's hand and held it tightly. "We will pray for you and Anna May." Tears welled in his eyes as he headed toward the door.

"Thank you for coming. I'm surprised to see you after what happened the other day." Jenny Marie winced. "I must apologize for Anna May's behavior. She's been blaming everyone, even some of our regular suppliers and customers."

I hugged her. "She has every right to be angry at such a tragic and senseless crime."

Jenny Marie smiled gratefully. "I spoke to my daughter about your condo. She's an interior designer, too, and she would love to see it sometime."

My eyes traveled around the room, searching for younger head of blonde hair. While I had never met Grace, I figured she resembled her mother and aunts. "I'd love to show it to her. Is she planning to stay for a few days?"

"She's in the middle of a very important assignment out East. I told her not to worry about missing the service. Anna May insisted on having it today." She paused and added, "Carrie Ann would have understood."

Sofia spoke. "My condolences to you and Anna May. We will keep you in our prayers."

One of the funeral directors made an announcement. "Ladies and gentlemen, may I have your attention please." The room became quiet, and he continued. "Father Cleary will be conducting a short service in the chapel, two doors down the hall. It will begin in ten minutes."

"Let's go." Sofia started walking faster. "We want to get good seats."

"This is not an arena." While I didn't think it was dignified to be moving so quickly in a funeral home, I noticed several other visitors also quickening their pace.

"I don't know about you, but I have no intention of standing any longer than I have to in these heels."

I followed her into the chapel, marveling at how she managed to elbow her way past the others. We found two places in the fourth row from the front. Sofia smiled as she sank into her chair. I focused on the altar where Anna May and Jenny Marie were talking with an older and much grayer Father Cleary. A tall, slender blonde woman approached the trio and began pointing toward the podium. She was strikingly beautiful with long, curly blonde hair. A man in a black, pinstripe suit approached and touched her on the shoulder. Carlo Fantin. She hugged him, and they stood close together for a while.

"Do you remember Melly Grace?" Sofia asked.

"The American cousin from Tennessee." How could I forget the Group of Four as they liked to call themselves? The three Godfrey sisters and the visiting cousin were inseparable during that spring so long ago.

"She broke up at least ten couples." Sofia whispered, but she had a definite edge to her voice.

"What are you talking about?"

"I'll tell you later. It's too long a story, and Father Cleary is ready to start the service."

Father Cleary stood at the podium waiting for everyone to get settled. It had been over twenty years since I had seen the dynamic priest who delighted in delivering fiery sermons and openly confronting "holiday Catholics" and rebellious teenagers. It was his way or the highway. The years had not been kind to the aging priest. His hair had thinned and grayed, and he was stooped in his posture. He appeared as a frail octogenarian with a pronounced tremor in his right hand. In a low and shaky voice, he made a considerable effort to deliver the two readings selected by the family: Ecclesiastes and the parable of the vine and branches. Afterward, he slowly made his way to a nearby chair.

Melly Grace nodded to Father Cleary and approached the podium. She wore a black suit with a short skirt and a black-and-white striped blouse. Her skin was flawless, and the honey-blonde curls looked very natural—similar in color to Carrie Ann's. Rimless glasses accentuated her large, blue eyes. From where I sat, she could easily pass for thirty-five. She began to speak in a low, melodious voice which held traces of a southern drawl.

"First of all, I would like to thank Father Cleary for leading us in prayer. How appropriate that he read from Ecclesiastes—one of Carrie Ann's favorite passages. She believed there was a season to everything in life; the challenge was to embrace all events, both positive and negative, and somehow maintain equilibrium.

"I feel privileged to have been her cousin and friend since childhood. I can still remember spending our summers together at the family compound in French River. She was a tomboy who loved and excelled at every sport. As the two children closest in age, we spent a lot of time together, and I often think of Carrie Ann as the sister I never had." Melly Grace glanced down and paused. Her right hand shook as she turned the page.

"As we grew older, there were fewer and fewer family get-togethers. We started writing monthly letters to each other. I did manage to spend a few months with her during our senior year in high school. I still have fond memories of our prom night, double dates, barbecues, and the summer spent as camp counselors in Algonquin Park. After university, we spent a year traveling and working in Europe. Carrie Ann dragged me to every museum and church listed in the travel guides. We must have visited hundreds of them." Melly Grace smiled and shook her head as several chuckles could be heard throughout the chapel.

"In adulthood, we maintained our correspondence and later switched to weekly emails and the occasional telephone call. I could talk about anything and anyone with Carrie Ann. That was her greatest gift. She was a wonderful listener who knew when to offer sympathy and when to offer solutions. She was nonjudgmental and would never scold or indulge in one-upmanship.

"In her chosen profession, she created sanctuaries and artistic masterpieces for her clients. She was passionate about everything and everyone in her life: her sisters, her extended family, her career, and her many hobbies and interests. She will always have a special place in my heart and the hearts of all who knew her.

"There is no explanation or justification for the violent and senseless way she was taken from us. But let us take solace in the fact that she has now entered another realm and will always be with us in spirit."

Melly Grace bowed her head and stood silent for a few seconds. She then walked toward the pew and sat next to Anna May and Jenny Marie. The two sisters embraced her, and Carlo patted her shoulder. I wondered why he sat with the family.

"That was some eulogy," Sofia whispered in a voice tinged with envy. "Who would have thought the dipstick had it in her."

I decided not to respond. While I loved my cousin dearly, there were times when I wanted to muzzle her. She was filter-free, a trait I sometimes envied, but not today.

One of the funeral directors approached the podium. He cleared his throat and addressed the group. "On behalf of the Godfrey family, I wish to thank all of you for coming to pay your last respects to our beloved Carrie Ann. You are all invited to join us for refreshments in the meeting room."

"I'm ready to go. What about you?" It had been a tame experience, and I didn't want to press my luck and risk the chance of running into Anna May.

Sofia sighed. "I guess you don't want to partake." She wanted to stay and sample some of the pastries and chat with the other guests. Like my mother and aunt, she made an afternoon of it whenever she paid her respects.

"You got it."

"All right, we'll go." Sofia headed toward the corridor. "I need to use the washroom. I'll meet you in the foyer."

I slipped out the back entrance and headed toward the donation desk. I couldn't help but eavesdrop on two older ladies standing in front of me.

"Isn't it wonderful that Melly Grace came up for the service?"

"I'm not surprised. She and Carrie Ann were very close. What did you think of the eulogy?"

"Well done! I hear she's a successful attorney. Someone said she made partner."

"I'm not surprised. Doesn't she look wonderful?"

"Hmm. I wonder if she had any work done."

"You would never know she was in her late forties."

"She can't be that old!"

"She and Carrie Ann were the same age. And I know that Carrie Ann planned to celebrate her fiftieth birthday next year."

"So that makes both of them forty-nine. I'm surprised that Melly Grace never married."

"If you think about it, none of the Godfrey women

seem big on marriage or family. The sisters are all divorced, and Jenny Marie is the only one who produced a child." The women reached the head of the line, wrote their checks, and headed for the exit.

When I reached the front desk, I made out the check to Genevra House, a local organization that offers support services for women experiencing abuse. Sofia waved me over. "There you are. I don't think we should go back to your condo or my place."

"Why not?" I asked.

"Don't you remember what our mothers taught us about wakes and funerals?" Sofia spoke in a sing-song voice. "It's bad luck to visit anyone right after a wake or funeral. If you do that, you bring death into the guest's home."

I shivered. "We don't need any more deaths. Where should we go?"

"Out to supper," Sofia said. "You love eating out, and I haven't been out in a while."

"Okay, but you pick this time."

"How about we try that new Greek restaurant out on Falconbridge Road. I think it's called Olympius."

"Olympia. Yes, I've heard wonderful things about their souvlaki and roast lamb." I glanced at my watch. "It's ten after four. I don't want to have supper this early."

Sofia's face brightened. "Home Depot is just around the corner from the restaurant, and we could spend some time there. I know it's not of your haunts, but—"

"It's one of yours. I don't mind hanging out there for a while."

As we drove away from the funeral home, I

breathed a sigh of relief. From now on, things could only get better.

Chapter 6

Sofia visited every nook and corner of the store and ended up buying a cart full of bargains. By the time, we left the store and headed for the restaurant, we were tired and hungry. The hostess seated us and gave us menus. Flushed with excitement, Sophia chatted about her bargains. As she spoke, she scrutinized the other patrons. Whenever we went out, Sofia was like a bee, jumping to every flower. If she could not physically table hop, her eyes would nervously dart around the room.

Our waiter approached. "Good evening, ladies. My name is Niko, and I am here to help you experience the best of Grecian cuisine."

"Hello, Niko," I said. "What do you recommend?"

"Our signature dishes are the chicken souvlaki and moussaka. Our catch of the day is the red snapper, and most of our seafood dishes are popular choices."

"I'll have the chicken souvlaki with the Greek salad. I'd like the squid as appetizer."

"You are as decisive as you are beautiful. I like that in a woman." Niko winked at me. "What about drinks?"

"A glass of your white house wine would be fine."

Niko raised his eyebrows at Sofia. "And you, ma'am?"

"I'll have the same as her," Sofia answered abruptly and turned her attention back to the two couples at the door.

After Niko left, I admonished her. “You could try to be more polite. He seems like a nice young man.”

Sofia’s lips formed a tight red line of anger. “He flirted with you. I just got a ma’am and you know how much I hate that.”

I decided to steer the conversation in a different direction. “In the chapel, you were talking about Melly Grace and all the trouble she created in the past. What did you mean by that?”

“I can’t believe you don’t remember any of it,” Sofia shook her head in amazement. “Melly Grace had already completed her school year in Tennessee at the end of May and decided to come up to Sudbury. Carrie Ann arranged for her to participate in all grad activities. She even got to attend the prom, her second prom of the year.”

“I’m sure that didn’t sit too well with many of the female grads.”

“You’ve got that right. When the boys saw Melly Grace and heard her southern drawl, they started lusting after her.”

And then I remembered. Carlo and Melly Grace had attended the prom together.

“Those two were pretty tight for most of the month,” Sophia said. “I heard he even went down to Tennessee to meet her family.”

“I wonder what came of that relationship.”

“The scuttlebutt was that she did the dumping.”

“Hmm.

“You’re interested in him, aren’t you?”

“Well, I don’t know…I guess…yes, I am. I thought…”

"You thought he was interested in you, but now you're not so sure, and you don't want to put the moves on him if he's still lusting after Melly Grace."

"That's about right." It was time to change the subject again. "I heard some of the ladies in the foyer talking about Melly Grace. They mentioned that she never married."

"I thought she'd marry young, like her cousins, but she turned out to be more career focused."

"I don't remember much about her, but she sounds very shrewd and used to getting her own way."

"The Godfrey women excel in that area. They always—" Sofia frowned as she watched the entrance. "I think we are about to be graced by their presence."

I followed her gaze and watched as the hostess seated Melly Grace, Anna May, and Jenny Marie. I sighed. "I was hoping for a pleasant meal."

Sofia picked up her purse. "We don't have to stay if you're not comfortable."

I had nothing to do with Carrie Ann's death, and I would not allow Anna May to intimidate me any further. I managed to plaster a fake smile on my face. "We'll leave when we are ready to leave."

As the evening progressed, the restaurant became more crowded and noisy. Sofia and I were quiet throughout most of the meal. We liked to eat in silence and then chat over coffee and dessert. I smiled as I watched Sofia try to figure out the ingredients in her blueberry dessert.

"This was not cooked. It was prepared yesterday and refrigerated overnight." Sofia took out a small notepad and started jotting down the ingredients. "I can taste a bit of vanilla, and there is a definite lemon flavor, uh…maybe two or three tablespoons of lemon juice. It's very light and creamy; I'm not certain, but it could be Cool Whip."

"You take a few bites, and presto you can figure out the recipe." I envied the gift that Sofia shared with all foodies worldwide. Our grandmothers and mothers also possessed the gift that had somehow bypassed me.

"I'll make it for next Sunday's dinner at my in-laws." Sofia made a face at my dessert. "New York cheesecake—pretty basic. I'm not even going to bother tasting it."

"Sorry, I'll order something more exotic next time."

"Well, well. Look who followed us here." Anna May was breathing heavily and speaking in a loud voice.

The Godfrey women were standing next to our table. Jenny Marie avoided my glance while Melly Grace nodded in my direction. "Hello, Gilda. It's been a long time."

"Hello, Melly Grace." My pulse quickened, and I felt my palms grow wet. "It's unfortunate that we must meet under these circumstances."

"Now that's an understatement," Anna May said. "Why don't you tell us how you really feel? We all know you had something to do with Carrie Ann's death." The other patrons were staring and listening intently.

"That's enough, Anna May." Melly Grace's blue eyes blazed at her cousin. She then focused her attention upon me. "I will be staying in Sudbury until Wednesday, and I intend to make very good use of my time. I will leave no stones unturned. I will meet with you tomorrow morning at ten. I want to know every detail—"

"I've already given my statement to the police," I said

Melly Grace smiled frostily. "I'm representing the family, and you are considered one of the prime suspects."

Sofia gasped. "You're out of line, Melly Grace. You don't have a license to practice law here in Canada. So back off. "

"Sara? Sofia? You haven't changed a bit since high school." Melly Grace dismissed her and addressed me again. "If you feel the need, by all means have your attorney present. I would expect that you have already spoken with him or her at length."

"There is no need for any attorney or any meeting with you," I said, lifting my chin defiantly. "I don't know what cozy little arrangement you have with the police department, but I will not be giving you any information."

Melly Grace laughed. "Cozy little arrangement. Can't you come up with something better than that? What was it that Carlo said about you?"

"Don't patronize me, Melly Grace Godfrey. I don't know your game plan, or what lives you plan to ruin this time, but I won't be part of it." I couldn't believe the words coming out of my mouth. And I had raised my voice at least one octave higher.

Melly Grace raised her eyebrows. "This time?"

Anna May roared. "She's talking about the prom, all your beaux, and high school!"

Melly Grace's eyes widened. "High school? Don't tell me you're still at that stage of development. You need to move on with your life, Gilda Greco. More importantly, you need to get a life."

Out of the corner of my right eye, I caught a glimpse of Sofia's shocked face. My hands curled into tight fists at my sides. I longed to pick up the steaming cup of coffee sitting right in front of me and hurl it at Melly Grace's blonde curls. I noticed a steak knife at the next table. It would be so easy to reach for it and throw it at Anna May's smirking face. I closed my eyes and forced my hands to remain at my sides. I took several deep yoga breaths and then opened my eyes. The Godfrey women were no longer at our table.

Sofia whispered, "Let's wait ten minutes and then leave."

"I won't give them that satisfaction." As I sipped my coffee, my eyes traveled around the room. I knew that I was the main topic of conversation. I didn't want to fuel more of that talk with a dramatic exit.

"What are you thinking?" Sofia hissed.

"Now, don't you start! I've had enough putdowns for one evening."

"Putdowns?" Sofia's eyes popped. "Those women attacked you. They're out for your blood."

"Maybe, but I don't think that I'm the only one under investigation." I felt strangely calm as I mentally dissected the scene. "I watched Anna May throughout that whole escapade. She didn't look too happy."

"She was drunk."

"She's afraid of Melly Grace. So is Jenny Marie."

"Jenny Marie is afraid of her own shadow. She's been depressed since her husband had that affair and left. Carrie Ann tried to help, but Anna May just bullied her."

"More information from Curves?" I managed a tight smile.

"I don't think I'll go tomorrow."

"Are you afraid they might talk about me?"

"I know they'll be talking about you." Sofia gestured around the room. "There are over forty people in this restaurant, and I am willing to bet they'll all go home tonight and tell at least one other person."

I signaled for Niko. When he approached, I smiled at him. "Niko, I would love another cup of this delicious coffee, and I think I'll try the crème brûlée." He nodded and left quickly.

Sofia eyes popped. "Two desserts in one evening!"

"Well, if everyone is going to talk about me anyway, I may as well indulge myself and get my sugar fix for the month."

Chapter 7

Tuesday, October 25, 2011

Under normal circumstances, I would still be fast asleep. But normal no longer existed for me. At five-thirty, I found myself on Highway 17 West headed for Manitoulin Island. I needed to get away from Sudbury and the Godfrey women. Last night's escapade had set me back, and I was still reeling from the after-effects.

As I passed the city limits, I felt myself relaxing. In the four months since I had moved back to Sudbury, this was the first time I was letting my hair down. What a luxury to disappear and not have to account for every minute of my time! I had considered not bringing my cell phone, but then realized it wouldn't make sense to travel without one. So, I compromised and turned it off before leaving.

Providence Bay was one hundred ten miles away: Northern Ontario miles with isolated, small towns and little traffic. I enjoyed driving on country roads, and I didn't consider it a long trip. My Guelph friends had a hard time understanding the Northern Ontario concept of a day trip. Growing up, we would spend seven hours on the road whenever we visited Sault Ste. Marie for the day. And from what I hear, that still goes on. Many Sudburians still spend that much time on the road when they visit Casino Rama for the day.

I inserted a Rolling Stones CD, and let the music fill the car. It took little over an hour to reach Little Current, the largest town on the island. I pulled over and stopped the car on the side of the road to check Karen's instructions.

Last week at the bank, Karen had mentioned that she was putting her cottage on the market. She was planning to relocate to Barrie to be closer to her adult children. I expressed an interest in the cottage and picked up the keys on the day Carrie Ann died.

Like Karen, the instructions were precise and direct. I followed Highway 6 and took in the splendid show of color created by the maple trees which dotted most of the island. Providence Bay had the longest beach on the island, and I couldn't wait to take a stroll on the boardwalk.

I had no trouble finding the cottage. It was much smaller than I had expected. There were two bedrooms and one bathroom. Typical of most cottages, but not that convenient if my family or friends from Guelph decided to visit. The cottage had a musty odor and old blankets and quilts covered the furniture. Karen mentioned including all the appliances and furniture, but I couldn't imagine keeping any of them. I sighed and thought about the renovations that would have to be done. As I brought in my cooler, coffee maker, and laptop, I tried to visualize the comfortable house that could replace this small, rustic cottage.

I put on a heavier sweater and decided to spend the day outdoors. A cool day, but the clouds were clearing, and soon the sun broke through, creating a spectacular view of Lake Huron. I spent the morning walking on the boardwalk and after a quick lunch, took out my laptop and settled into a comfortable chair on the porch. I started to plan the PowerPoint presentation for the grade ten career classes. While ReCareering catered to an older clientele, I didn't mind facilitating workshops and seminars at the local high schools in Sudbury. I managed to get halfway through the presentation before my eyelids started to get heavy. When I woke up, the sun had started to set.

The ride home was an uneventful one, a few more cars than the morning, but nothing to delay my arrival. I had told no one about my solo adventure, and there had been no way for anyone to contact me.

I smiled contentedly as I neared the city and caught glimpses of the Big Nickel, that famous landmark associated with the city. I recalled the many times I had visited the large coin, climbing the rocks and sneaking in the back way. When it first opened, there was no fence or extra staff to supervise the grounds. And then I thought of the other attractions in the city—Science North, Bell Park. Maybe it was time to revisit them again and show them off when my southern Ontario friends visited in the spring.

When I arrived at my condo, the telephone rang, and the message light flashed ominously at me. I groaned. I would be spending the next hour responding to all my relatives' concerns. Or I could put it off until tomorrow. Without bothering to check call display, I picked up the telephone and managed to say hello.

"Where have you been?" An irate, masculine and vaguely familiar voice accosted me.

"I'm sorry…who's calling…"

"Carlo Fantin. Have you forgotten me already?" Anger tinged every word, and there was a sarcastic edge to his voice. “But I guess with your busy schedule, you can’t keep up with regular, everyday occurrences like murder investigations.”

“You sound angry and put out.”

“Two murders in one week have a way of doing that to me.”

“Two murders!” My heart plummeted. “What are you talking about?”

“Where have you been, Gilda?” Carlo spoke more gently.

“I went to the island.”

“What island?”

“Manitoulin Island. I went to Karen Anderson’s cottage. She works at the bank in my plaza.”

“Yes, I know Karen.” Carlo sounded relieved. “I’m glad you spent some time with a friend. It’s a bit cool, but I know the island is beautiful at any time of the year.”

“I went by myself. Karen and her husband are thinking of selling it, so I decided to check it out.”

Carlo paused. “You must have gotten to know her neighbors. It’s always a good idea to check out who’ll be sharing the waterfront with you.”

“I didn’t meet them. Most people locked up their cottages last week. The place is usually deserted between October and May. At least, that’s what Karen tells me.”

“You must have seen someone.” I could hear an intake of breath on the other end and I tensed, expecting Carlo to lash out at me. “Did you stop for gas? Where did you eat?”

“This is starting to sound like an inquisition, and I’m not too crazy about your line of questioning,

Detective." My heart beat faster as I gripped the phone. "I filled up with gas last night, and I brought a cooler with food."

"Coffee?" he barked.

"I love my espresso, and I don't go anywhere without my own coffee maker."

"Great. Just great," Carlo groaned.

"You're beginning to make me nervous."

"Good! It's about time you realized how serious this situation really is."

"What are you talking about?"

"Melly Grace is dead."

The information hit me like a blow to the stomach. "Oh, my God! What happened?"

"You know I can't give you any details."

I persisted. "She was alive last night when I left the restaurant. I don't know—"

Carlo interrupted, "I've heard many versions of what happened last night." Another pause and then he asked, "And what time were you up and about this morning, Gilda?"

"I don't know what you've heard, but the Godfrey women verbally attacked me." I paused to take several breaths and then continued, "I don't remember what time I got out of bed, but I left around five-thirty, and I arrived at the cottage two hours later."

He persisted. "Did you call up your mother or see Sofia? You must have phoned Karen and picked up the key before you left."

"No, I got the key when I visited her office the day Carrie Ann died. There were several older couples walking on the boardwalk, but I didn't have conversations with any of them. You're the first person

I've spoken to—"

"I'm going to terminate this conversation right now. For your own protection, I suggest you find yourself a lawyer and come downtown as soon as possible." He hung up.

I sank into the leather couch and held my head in both hands. The telephone rang. This time I checked call display. I breathed a sigh of relief as I picked up the phone.

"Where have you been?" Sofia asked in an exasperated tone.

"I guess no one says hello anymore."

"So you know. Who told you?"

"I just finished speaking with Carlo."

"How was it?"

"Terrible. He advised me to get a lawyer."

She swore under her breath. "I wish I had talked to you first. Then you would have been prepared."

"I told him the truth. I have nothing to hide."

"Then why would he say you need a lawyer? And you still haven't told me where you've been."

"I'll answer your second question first. I couldn't sleep. I got out of bed and decided to get out of town. I drove out to Manitoulin Island and spent the day alone at Karen Anderson's cottage. I've been gone the whole day, and there's no one who can vouch for me. And that's why Carlo thinks I need a lawyer."

"This is beyond damage control," Sofia muttered.

"This is murder. And I think someone is trying to set me up."

Sofia spoke briskly. "First things first. Tomorrow morning call Henry Keenan. He's the best criminal lawyer in town and, thank God, you can afford it."

"Isn't it wonderful how handy a lottery win can be." I bit down on my lower lip.

"You sound strange." Sofia lowered her voice. "Go ahead and cry. Let it all out. You'll feel better."

I stopped biting my lip and sobbed uncontrollably for a few minutes. I sniffed and blew my nose. "Thanks."

"Do you want me to come over?"

"No, I have a splitting headache, and I plan to go to bed very soon. I'll check my messages tomorrow, but I think I'll call my mother now. I wonder if she knows."

"Everyone knows. They reported Melly Grace's murder this afternoon, and word has spread like wildfire."

"Who told her? And what did they tell her?"

"My parents gave her an edited version, and Maria and Rosa gave her all the details about last night at Olympia. Rosa's son and girlfriend were sitting a few tables away from us, and they heard and saw everything. She has been listening to the radio, and I'm sure she's called you a number of times."

Would it ever end, I wondered. "I'll call her right now."

"I wouldn't do that if I were you," Sofia said. "My parents and I took supper over there, and before we left, she took a sedative and went to bed. Tomorrow morning, we'll all come over and have a family powwow at your place."

"I'm willing to bet you've even baked something for the occasion."

"Well, you know how I like to bake in crisis situations. This afternoon I baked double batches of blueberry and banana muffins. What we don't eat, you can freeze." Sofia cleared her throat. "We'll be there around ten. Good night and sleep tight."

I felt a bit ashamed about my earlier thoughts. I was fortunate to have family and relatives who would drop everything to help me through this nightmare. And what a nightmare it was turning out to be.

Chapter 8

Wednesday, October 26, 2011

I watched on the flat screen as Sofia led the solemn, slow-moving group past the entrance into the foyer. My mother and aunt were wearing head-to-toe black and clinging to each other. Uncle Paolo followed behind, head down. I waited for the knock at the door and then opened the door to let them in. My mother burst into tears, and both Uncle Paolo and Aunt Amelia had to help her sit down.

"Please, Ma, don't cry. It's going to be all right." I forced a smile and bent over and kissed her.

"Things will only get worse." Head down, she continued to cry into her handkerchief.

"I agree," Aunt Amelia said. "There have been two murders, and I'm certain there will be a third. Everything comes in threes."

"Why not four murders? There are two more sisters, and they're both blondes. This is a season for killing blondes," Sofia joked as she arranged the muffins and fruit on the table.

"Sofia! That's terrible. Don't even joke about it." I was taken aback by her comment.

"Sofia, what's gotten into you?" Uncle Paolo gasped in disbelief. "What if someone else had heard you?"

Sofia rolled her eyes. "Just kidding! It's pretty bad when you have to muzzle your comments in front of family."

Yes, isn't it, I thought. Although I did not approve of her comments, I envied her ability to speak so bluntly. It made life a lot easier and less stressful.

Sofia stood back and surveyed the table. She had artfully arranged the food and flowers to create an autumn burst of loveliness. Aunt Amelia and Uncle Paolo smiled and nodded in approval as they sampled the banana and blueberry muffins. My mother poured coffee into the small, espresso cups and carried the tray into the living area. The angry moment had passed, and now everyone focused on the food.

"Sofia, these muffins are delicious." Uncle Paolo had both types of muffins on his plate and alternated between them. "Much as I hate to agree with your mother's Aunt Renata, I have to admit she was right. The blueberry muffins are the best."

Aunt Amelia laughed. "I never thought I would hear you say anything nice about her."

We all joined in the laughter as each of us recalled the year that Aunt Renata decided to spend the winter in Canada. She did nothing but complain about the weather and the lack of stimulating activities. Recently widowed, she had decided to travel and visit her many nieces and nephews in Canada and the United States. She had not bargained for a harsh, cold winter and bouts of influenza. I visited Sudbury once during that time, so I hadn't experienced the full impact of that woman's selfishness and self-absorption. "I still don't understand why you all catered to her. You treated her like a guest for four whole months. I wouldn't have had the patience for it."

"We felt sorry for her," Sofia said. "Her children had all moved to northern Italy, and she lived all by herself in that large, rambling house in Calabria."

"She drove everyone away," my mother explained. "And she had such a sad ending in Italy. I heard that very few people attended the funeral. Maybe we should have gone, Amelia."

"It wasn't a good time for either one of you, Aunt Assunta. You had just lost a husband, and Ma had that cancer scare." Sofia put down her coffee cup. "Enough about Aunt Renata. We have more important matters to discuss."

Sofia nodded in my direction. "Did you call Henry Keenan?"

"I'm meeting with him early this afternoon."

Sofia continued, "Do you want me to come with you?"

"No, I'm fine." I really wasn't fine, but I didn't want to alarm everyone. Somehow, I would muddle through this mess.

Uncle Paolo cleared his throat. "Gilda, you need to start thinking very carefully about every move you make." He waved his hands. "We feel you should move in with Sofia or your mother."

"Are you putting me under house arrest?" Did they think that I could be involved?

"You're alone and you never have any…what is that word…" My mother started to cry again.

"Alibi, *zia*." Sofia shook her head. "She's right. You don't have an alibi for the two murders, and you've had dealings with both of the women."

I spoke in a choked whisper. "I'm not a murderer."

My mother continued to cry as Aunt Amelia comforted her. Sofia started arranging muffins and fruit on a smaller tray. She picked up the tray and pointed toward the balcony. I followed her outside. She waited until I closed the sliding door before speaking. "We know you're not a murderer. But the rest of the world is not convinced. Even Carlo has his doubts."

"What do you mean?" Where on earth was she getting all this information? "Ah, don't tell me, more news from Curves. I guess you went there this morning."

"I missed yesterday, but I went in today. The women couldn't stop talking about the murders and Carlo Fantin." She paused and took a sip of coffee. "I don't know how much you are prepared to hear."

"Give it to me straight. I need to know what's going on."

We sat and started eating the fruit.

"Carlo lost his cool yesterday when he found out about Melly Grace's death," Sofia said.

"There aren't too many grisly murders in Sudbury. Two in the same week involving friends of his—"

Sofia interrupted, "He has a reputation for being calm and always in control."

"I guess losing Melly Grace upset him." At the funeral home, they had sat very close together, and his face had softened whenever their glances met. "Maybe he still carries a torch for her."

"One of the officer's wives dismissed that theory," Sofia said. "She suggested he was upset because you were in the picture." She took a deep breath and continued. "After the news bulletin went out, Carlo received a number of calls from people who claimed they were at Olympia on Monday night. They gave very interesting accounts about what happened that night. I don't know if you—"

"Spill it, Sofia."

Her eyes traveled toward the lake as she paused to find the right words. "Eight different women called and told Carlo that you looked angry enough to kill that night. One of them even said that you threatened Melly Grace."

"These people are lying!" My breath caught, and I struggled to slow down my heartbeat. "Sofia, you were there."

Sofia gave me a sad smile. "You stared a bit too long at that steak knife, and you clenched your hands. That's what people remember."

I thought back to that night and remembered the murderous thoughts that had gone through my mind. Was I that transparent? A detail came to mind. "How could all those women claim that they saw me looking at the knife? The Godfrey women were standing very close to our table and blocking everyone's view."

"Those eight witnesses are all somehow connected with Anna May," Sofia said. "One of the wives mentioned that Anna May could have talked the women into calling Carlo."

"What is Anna May's problem?" I hadn't seen the woman in years, and suddenly she's accusing me of two murders.

"Don't you remember how she was in school?" Sofia asked. "She couldn't handle it when anyone else attracted more attention."

The teenage Anna May was a far cry from the overweight, middle-aged woman who was unraveling before us. If Anna May got that upset whenever she encountered a more attractive woman, she must be in a constant state of agitation. Something else was behind this harassment. "I wonder if Anna May is somehow involved in both murders?" I was surprised to hear myself thinking out loud.

Sofia's eyes widened. "Why would you even think such a thing?"

"Just a gut feeling, I guess." It was a far-fetched theory, but one that was starting to make sense. Why else would she be so quick to pin the murder on me? We had no history, none at all.

Sofia shook her head. "Three Sisters Decorating revolved around Carrie Ann's creative talent. Without her, Jenny Marie and Anna May don't have a meal ticket."

"Carrie Ann wanted to leave. Maybe Anna May caught wind of that and lost it." I thought back to my own unpleasant encounters with Anna May. It wouldn't take much to unhinge her.

Sofia frowned. "I can't even imagine Anna May wanting to kill her sister, and what would she be doing lurking in that alley behind your office? It doesn't make any sense." She shuddered. "I hate to say this, but I agree with our mothers. I think there may be another murder."

I changed the subject. "Back to Curves. Spill the rest of it."

Sofia frowned but quickly regained her composure. "Oh, yes. They were also talking about how similar the two murders were. Both women either hit their heads or were hit by blunt objects, and there was extensive neck bruising. They were neatly arranged in the Dumpsters.

They weren't just thrown in haphazardly."

"Neck bruising?" All I could recall was that pale, lifeless face. "I didn't see any of that on Carrie Ann's body."

"Well, for starters, we weren't looking for it. And remember she had that scarf covering most of her neck. It would have been very easy to hide any signs of strangulation. Melly Grace was another story. The police officers had to turn away."

"They were killed by a woman," I said. "Or a woman assisted in the murder."

Sofia gasped. "That's not the impression you want people to have."

"But don't you see how much sense it makes? The signs of strangulation were covered, and they were neatly arranged in the Dumpster. No man would go to all that trouble."

"A gay man might or one suffering from OCD," Sofia said.

I nodded in agreement. "The woman would also have to be a bit obsessive and concerned with appearances."

"That covers about ninety-five percent of the women we know," Sofia joked.

I laughed and threw up my hands. "That's it. I have had enough. My Nancy Drew moments are over." I glanced over her shoulder and noticed that my mother had stopped crying. "Do you think it's safe to go back in?"

Sofia pointed toward the living room. "Yesterday, I spent most of the day calming them down. They aren't going to let up until this is all settled, and that may take a while."

"So what's the plan?"

"I think it would be a good idea if I moved in with you." Sofia held up her hand to stop me from interrupting. "I know you like your space and need more privacy than the rest of us, and I am prepared to accommodate that. Peter and Paul are away at school, and Andrew is still in Italy."

"When is Andrew coming back?" It had been a while since I had seen him. Was his uncle's estate taking this long to settle?

Sofia sighed. "There are complications. You know what it's like in Italy with all that bureaucracy. It takes forever to get anything done." She changed the subject. "Back to me moving in. I won't be spending too much time here. I'm up to my eyeballs with the Autumn Tea, so this would only be a pit stop for me."

"I got the impression they wanted me to have a constant companion." What was the point of Sofia moving in if she was going to be out all the time? Especially the week before the tea. Knowing Sofia, she would be running around town collecting door prizes and attending to every last detail. From what my mother had told me, I've gathered that Sofia threw herself into all these church activities and micromanaged everyone.

"We would do a few things together," Sofia said. "But we don't have to be attached at the hip and share any of this with our parents. It will make them feel happy and secure to know that I'm staying here."

"You're really good at dealing with them." I couldn't get over how well she handled these crises. And when there was a tense moment, she smoothed things over.

"I've had lots of practice. Years and years of it.

Now, let's go back in and break the good news to them."

Chapter 9

Henry Keenan had a constipated and ineffectual look about him. It was hard to believe he was the best criminal attorney in Sudbury and a force to be reckoned with in the courtroom. With his untidy mop of white hair, wire-rimmed glasses and rumpled clothes, he could pass for an aging university professor. I wondered if he owned a dark, pinstripe suit. If he didn't, I would buy one for him. Whoa, I thought. One step at a time. I haven't been formally accused, and I'm already planning the courtroom scene. I closed my eyes and willed myself back into the present moment.

Henry spoke in a low monotone, and I had to strain to hear him. "I'll be checking in with the police. I want to get a full transcript of your initial statement. Try to avoid talking about the murders with the press, friends, and relatives. I'm familiar with the case, but I will need some time to get a firm grasp on your involvement." He paused and then continued. "Questions?"

"Will you hire someone to investigate other suspects?"

Henry peered at me and frowned. "What other suspects?"

"Anna May Godfrey."

"You have proof Anna May Godfrey killed her sister and cousin?" His eyes darkened with annoyance as he raised his voice. "Please share this information with me."

"Well, not exactly. I've heard a few things about her and her business dealings, and I've had a couple of unpleasant encounters with her—"

"Let me get this straight." Henry stood up to his full height of over six feet. His eyes fixed on mine. "You want me to conduct a full-fledged investigation of Anna May Godfrey based on hearsay information and your own feelings toward her."

He didn't need a dark pinstripe suit to intimidate anyone. He had a presence and demeanor that could quell all opposition within a radius of one hundred feet. My knees shook as I got up. "Well, I guess when you put it that way—"

"And what other way is there?" His lips curled into a snarl. "Murder is serious business, and in case you haven't noticed, this is a law office, not a principal's office. I don't deal with idle gossip and cat fights. You may wish to reconsider. No, I'm reconsidering. In all honesty, I don't think we're a good match."

"Thank you for your time, Henry." I didn't bother shaking his hand. I left and headed for my car in the parking lot behind the building. I sat for several minutes and considered my options for the rest of the day. I could take out the Yellow Pages and try to find another lawyer or call Sofia for advice, or I could conduct my own investigation. That last option excited me.

I needed to take charge and get actively involved. Throughout my teaching years, I had been told my research and organizational skills were exceptional. It was time to put them to work outside the classroom. I leaned over and grabbed the telephone book from the back seat. I flipped to the Investigators section and skimmed through the list. Four of the six listings had 800 numbers. I focused on the remaining two with local numbers. Nickel City Security caught my eye. When I checked the address, I recognized the street. One block behind the ReCareering office. I left the downtown area and headed toward the south end of the city. I decided to drive a bit farther and park in the plaza rather than using the back alley which separated my office from Nickel City Security. Under normal circumstances, it would have made more sense to use the alleyway, but I wasn't taking any chances. I didn't want to run into any of the other tenants or anyone else poking around back there. It would be a while before I could walk confidently in that back alley.

I took my time walking to the office, located at the far end of the plaza. I opened the door to a very untidy and crowded outer office. Boxes were piled on the floor, and groups of files lay on chairs, desks, and cabinets. I wrinkled my nose as I caught whiffs of stale cigarette smoke, French fries, and aftershave. The door to the inner office was closed, but I could hear someone talking in the other room. I knocked tentatively on the door, and a male voice bellowed, "I'm on the phone. Give me a few minutes."

One chair had several files on it, so I gathered the files and sat down. As I went to place them on the desk, I noticed the name on the topmost file: Anna May Godfrey. My heart pounded, and my hand trembled. It would be so easy to stuff the file under my jacket and leave. No one had seen me come, and it could be days before the investigator realized the file was missing. I debated the issue for a few more seconds, and as I rose to leave, the door opened, and a short, balding middle-aged man emerged.

He managed a tight smile and offered his hand. “Hi. Jim Nelson.” He waved his hand. “Sorry about the mess. My receptionist quit last week, and I’ve been manning the office solo since then.” He noticed the files I was holding. “Here, let me take them. Sorry, I had to use all the chairs. I have my own system. I know. Bizarre and unorganized, but it works for me.” He frowned as he glanced at the folders and then placed them on the desk. “What can I do for you, pretty lady? Need to have a special man followed?

“No, nothing like that. My name is Gilda Greco, and I would like to hire you to conduct a full background and criminal check.”

“Sounds interesting.”

“It’s a woman,” I blurted out.

“That’s fine. You can swing anyway you want. I don’t pass judgment.”

I tried again. “I want you to investigate Anna May Godfrey. I want to know everything about her personal habits, financial affairs, and any criminal involvement. I think she may be involved in a murder case, and I need to clear up a few questions.”

“You think she murdered someone?”

“Yes. And I know you can get that information for me very quickly.”

“You saw the file.”

“I didn’t open it.”

He breathed a sigh of relief.

“I am assuming that Carrie Ann hired you and was coming over here the other day to pick up this file. I have a strange feeling she didn’t make it here.”

He shrugged but said nothing.

"That file incriminates Anna May, and you're afraid to hand it over to the police."

"I'm not afraid of Anna May or anyone else for that matter," he said, leaning back in his chair. "I like living on the edge. As for incriminating Anna May, that is subject to interpretation."

"What did you say when the police called the other day?"

"No one came."

"That's odd." How could they have missed this office?

Jim smiled and shook his head. "This office is well hidden, and people tend to forget it exists. That suits me and my clients just fine. We don't need the exposure." He raised his eyebrows. "And who would expect a classy interior designer to visit a seedy, rundown investigator's office?"

Despite appearances, he was sharp and on the ball. He was not about to volunteer information, but he would co-operate with the police.

"Thank you for your time, Jim." I didn't give him any time to respond. I got into my car and took out my phone. I called the police department and asked for Carlo Fantin's office.

He answered after one ring. "Fantin here."

"Hello, Carlo. It's Gilda. I've been doing my own investigating—"

"What! I told you to get a lawyer."

"I tried to get a lawyer. I visited Henry Keenan, and I wasn't impressed. Neither was he."

Carlo laughed. "That doesn't surprise me considering his connection with the Godfreys."

"What connection?"

"You mean you didn't know that Henry was Anna May's godfather?"

I couldn't help giggling. "Now I know why he was so incensed when I suggested that Anna May might be a suspect in this case."

"You did *what*?"

"I'm glad it didn't work out. If it had, I would never have found the file on Anna May."

"What file? What have you been up to?

"I'll start from the beginning, and I would appreciate it if you would save your comments for the end."

"Yes, Miss Greco."

I gave him a quick summary of what had happened at Nickel City Security.

"Did Jim see Carrie Ann before she died?"

"No, she was on her way to see him after she spoke to me. She never made it."

"What else did Mr. Nelson say?"

"Not much. I gathered he wasn't going to share the file with me. But he might if he an officer shows up with a search warrant." I couldn't resist adding, "It's too bad your officer didn't visit him last week."

"We'll move on that today." Carlo switched to detective mode. "I have a bone to pick with you. Why didn't you tell me that Jean Taylor dropped by your office the night Carrie Ann died?

I was caught off guard. "I didn't remember till later and, after all that's gone on, I didn't get a chance to tell you. I'm not sure when she was there."

"Between seven and seven-thirty," Carlo said. "When I called Karen Anderson last night, she mentioned seeing Jean as she left the bank on the day

Carrie Ann died. Jean stood there with a plant. Karen offered to put the plant in her office, but Jean insisted on giving it to you personally."

I chose my words carefully. "She gave it to me after yoga class."

"Hmm. I wonder why she didn't mention her visit when I called last week. I've left several messages on her machine, but she hasn't called back." He changed the subject. "I'm sorry about last night. I shouldn't have spoken so harshly to you. I appreciate this tip, but leave the investigating to us. It's too dangerous for you to get any more involved."

"I'll try to stay out of it, but it's frustrating to sit back and let someone set me up time and time again."

"If it's any consolation to you, no one here thinks you had anything to do with either murder. And to make sure that no more questions would be asked, I found two people who could vouch for you when you took off and went to the island."

"Who are you talking about?"

"I got the address for Karen's cottage when I spoke with her last night," he explained. "This morning, I left at five-thirty and drove out there. I walked along the boardwalk for a while and met up with an older couple who identified your picture."

"What picture?"

"The one on your business card." He added, "They saw you between eight and nine o'clock on Tuesday morning. There's no way you could have been anywhere near the restaurant when Melly Grace was killed. That's enough to put an end to any suspicions about your involvement."

My eyes welled with tears as I heard the relief in

his voice. I couldn't believe he went to all that trouble for me. "I don't what to say, Carlo. Thanks—"

"You're welcome. And please leave the investigation to me."

"I just want to share one theory with you."

"Gilda!" Carlo expelled a loud sigh.

"Hear me out. Either two women are involved or a man and a woman."

"Hmm. Interesting. Continue."

"There's no way one woman could physically lift either Carrie Ann or Melly Grace and arrange them so neatly in the Dumpster. And very few men would bother fussing with hair and scarves."

"Any other suspects in mind besides Anna May?"

"That's where I'm stuck. Anna May couldn't do it on her own, but she is capable of bullying someone else into helping her. She hasn't changed much since high school."

"What about Jenny Marie?"

"I don't think she has the stomach for it. I think that the file will reveal a number of unsavory characters who have dealings with Anna May. I wouldn't put it past her to hire one of these people."

"Now, why would Anna May be involved with unsavory characters? Don't you think that's a bit far-fetched?"

"Not based on what I've heard about her company's financial problems."

"Where are you getting all this information?"

"Well, it's…uh…I've heard…uh…it's second-hand information that Sofia has given me."

"And where did Sofia get this information?"

"At Curves." He needed to know about the leak,

but I didn't want to come right out and say it.

He laughed. "Gossip from Curves. I'm surprised that you would even consider it."

"Get the file and check it out. Something will come of it, I am certain of that."

"I will do that. But promise me that you'll stop investigating."

"I won't do any more investigating today. That I can promise you."

"Smart, beautiful, and stubborn. You haven't changed a bit, Gilda Greco." He lowered his voice. "After all of this is over, I'm taking you out to dinner."

Chapter 10

I switched to an Enya CD and opened the car window, breathing in the crisp, autumn air as I hummed along to the hauntingly beautiful lyrics. I was in no rush to get back to the condo. Sofia was moving her stuff over, and I knew she would be rearranging furniture in the guest bedroom. I didn't like being around when she fussed like that.

I drove without any destination in mind. Before long, I realized that I had reached my mother's street at the west end of the city. Gatchell. Sudbury's Little Italy. It was still a working class community, with smaller lots containing houses built before the 1940s. Many of the homes had been restored by the Italian immigrants who had settled the area. I was surprised to find myself heading toward my childhood home, but then I realized that's where I went when I had good news to share.

Growing up as an only child, I had a very close bond with both my parents. As my mother's health became more precarious and fragile, my father and I started to shield and protect her from any unpleasantness. After his death, I continued to protect her as much as I could. I know my disastrous early marriage had affected her, and I tried not to upset her with any other news. I had even kept my brief cancer scare a secret. I had confided in my Guelph friends. I saw no point of involving my mother or any of the Sudbury relatives.

I wanted to reassure my mother and talk about Carlo. I took special delight in seeing those dark, hooded eyes light up, and the drawn face become more animated and alive. It reminded me of lighting up the Christmas tree for the first time in December. It didn't happen too often, but when it did, it was memorable.

I pulled into the driveway and got out of my car. As I opened the door, I was greeted by one of my favorite childhood aromas, a combination of fresh tomato sauce and fragrant dessert, cooking and baking together. I called out, and my mother appeared at the door. She smiled and hugged me close. "Something good has happened. I can feel it in my bones."

"I have a surprise for you."

"You've found someone!" She clapped her hands. "We'll have him over to dinner tonight…no, tomorrow would be better. I need more time to prepare. I'll get Amelia and Sofia to help."

"Hold your horses, Ma. At this rate, you'll have me married before Sunday. Let me come in and sit down before you start calling the priest."

She nodded and led the way into the kitchen. She grabbed a place mat and started to set a place for me. "You'll stay for supper. The sauce is almost ready. I've made meatballs. We'll have the linguine."

I shook my head. After all these years, my mother still insisted on treating me like a guest and serving me. "That would be lovely, Ma. Just the two of us. We haven't done that for a while."

She busied herself around the kitchen and would occasionally give me an expectant look.

"It's Carlo. Carlo Fantin. He wants to have dinner with me as soon as the investigation is over.

She raised her eyebrows. "He doesn't think you had anything to do with the murders?"

"He never did. Everything is just too obvious. Whoever is setting me up is doing a very poor job of it." I told her about his drive to Manitoulin Island.

She frowned. "But why are you being set up? Who would do such a thing?"

"I don't know," I shrugged. "No one does."

She made the sign of the cross. "I agree with Amelia. I think there will be another murder and soon. I'm so glad Sofia is staying with you. At least, you will have an alibi."

"I don't think she needs to stay with me for too long. She has her own life, and I'm sure she'll want to move back to her house when Andrew returns from Italy." I tried, but I couldn't recall the last time I had seen Andrew.

My mother shook her head. "It's not about the estate. Andrew is never coming back to her."

"What are you saying?"

"Sofia and Andrew have separated," she explained. "After you gave her that million-dollar gift, he moved back to Italy. I hear he's found himself a much younger woman to keep him company."

Unbelievable! Sofia had spoken a great deal about her twenty-fifth wedding anniversary party coming up next spring. I remember one lunch where all she did was discuss the menu. How could she not say anything?

"Did you think that marriage would last?" my mother asked. "I didn't think it would last a year."

"They had to get married that summer. Don't you

remember?"

"Of course I remember. I also remember that Sofia lost that baby after one month of marriage. He wanted to leave then."

"Sofia didn't want to hurt her parents. You know how Uncle Paolo and Aunt Amelia can be."

"It wasn't working, and everyone knew it. They could even have gotten an annulment at that time. Monsignor would have helped them."

"This doesn't make any sense," I said. "Sofia stayed in that marriage to please her parents."

"No, Sofia stayed in that marriage to please herself. She liked being married, and she didn't want the single life." Her eyes bored into mine.

I felt myself reddening. I didn't want to talk about my own walk down the aisle.

"I was upset when you ended your own marriage." She paused. "But you didn't have any other choice. I would have done the same."

Another shock. "You never told me that before."

My mother spread out her hands. "You didn't give me a chance. I still remember that call I got from you. You had already left Sudbury and made it clear you weren't coming back. And Luigi had taken off for God knows where." She shuddered. "He *had* to leave. No way could he stay here with that problem."

"Luigi doesn't have a problem. He's gay, that's all."

"That's enough." She sighed. "I still don't understand why you didn't figure that out before you got married."

There were so many signs, but I chose to ignore them. At age twenty-nine, I had too many bridesmaid dresses in my closet. I was tired of waiting for Mr. Right, so I decided to settle for Mr. Right Now. Luigi Battista and I taught at the same school. We were both introverts and loved to spend our leisure time reading, going to movies and theatre, hiking and cross-country skiing. He also felt the pressure to marry, but thought he could have his cake and eat it too. He married me, but continued to seek the attention of other men. One man in particular, Claude Noel de Tilly, wanted a more exclusive relationship, and Luigi gave in to him.

I managed a smile. "You're right I should have known better."

She came over and hugged me. "It's over." She frowned. "Does Carlo know about Luigi?"

"It hasn't gotten to that stage yet." I was still embarrassed about that brief period in my life and didn't want to discuss it with him or anyone else for that matter. But I must admit, I didn't mind today's talk with my mother. It had cleared the air. I decided to take a page out of Sofia's book and change the subject. "Sofia put up with a lot from Andrew. All that philandering and heavy drinking. And to top it all, he delighted in putting her down in public. I couldn't stand for such behavior."

My mother shrugged. "Sofia likes being married, and she's not too crazy about being on her own."

"She's in denial. Just the other day, she was telling me that the four of them might go skiing in Quebec during the Christmas break." I thought of my nephews. How would they react to the divorce? "What about the boys? Do they know what's going on?"

My mother shrugged. "They've found girlfriends in the States, and they're not planning to come up until the spring. Sofia knows all of this, but like you said, she's in denial."

"I must say she's put on a very good front."

"So do you, Gilda. You girls don't fool us for a minute. Amelia and I always know when something isn't right." She sighed. "Enough about Sofia! I want to hear about Carlo."

"Well, there's not much to tell. We had a very pleasant telephone conversation today, and I gave…I think he has another suspect in mind." I decided to stretch the truth and tell my mother that Carlo suspected Anna May. She would be horrified if she knew I had visited a private investigator.

"Who?"

"Anna May."

"The sister? I hope not. I still remember how much pride Mrs. Godfrey took in those girls. Anna May was so pretty and plump." My mother's eyes filled with concern. "And then she lost all that weight and became skinny, too skinny."

"She's more than plump now," I said. "I think she's put on at least fifty pounds since high school, and it's not a healthy weight for her."

Before my mother could answer, the timer rang, and she removed a perfectly formed sponge cake from the oven. She placed it next to the other two that were cooling on the side cupboard.

"What's with all the sponge cakes? Are you planning to freeze them?"

"No, these are for Sunday's tea at the church. Amelia, Rosa, and Maria are also baking them. Later tonight, Sofia's coming to wrap these cakes and place them in those fancy hat boxes that she likes to make."

"I saw her working on them the other day. I still don't understand the concept."

"A few years ago Sofia saw one of those special Oprah shows around Christmas time. One of the gifts was a sponge cake wrapped and placed in a fancy hat box. A woman in New York makes a bundle sending these cakes to people. Last year, Sofia thought it would be a good idea if we introduced these cakes at the Autumn Tea. We made ten of them, and everyone loved them. This year, we'll have forty of them."

Sofia could give Martha Stewart and Nigella Lawson a run for their money. "I don't know why she's never tried catering or interior design or some other creative venture. She would have done very well."

"She's happy staying at home and taking care of her family," my mother said.

"Andrew's departure is going to throw a monkey wrench into her life plans," I said. "And Peter and Paul won't be spending too much time up here either. Ready or not, she's got an empty nest to deal with."

"Like the rest of the mothers in the world, she'll adapt and learn to cope." My mother sat across from me. "Enough talking. Let's eat now."

I had been so intent on the conversation I hadn't noticed that my mother had made the salad, finished setting the table, and prepared two steaming plates of pasta and meatballs.

I savored every bite of my favorite comfort meal. At the end, I turned to my mother and said, "It never tasted this good. What did you do differently?"

She smiled. "I may add more or less of a particular spice or ingredient, but my recipes haven't changed much over the years."

While that was true, there was something else that my mother shared with Sofia and all the other foodies. They cook with love and passion. That's what makes the difference. I could make any of these meals, but I don't enjoy cooking. It's a task, another to-do item on my list. And I never focus exclusively on whatever is cooking or baking in the oven. I'm reading a book, working on the computer, or talking on the phone while I'm preparing a meal. Thank God for timers!

"And now for dessert."

I groaned. "I'm stuffed. I couldn't possible take another bite of anything."

She went downstairs to her large, well-stocked institutional-sized freezer. She returned with an aluminum foil wrapped log and proceeded to cut generous pieces of her Neapolitan ice cream cake. She smiled mischievously. "I think you can manage a few more bites."

"You know I can't resist that cake." I tugged at my waistline. "I'm glad I'm going to my yoga class tonight."

"Yes, it's good for you, and you need it."

"Are you saying I'm too fat?"

"Now, don't start that nonsense with me. If anything, I think you're too thin. I don't know anything about this exercise class, but I know you enjoy going there with your friends. That's what I think is so good about it."

After we finished eating, I put the dishes in the dishwasher and washed some of the larger pots and pans while my mother tidied and prepared the kitchen for tonight's Cake Fest. As I scrubbed the pots, I dreamed of my future date with Carlo.

Chapter 11

I made a quick stop at the condo to change my clothes. When I went into my bedroom, I found a note pinned to my mirror. *I'm picking up a few things at the mall and then going to your mom's. See you later. Sofia.* Just as well. Part of me wanted to bring up her marital problems, but another part didn't want to know the details. I would wait until Sofia told me about Andrew. At some point, she would have to admit to the breakdown of her marriage.

I changed into my black yoga pants and *Life is Good* T-shirt. I threw on a matching jacket and headed toward the studio. My heart fluttered as I drove into the parking lot. While I worried about seeing Jean so soon after that unpleasant telephone conversation, I looked forward to a relaxing yoga session and reconnecting with my friends. When I got inside, I found Erin Haskell, Jean's partner, huddled with Sarah Clarkson, one of the part-time yoga instructors. They appeared to be arguing, though their voices were low. I went into the main exercise room and searched for Adele and Laura. They waved me over.

I could feel myself becoming even calmer as I approached. Adele and Laura were my best childhood friends. After elementary school, our paths had diverged. In spite of the winding roads we had taken, we had still managed to connect several times a year.

Since returning to Sudbury, I made an effort to meet with them more often.

After I had put my yoga mat down, Adele spoke, "How are you doing?"

Laura moved in closer and patted my shoulder.

"Much better. I'm sorry I didn't return your calls."

"Not to worry," Laura said.

"What's going on?" I asked. The other students were all whispering and pointing at Erin and Sarah.

"Jean took off last Friday and hasn't been seen since," Adele whispered. "Sarah and Erin covered most of her classes, but they still had to cancel some of them. Jean hasn't called, and her cell phone is off. Erin is not a happy camper. She'll be leading tonight's class."

Laura groaned. "We're in for a killer session tonight. My abs will be feeling it for days."

While I welcomed the change this evening, I preferred Jean's calmer, more soothing sessions that included twenty minutes of meditation. Erin was also a Pilates instructor and liked to include abdominal work in her yoga sessions. I cleared my throat. "Does anyone know where Jean went?"

"She left a message saying she had to get out of town for a while. Sarah thinks she might have gone to her aunt's cottage near North Bay. That's where she goes to unwind. But she doesn't stay there for more than a couple of days. It's been six days and no sign of her yet." Laura frowned. "But she went alone. I wonder if she's having marital problems."

I perked up. "She went alone?"

Laura nodded. "One of the ladies saw her husband at the grocery store yesterday."

My mind spun with possibilities. Jean had probably

left after speaking with me Friday morning. I wonder where she was when Melly Grace was killed Sunday morning. And what about her husband's whereabouts? While I longed to sneak out and call Carlo, I knew that would just arouse suspicion. If I waited, I could gather more information about Jean and her whereabouts.

Erin walked by us and made her way to the front of the room. She managed a smile. "Sorry, folks. We've had a bit of a snafu this week. But let's not let that get in our way." She took several deep breaths. "Let us begin. Lie on your backs—"

Erin did not revert to her Pilates moves; instead she guided us through a calm, well-structured class. There was something immensely comforting in the precision of her instructions: "*Inhale and raise both arms straight out from the shoulders parallel to the floor with the palms facing down"... "Exhale slowly while turning the torso to the left"... "One more long, luxurious inhalation, one more complete exhalation.*"

I loved listened to the soft, soothing Sanskrit names—*balasana, garudasana, tadasana, savasana*—that described the different poses. Much more interesting than simply hearing child pose, eagle pose, mountain pose, or corpse pose.

Erin might have been stressed earlier, but she radiated calm at the end. She bowed to all of us. "*Namaste*."

"That wasn't bad at all," Laura said.

"It's almost as soothing as Jean's sessions," Adele added. "Though last week, she wasn't at her best."

"What do you mean?" I was surprised to hear Adele criticize Jean.

Adele's eyes widened. "Don't you remember how

flustered she got during the sun salutations? She kept doing all the poses on the same side. And she didn't include a single Downward Dog pose. That's so unlike her."

"She left the room for a good ten minutes," Laura added.

I thought back to last Wednesday night, but could remember none of this.

Adele and Laura laughed. "You were out of it, too. You went through the entire session in some kind of trance. And afterward, all you could talk about was the open house." Adele winced. "Sorry! I didn't mean to bring it up."

"It's all right, Adele. I don't remember any of this stuff going on with Jean. I guess I was too wound up." I changed the subject. "So, are we on for Tim Hortons?"

Both women nodded enthusiastically. We took several minutes to freshen up and then walked over to Tim Hortons. We often joked that we should be having herbal tea, but somehow the aroma of coffee always won us over. I was glad to see that the restaurant was not too crowded. I was hoping to learn more about Jean and didn't want anyone else overhearing our conversation.

We ordered our coffees and made our way to a table near the window. Adele and Laura glanced at each other and then focused their attention on me. I could tell they were curious about the events of the last week. I gave them a brief, edited version. They were relieved to learn that the police did not consider me a suspect, but were surprised to hear that Sofia had moved in with me.

"How long is she staying?" Adele asked.

"A week or two," I said. "I can't see her staying

any longer than that."

Adele and Laura exchanged glances but said nothing.

"Spill it." It wasn't like my two oldest friends to not offer an opinion.

"It's just that you two were never that close," said Adele. "You had different sets of friends."

Laura piped in, "And you weren't in each other's bridal parties."

"Sofia was pregnant with twins," I said. "I couldn't ask her to put on a bridesmaid dress."

"But she could have asked you when she got married," Laura said. "You were single and *not* pregnant."

It still rankled a bit, even after all these years. While we hadn't been close, I did expect to be part of Sofia's bridal party. And I know my parents, Aunt Amelia and Uncle Paolo were very upset with Sofia. Angry words had been tossed about, and I remember being so grateful that I was leaving for teachers' college shortly afterward.

"Did she ever talk about it with you?" Laura asked.

Thinking back, I don't remember seeing much of Sofia during the early years of her marriage. She spent the holidays with Andrew's family, and whenever our paths crossed, there were lots of people around. We didn't get close until I won the lottery.

Laura changed the subject. "I wonder when Jean is coming back."

Good! We were talking about Jean again. I knew Laura and Adele would have the goods—if there were any—on her.

"It sounds like she hasn't taken too many days off

in the past. As far as I'm concerned, she's entitled to time off." Adele yawned and glanced at her watch.

"I hope she's not having marital problems. That would be so hard on her, especially with Michael being so young." I thought of all the students I had taught. Whenever there was a divorce in the family, the children started acting up in class, and some even turned to drugs and alcohol for comfort.

"Once a teacher, always a teacher," Laura teased. "I think she'd be more concerned about her husband's reaction. Michael Senior didn't do too well after Carrie Ann left him."

"Let's hope he doesn't sink into another depression," Adele said. "Back then, he was down for almost two years."

"Wasn't there anyone around who could help him?" I wondered about the man who had married Carrie Ann.

"People did try, but he wouldn't let them in," Adele said. "Only Jean and Mrs. Godfrey were able to get through to him. It took a while, but Jean didn't give up and he finally married her."

"It was good of Mrs. Godfrey to get involved." I wasn't that surprised to hear that she had helped her ex-son-in-law get back on his feet. She did not have a single judgmental bone in her body and gave everyone the benefit of the doubt.

"She was a good soul," Laura said. "Carrie Ann and Jenny Marie are a lot like her. Now, Anna May is another story."

We laughed.

"Anna May used to be like her," Adele said. "I could never get over how much she changed once she got to high school. She lost all that baby fat and her pleasant personality. I think it was all those diet pills she took. And I wouldn't be surprised if she got into some heavy-duty drugs."

I had also heard the rumors about the pills and wondered about the drugs. While I had few memories of Anna May during elementary school, I could vividly recall her mean girl antics during her high school days. She would not hesitate to malign any girl who attracted the attention of her boyfriend of the week. "I guess being thin was that important to her." I thought of some of my former students who also dabbled in drugs. A slippery slope and very few emerged unscathed from their experiences.

"It got her a lot of male attention," Laura said. "But the guys never stuck around too long. Even that husband of hers took off on her after only a year of marriage."

For the second time today, I recalled my own short-lived marriage. I decided to bring the conversation back to Jean. "Those Godfrey women weren't too lucky in love. But I heard that Carrie Ann and Michael Taylor were still on friendly terms."

"That's all Jean's doing," Adele said. "On his own, Michael wouldn't even talk to Carrie Ann. He carried a grudge for the longest time. But Jean wasn't about to give up her connection with the Godfreys. She owes them too much."

"What connection?" I asked.

"I keep forgetting that you've been away for so many years," Adele said. "I'll give you the short version of Jean's life. Mrs. Godfrey practically raised Jean after her mother died in a car accident. The

Merriweathers lived on the same street as the Godfreys, so Jean could go back and forth between the two homes. She moved in during her teen years. Her father had remarried, and she didn't get along with her stepmother."

No wonder Jean was so upset. The Godfreys were family to her, the only family she had really known.

Laura continued the story. "Jean went to Western—just like all the Godfrey girls—and then she came back to Sudbury. She worked as an addiction counselor but burned out after a couple of years. She took up yoga and found she enjoyed it. She got herself certified, and Mrs. Godfrey and her father gave her the money to start her own studio."

I leaned closer to Laura. "What about Michael? How did she get involved with him?"

"Jean had a king-size crush on him while he was married to Carrie Ann," Adele said. "After he got divorced, she brought soup and casseroles over to his place. She made sure he took his meds and got him hooked on yoga. They went out for almost ten years before he popped the question."

The puzzle pieces were starting to fall into place. Michael Taylor must have been devastated when he found out that Carrie Ann had died. And Jean must have been devastated to learn that he still cared so much for his ex-wife. Or maybe Michael was feeling guilty about killing Carrie Ann. Jean would have picked up on his negative feelings. She was intuitive and seemed to know when others were hurting.

"Earth to Gilda. Earth to Gilda." Adele and Laura were waving frantically in my face.

"Sorry! I was just thinking about Carrie Ann and

how—" I paused. I didn't want to share any of my theories with them. I longed to get home and call Carlo. And then I remembered that I had already spoken with him this morning. I would wait until tomorrow.

"Omigod! You're thinking of her dead body in that Dumpster." Adele put her hand on top of mine. "We didn't mean to bring that up."

They had just reminded me of that scene, but I was okay with it now. I was more concerned about finding the killer. Two women had died unnecessarily and I wanted justice done. I glanced at my watch. "It's been a long day. I'm beat and ready for bed. I've got two days of workshops ahead of me."

"You're still going ahead with them?" Laura's eyebrows shot up.

"There's no reason to cancel. I'm ready to move on." I hugged both of them and headed toward my car.

Chapter 12

Thursday, October 27, 2011

The alarm woke me up the next morning. I groaned when I saw it was only six-thirty, but I needed to get up early if I wanted to get everything done. First things first. I would send off an email to Carlo. I had drafted it last night. I'm not at my best in the morning and could accidentally send a message filled with grammatical and spelling errors.

I gave the message one last glance before sending it. *Hi Carlo, Hope that all is well. I thought you might be interested in the latest regarding Jean Taylor. Last night, I went to my yoga class and heard that Jean has been out of town since last Friday morning. No one seems to know where she is, but one of the other instructors thinks she might be at her aunt's cottage near North Bay. Her husband is still in town. Gilda*

I took my time getting ready. I decided on business casual—black pinstripe pants with a black sweater and my new purple leather jacket. I added a multicolored scarf and fussed with it for a while. I had thirty minutes to kill before leaving for the school. I made myself a smoothie and sat down to drink it.

"You're up early." Sofia's voice carried from her bedroom. "Do you have an appointment?"

"I'm going out to St. Benedict's for the grade ten

career workshops."

She cast me a questioning look. "I thought you canceled."

"No reason to do that. I'm ready to get back into the swing of things. I'll be doing more workshops tomorrow at Marymount College. I think I'll start going into the office on Monday." I couldn't help smiling as I watched the changing expressions on Sofia's face.

Sofia folded her arms across her chest. "What's going on? Yesterday, you were a mess."

"Well, for starters I discovered a file on Anna May."

"And you waited this long to tell me." She scowled at me.

"I haven't seen you since yesterday morning."

She waved her hand impatiently. "Tell me everything from the beginning."

I gave her a condensed version of what had occurred yesterday.

"I'm sorry about Henry Keenan. I didn't realize he was Anna May's godfather." She shuddered. "I can't believe you went to an investigator's office by yourself. I hope you didn't share that with your mother."

"Of course not, Sofia."

"I wish you would have called me before you visited Jim Nelson." Her eyes narrowed to slits. "I would have come with you and taken that file."

"I considered it, but—"

"Took too long to decide and then Jim appeared." She finished the sentence and added, "It would have helped to know what you're up against."

"What do you mean?"

"Carrie Ann must have had a good reason for

investigating her own sister. Anna May might have been involved in some kind of criminal activity."

I had woken up feeling very positive, and now Sofia was dampening my spirits. "I'm sure that Carlo will let me know if there's any cause for concern."

"His priority is solving those two murders," Sofia said. "And another thing. I don't think you should have sent Carlo that email about Jean Taylor. That could come back and bite you."

"What do you mean?"

"Do you want another one of those calls from Jean?"

"How would she find that out?" And then I remembered about the chatty policemen's wives.

"What's done is done. Just be careful from now on." She made a face at my smoothie. "All this murder talk is making me hungry. I'll need something more substantial. Pancakes. That'll do it. Do you want any?"

"No, I've got to be going. I want to meet with Mirella before class starts."

Sofia yawned. "How about a movie tomorrow night? I'd like to see the new George Clooney film."

"Sure. Have a good day. I'll see you later." Tonight, Sofia would be having another Cake Fest, and I would be having a nice dinner with Mirella and her crowd. Our paths wouldn't cross until tomorrow. Just as well.

It didn't take long to reach St. Benedict's. I reported to the main office and was pleased to find a pretty young student waiting for me. She accompanied me to Mirella Rossi's classroom. Mirella and I had attended teachers' college together, and we had kept in touch through Christmas cards and occasional visits. I hoped to see more of her now that I had moved back to Sudbury.

Mirella hugged me tightly. “Are you sure you’re up to this today?”

“I’m fine. I’ll just take a few minutes to set up.” I had brought my own laptop, projector and extension cord along with the handouts in a weekender bag. I started to set up on one of the front tables.

“Always so organized! You put the rest of us to shame.” She lowered her voice. “I need to warn you. The kids are excited about you being here, but not because of your presentation. They know all about your lottery win and connection to the two murders. I’ve told them to stick to the subject of careers, but they may try sneaking in other questions.”

“I know what adolescents are like. I don’t mind their questions.”

Mirella waved her pen. “I’ll be sitting at the back. If things get out of hand, I’ll step in.”

I started to complain, but then thought better of it. I couldn’t very well tell her to back off in her own classroom. The warning bell rang, and the students started to file into the classroom. Mirella greeted them, and many of them eyed me with interest. I was fresh meat.

I finished setting up and testing the equipment. I made my way to the back of the room as “O Canada” started to play on the public address system. A short prayer and lengthy announcements followed. The students started to fidget, and Mirella had to reprimand a few of them. I thought back to my own teaching days. Why did administrators feel the need to overwhelm the students with trivia first thing in the morning?

Mirella waited until everyone settled down before speaking. "This morning, we have a special guest with us. A few years ago, more than we care to remember, Gilda Greco and I attended teachers' college at Western. We met in the Business Education class and have been friends ever since. Gilda started her teaching career at Marymount College and then moved to southern Ontario. She has taught in different schools throughout Halton, Dufferin Peel, and Wellington counties. As many of you know, she won Lotto 649. She has just opened her ReCareering office and will be offering her career counseling services to the Sudbury community. We are very fortunate to have her with us today. She will be talking to you about Career Exploration."

I made my way to the front as polite applause accompanied me. Instead of starting with the PowerPoint presentation, I decided to turn the tables on these fifteen-year-olds and put them on the hot seat. "Good morning, everyone. I'm very happy to be here. I've been out of the classroom for almost two years and loving every minute of it." I smiled at the puzzled expressions on their faces and relaxed. "I left teaching forty-three days after I won the nineteen million dollars and did everything I always wanted to do. I racked up thousands of air miles travelling through five of the seven continents. I intend to visit Africa next year. I paid off the credit card debts and mortgages of my friends and relatives and gave to my favorite charities. And then I got bored. That's right. I got bored spending money. So, I decided to explore different career directions and ended up taking an online Career Development Practitioner program offered through

Conestoga College."

The students were listening to me intently, and I knew they were waiting to hear about the aborted Open House and the murders. When I made eye contact with Mirella, I saw her frowning and nervously glancing around the room. I took a deep breath and continued. "I want each of you to close your eyes and imagine winning nineteen million dollars, but with one catch. You won't have access to the money until age twenty. What plans would you make today if you knew that you would be rich in five years' time? I'll give you a couple of minutes to think about it, and then we'll go around the room. I want to hear your answers."

I could feel the tension in the room. One student got up and went to speak to Mirella who listened and then shook her head. I smiled. The girl had hoped to leave the room for a prolonged washroom or smoke break. Not too much had changed since I had left the classroom.

I waited several minutes and then nodded toward the first student on my left. She spoke about her dream of becoming a doctor and working in developing countries. I jotted down notes as we went around the room. There were close to thirty students in the room, and many of them spoke of very lofty goals that included attending prestigious American universities. Lots of doctors, lawyers, CEOs, and other professionals in the group. A few wanted to become rock stars, models and other entertainers. Two students talked about dropping out and doing nothing until they got their money.

I launched into PowerPoint, asking questions throughout the presentation. I also included some handouts that required their input. We didn't get through all the slides and handouts. The bell rang, and the students started to get up.

"Sit down everyone. We're not finished yet." Mirella made her way to the front of the classroom. "Thank you, Gilda, for coming today. You've given these students food for future thought. We hope to have you back soon." There was scattered clapping, and then the students quickly left the room.

"Sorry about that. I should have signaled you five minutes before the period ended. I must say I got caught up in your presentation. Lots of good stuff here." She pointed to the handouts which she had also filled out. "Do you need a break before the next group arrives?"

"No, thanks. I'll be fine."

The next class went smoothly, and I managed to show all the slides this time. Again, there was no time for questions. Afterward, I followed Mirella to the staff room. I reconnected with some friends from my early teaching years and met several of Mirella's younger colleagues.

Before the end of the lunch break, Mirella introduced me to Barb Patterson, the other Careers teacher. The younger woman shook my hand enthusiastically and talked a mile a minute about her challenging afternoon classes. I hid a smile. After twenty-five years of teaching, I figured I could handle one hundred and fifty minutes of high-energy students.

I stuck to the same agenda as the morning, but managed to finish with enough time for questions. While most of the questions centered on specific careers, one young man in the last period class stood and made direct eye contact with me as he spoke. "Who do you think murdered those women?"

I heard Barb Patterson gasp. "John Bruni, that question is inappropriate. You're putting Miss Greco in a very difficult position."

Over thirty pairs of eyes were fixed on me. I could ignore the question, but decided to answer it. "It's all right, Ms. Patterson. I'll answer John's question." I smiled at the young man. "The police are handling the investigation, and I am confident they will get to the bottom of it."

John shook his head. "They're stumped. My uncle's a cop. I overheard him talking on the phone. He thinks a professional was involved. Fantin's hoping that—"

"That will be enough!" Barb raised her voice as the bell rang. The students left before she could say anything else.

I went over and hugged her. "It's all right, Barb. John was just curious. If I remember correctly, he talked about going into law enforcement. These two crimes must be very exciting for him."

Barb sniffed. "I specifically told them not to ask about the murders. I'm willing to bet that everyone in Mirella's classes cooperated."

"And so did everyone in your period four class."

Before Barb could answer, the P.A. interrupted with an announcement. "Would all fall coaches please come to the conference room. Our meeting will start in five minutes."

Barb groaned. "That's me. I'm sorry to leave you, Gilda, but—"

"Not to worry. I'll just collect my stuff and go see

Mirella." As I disconnected the projector and gathered my extra handouts, my head spun with possibilities. Anna May could have hired someone to do her dirty work. Hopefully, Jim Nelson's file would point to the killer. I met up with Mirella in the staff room. We sat and chatted for a while and then made our way to Apollo Restaurant where we enjoyed drinks and an excellent Greek dinner. We chatted about our travels, books, and the latest celebrity gossip.

Chapter 13

Friday, October 28, 2011

I hoped to touch base with Sofia, but she had already left for Curves by the time I woke up. We hardly saw each other, and should another murder take place, she wouldn't even be able to provide me with an alibi. This living arrangement didn't make any sense at all.

I took my time and had a leisurely breakfast. I didn't have to show up at Marymount College until ten o'clock, and I would be visiting only two morning classes. Afterward, I would check the mail and phone messages at the ReCareering office. I wanted to make sure everything was in place for Monday. As for the open house, well, that would be postponed indefinitely.

I left her a note.

Sofia,

I'm going to the office later this afternoon. I'll grab a quick bite and meet you at Silver City Cinema around 6:30.

Gilda

The classes at Marymount went off without a hitch. I stuck to the same agenda as the previous day, but I must admit I was bored by the end of the last session. I never liked teaching the same lesson twice in the same day. As for teaching it six times in a row, well that was beyond boredom. I decided not to linger too long at the school. I didn't recognize any of the teachers on staff. Some of my former colleagues had retired, and the rest had transferred to other schools within the board.

As I drove toward the ReCareering office, my heart started beating faster, and my hands gripped the steering wheel. I could drive right by, but if I put it off today it would be so much easier not to go in on Monday. When I arrived at the plaza, I took several deep breaths and sat quietly in the car. I grabbed the extra handouts and then entered the office. I was greeted by Sofia at the reception desk and the tantalizing aroma of roasting chicken.

"It's nice to see you smile like that again," Sofia said.

My eyes traveled around the room. Sofia's desk was clear with two neatly arranged piles of messages. Chairs and tables had been moved back and all signs of the open house had disappeared. "You didn't have to do all of this. I would have taken care of—"

"It's my job, remember. And I've been feeling a bit guilty about not spending time with you. This Autumn Tea is a lot of work." She sighed. "I'll be glad when it's all over."

"You can take Monday off if you want."

"I can't leave you alone on your first day!" Sofia's eyes widened. "I'll be fine once I get a good night's sleep, which I intend to do on Sunday."

"What time did you get in last night? Not that I'm checking up on you, but it seems like you've been putting in a lot of late nights." Having never organized a tea, I had no concept of the work involved. I couldn't imagine the other women in the CWL putting in those late hours. And that suited Sofia to a tee. From what my mother had told me, the Autumn Tea attracted women from as far away as North Bay. Afterward, Sofia received and enjoyed all the accolades.

Sofia shrugged. “I tried not to make too much noise.”

“I didn’t hear a sound,” I said. “It must have been past midnight.”

“After I packed the cakes into the boxes, Maria insisted on making another dessert. She gave me two generous pieces. We’ll have it later.”

“Thanks for making dinner, but I didn’t want you to go to any trouble. You’re my guest, and I should be cooking, not the other way around.”

“I love cooking. You don’t. End of story.”

The door opened, and Karen Anderson stepped inside. “Welcome back. Roast chicken. What a lovely aroma! I may just drop by Swiss Chalet on my way home.” She spoke directly to me. “I’m glad I caught you. Aaron and I are thinking of driving out to the cottage tomorrow.”

I rummaged through my purse and found the key. “Sometime next week, I would like to meet with you and your Realtor.”

“Take your time,” Karen said. “You’re just opening up here, and you’ve had a lot on your plate lately.” She added, “Feel free to spend some more weekends out there. After this weekend, we won’t be going again.”

I was grateful for the reprieve. I didn’t want to leave her hanging, but I also wanted to do more research on cottage prices and get Sofia’s opinion about the renovations.

"I'm glad to see you back. When are you planning…?" Karen didn't get a chance to finish her sentence.

"Stay out of my life, bitch!" A blast of cool air accompanied a loud, vaguely familiar voice.

Jean Taylor stood in the doorway, clutching a pair of scissors in her hands. The normally well-groomed yogini wore baggy gray sweats. Her blonde hair hung in disarray and looked like it hadn't been washed in days. I heard Karen gasp and saw Sofia move toward the door. Jean's angry eyes surveyed the room, and then she walked briskly toward the lucky bamboo plant she had given me last week. She savagely cut the stalks and threw them on the floor. "May you have decades of bad luck." She slammed the door and ran out.

"Unbelievable!" Karen curled her lips in disapproval. "I'm so glad Mrs. Godfrey is not alive to see this shocking display. That young woman needs help. I have half a mind to call her husband." Karen addressed me. "Do you want to get the police involved?"

"I don't know." Somehow, she must have heard about my call to Carlo.

"Why don't we think about this for a while?" Sofia said. "Let's give Jean time to cool off."

Karen frowned. "Fine, but if you don't feel comfortable phoning Carlo, I don't mind doing it." She glanced at her watch. "I need to get back. Have a good weekend. See you next week."

Every cell in my body buzzed in alarm. I now feared the gentle yogini who had taught me how to meditate. "What's Jean's problem? All she has to do is answer a few questions."

"Jean doesn't have a poker face. I'm sure Carlo could catch her in a lie." Sofia shook her head. "I still can't believe she's been practicing yoga for what ten…fifteen years."

I exhaled as a dreadful realization came over me. "Do you think she had anything to do with the murders?"

"Maybe not directly. But she might know who did."

"I wonder where her husband was when Melly Grace was killed?"

"They went to her aunt's cottage in North Bay," Sofia said. "I heard it at Curves this morning. He spent several days in North Bay and then came back to Sudbury late Tuesday night. Jean got back yesterday. Her aunt corroborated the story."

None of this made any sense. If Jean and Michael had alibis, there was no need for all this drama. Unless the aunt was covering for them. Knowing Jean, she could not handle the subterfuge. Everything about her life was an open book. She had no secrets, and she refused to keep them for others.

The oven timer rang, and Sofia headed toward the kitchen. She called out, "I'll finish making the salad and setting the table. You might want to check through the messages and call the ones I've highlighted. They sound keen."

I checked through the smaller pile of messages and zeroed in on the interested clients. I called and left messages on their machines. Thankfully, no one was home. I wasn't in career counselor mode.

I decided to clean up the mess that Jean had left. As I made my way to the utility closet, I overheard

Sofia whispering to someone on her cell phone. "No, I told you I can't leave her! You should be able to deal with it yourself…I don't know why you need me there…No, and that's final."

I was tempted to tell Sofia to go to the church, but I didn't want to be alone tonight.

I got the broom and went back and swept the area clean. I dropped the stalks in the garbage can. Jean had not destroyed the pretty glass container filled with stones. The glass would have stuck to the carpet and made it difficult to clean. I took it over to Sofia. "Do you want this glass container?"

"I have no use for it, but one of the other CWL ladies might want it. Leave it near the front. I'll put it in my car when we leave." She pointed to the table and bowed. "Dinner is served, madam."

The table was set with a royal blue damask tablecloth, cloth napkins and white dishes. As I took in the large casserole dish with roast chicken and potatoes, I realized how I hungry I was.

We sat down and ate companionably. After we finished eating the chicken and salad, Sofia produced two small bowls filled with apple crisp and topped with scoops of vanilla frozen yogurt.

"When did Maria start making apple crisp?" I thought of the lovable, but grossly overweight, woman who could eat half a cake in one sitting. It wasn't like her to bake with oats and other healthy foods.

"Her granddaughter is visiting for a while," Sofia said. "She decided to take a year off before starting her master's program. Belinda's put Maria on a strict diet and won't allow her to cook or bake any fattening foods."

It would be easier to tame a tiger than put an older Italian woman on a diet. I did not envy Belinda that monumental task. "How's that working for them?"

Sofia laughed. "Maria goes over to Rosa's and indulges her sweet tooth before each meal. She's hidden some chocolates at the back of her closet. Belinda hasn't caught on yet."

I tried to picture Belinda, but I hadn't seen her in years. And I found it hard to believe that she would want to live in her grandmother's traditional Italian home after being on her own for four years. "What's Belinda doing with herself these days?"

"She broke up with her boyfriend in St. Catharines and decided to spend some time away from him. She needs a job." Sofia put her cup down. "And that's where you come in."

"She can drop by on Monday for an appointment."

"She doesn't need counseling. She wants—or Maria wants—you to offer her a job."

"What on earth would she do?" While I understood Maria's need to get Belinda out of her kitchen, I didn't think her granddaughter would enjoy any make-work projects I gave her.

"She could do my job," Sofia said softly and averted her face. "I hadn't planned on staying more than a month, but I wouldn't mind leaving sooner than that."

"How much sooner?"

"It would take me a day or two to train Belinda," Sofia said. "She's better qualified for the job. She's got that degree in psychology."

I had known from the beginning that Sofia didn't want to do reception work, but I figured she would want to stay and help out for a while. Part of me wanted to pry further, but I decided to let it go. "I'll give Belinda a call tomorrow."

I helped Sofia load the dishwasher and clean the small kitchen. In no time at all, we were on the road and driving to see *Ides of March.*

Chapter 14

Saturday, October 29, 2011

"Do you always dress up to work out by yourself in the exercise room?" Sofia asked as I came out of my bedroom.

Last week, I had splurged and bought myself a Lululemon yoga outfit. A bit pricy, but worth every penny. And now I knew what to buy Sofia for her next birthday. "How was Curves this morning?"

"A bit boring. There weren't too many of the regulars around."

"No more news or interesting tidbits from the police department."

"No. Should there be?" Sofia sounded annoyed.

I wondered at her change of mood. Last night, we had enjoyed the movie, and afterward we had come home and chatted until midnight. It had felt normal, well almost normal after the incident with Jean yesterday. "Is everything all right. You sound a bit off?"

She forced a smile. "Just some last minute jitters."

"You've been organizing these teas for years."

"Yeah, well I'm just tired. I haven't been sleeping too well." She changed the subject. "I'm glad we're going to the spa this afternoon. I'll meet you there at one fifteen. I have several errands to run." She got up and headed for the door.

"See you later," I called out, but I doubted she heard me. When Sofia was on a mission, she put on her blinders and ignored everything and everyone around her.

I went down to the exercise room and inserted a yoga DVD. I spent the next ninety minutes stretching and meditating. Afterward, I swam in the pool and chatted with a few of the younger neighbors who used the facility on weekends. It was good to connect with normal people who had no interest in or experience with murders.

I took a long, luxurious bath and then dressed and drove over to the Lodge, Sudbury's newest spa. The other night, Mirella and her friends had raved about the different spa therapies and packages offered. Sofia and I decided to have manicures and pedicures today. We would leave the hydrotherapy, reflexology, and more exotic treatments for another day.

I found Sofia waiting in the large foyer. It was annoying to always find her waiting or arriving early. How could such a positive trait become so undesirable and unwanted? I took a deep breath and resolved not to apologize for keeping her waiting. "Hi, I guess you got everything done and decided to come here early."

"I didn't realize I was that early." She glanced at her watch and continued, "Had I known, I could have completed another errand. There's so much to do before tomorrow's tea."

"And of course you have to do it all. Let someone else take over for a change. It doesn't always have to be done perfectly and by you."

"I enjoy doing it." Her lips formed a tight red line

of anger. "I know it's hard for you to understand because you think all creative and domestic tasks are chores."

"You got that right. You're the domestic one."

"And you are the dynamic one." Sofia's voice had an edge to it.

"Where did that come from?"

"From nowhere. From everywhere."

I needed some kind of distraction or Sofia would pick at this all afternoon. I couldn't think of anything to say, so I picked up the latest *People* magazine and started reading it. Sofia sat there, saying nothing and watching the entrance.

I barely got the first page of the Brangelina story read.

"Hello, and welcome to the Lodge. My name is Natalia Gorsky, and I am the owner." A tall, blonde woman dressed in head-to-toe ivory and beige tones stood before us. She shook both our hands and smiled at me. "Please excuse me for staring. Have we met before?"

I still wasn't used to all the attention that had been generated by my lottery win, and I didn't feel comfortable bringing it up with new acquaintances. In this case, I had a convenient backup. "I attended last month's Chamber of Commerce breakfast. I enjoyed listening to your story." I added, "My name is Gilda Greco, and this is my cousin Sofia DiMatteo.

Natalia nodded and moved on to speak to other clients.

Sofia shook her head. "I don't think you satisfied her curiosity. She'll make a point of finding out all about your illustrious past. Once she finds out about the lottery win, she'll lay it on extra thick."

"How do you know so much about Natalia? Don't answer…Curves, right?"

Sofia laughed. The mood had passed. "No, she's been around for a while, five or six years."

"I thought she left Russia about ten years ago or so. I'm certain she mentioned that in her speech."

"She made a pit stop in the Parry Sound area for about three or four years. She likes to gloss over those details and not call too much attention to her marriage of convenience."

My gaze followed the tall, graceful figure that walked confidently through the foyer. "I find that hard to believe."

"Let me give you the unedited version of Natalia Gorsky's life," Sofia said. "About ten years ago, a widower from the Parry Sound area was searching for a younger bride. Someone suggested he import a Russian woman. He responded to an ad in the *Toronto Sun* and started a correspondence with Natalia. At the time, Natalia was in her late twenties and very plain looking. She hadn't been able to find a husband in Russia and was desperate to leave for Canada, the United States or any other country that would take her."

"I can't imagine Natalia that desperate," I said. "She is so beautiful and articulate—"

"That's how she appears now," Sofia said. "She married the older gentleman as soon as she arrived, but she quickly became frustrated by his sedate and comfortable lifestyle. She had been an accountant in Russia, but realized that her credentials would never be recognized in Canada. She trained as an aesthetician and worked in several spas in Parry Sound and Barrie.

She even took clients after hours in a makeshift home salon and got into all kinds of other moneymaking schemes. She worked sixty- to eighty-hour weeks and saved every penny."

"What did her husband say?" While I had been impressed by Natalia's speech, I was even more intrigued by her back story.

"He didn't say too much. I think he might have misrepresented his own situation and led Natalia to believe he lived very lavishly. Three years after they married, he was diagnosed with pancreatic cancer."

"How did she handle the caregiver role?" While I couldn't visualize her attending to her husband's needs, I didn't think she was capable of ignoring or abandoning him either.

"His adult children took over and left her out of the picture. After he died, she received a small financial settlement from the estate. She wanted to contest the will, but was advised not to by her lawyer. She decided to move on and—"

"Arrived in Sudbury with just two suitcases and a dream." I remembered the rest of her story.

"That's what she likes to say. It sounds more dramatic and makes her appear more interesting."

"How did you find this out?" While Natalia had shared many of her challenges at the Chamber breakfast, she had not mentioned the older gentleman. She would not want that particular story out there.

"The Godfreys had taken Natalia under their wing and helped launch her career in Sudbury," Sofia said. "Anna May spilled the beans one evening after a few too many drinks. The news spread like wildfire after that."

“I can’t imagine Anna May going out of her way to help her or anyone else for that matter.”

“Natalia met the Godfrey women at one of those spas in the Muskokas,” Sofia explained. “She impressed Mrs. Godfrey, and the two communicated regularly by mail and telephone. You remember Mrs. Godfrey. She was a kind soul who took in foster children and all kinds of strays. Natalia needed a soft place to land. When she moved to Sudbury, she stayed with Mrs. Godfrey for over a year, and the rest…well, I’m sure you must have heard Natalia’s edited version about angels, the kindness of strangers, and the power of love. That angel she talks about was Mrs. Godfrey. Bruce Steele is her life partner. He financed all of this.” Sofia waved her hand to take in the entire spa area.

As I digested this information, I noticed that Sofia had paled considerably and shifted her gaze to a fixed spot behind me.

“Well, look who’s here. Gilda Greco, you turn up everywhere, like a bad penny.” Anna May’s eyes were brimming with anger. “And followed by your lackey of a cousin. You two must be joined at the hip. I hear you’re even living together.”

“It looks like you’re following us around.” Sofia raised her voice as she clenched her fists. “There’s an ugly name for that—it’s called stalking.”

“Me following you.” Anna May laughed. “I don’t think so, ladies. I have been a regular client here since the Lodge opened. I don’t recall seeing the two of you around. It seems every time I run into either one of you, someone in my family dies shortly afterward. That’s some coincidence. Some people might even call it cold-blooded murder.”

The receptionist and several clients in the foyer watched in shocked silence. Sofia's eyes flared with anger as she moved closer, ready to pounce on Anna May. I tried to restrain Sofia with a gentle pressure on her arm. My heart pounded, and my brain tried to make sense out of Anna May's comments. Anna May was either slightly deranged or under some influence. She had wildness in her eyes and high color on her cheeks. She was wrapped in a black, cashmere cape which hid her girth and gave her an elegant air. She resembled the teenage Anna May who had modeled for many of the area fashion shows. I groaned inwardly at the growing crowd of women that had suddenly materialized. I didn't recognize anyone, but I had a sinking feeling they all knew about me.

Natalia reappeared and positioned herself between Sofia and Anna May. "Ladies, I will not tolerate such disruptive behaviour in my salon." She glared at Anna May. "You may have been a valued client in the past, but that could change if you continue to shout and upset everyone. Do I make myself clear, Anna May Godfrey?"

Anna May lowered her gaze. "I'm sorry, Natalia." She pointed to both Sofia and me. "They provoked me. They are cold-blooded killers who are systematically killing off my family."

Natalia frowned. "I don't know who started this, but I think it would be in the best interests of all concerned if the three of you left my salon."

Anna May's mouth fell open. "You're kicking me out? After all that my mother and Carrie Ann did for you and the many clients we sent your way." Her bloodshot eyes glinted at Natalia. "You will live to regret this. I'll make sure the Lodge becomes a ghost town. Keep this up, and you'll end up back in Russia."

Natalia paled but maintained her composure. "Leave my salon and never return again."

I kept my head down and followed Sofia out of the salon. I didn't speak until we reached our cars. "What a scene! We'll never be able to return here."

"Anna May showed her true colors, and I wouldn't be surprised if most of those ladies thought she was deranged," Sofia spoke matter-of-factly.

"I agree that she appeared deranged, but you didn't help matters when you started yelling at her."

"Anna May is a royal bitch, and she might just end up on the chopping block."

"You're beginning to sound like Anna May, and it's scaring me."

"Just kidding."

"I don't like that kind of kidding. Two women have died, and people keep pointing the finger at me…at us."

"Where do you get off…?"

"Don't get defensive on me. Anna May considers us a unit, and somehow she feels we are in cahoots against her and her family."

Sofia yawned. "I guess we won't be getting manicures and pedicures today. I think I'll head back and help out at the church. What are you going to do?"

I sighed. "I might go online and check some cottage listings. I intend to make Karen Anderson an offer. Maybe we could go out there next weekend. I'd like your opinion about the renovations."

Sofia nodded in approval. "That sounds like a plan."

Chapter 15

I entered my building and groaned when I saw the sign on the inside door. The video surveillance system was down again. This was the third time in less than a month. Why couldn't they fix it properly?

What a relief to be rid of Sofia! But I didn't want to spend the rest of the afternoon checking real estate prices. That could wait. Karen was in no hurry to finalize the sale.

Instead, I curled up in the over-sized recliner with Sue Grafton's latest novel, *V is for Vengeance.* Not exactly the best choice considering what had just happened at the Lodge, but I needed to distract myself, and strangely enough murder mysteries were my favorite—that is, other people's murder mysteries. I read all afternoon and stopped to have dinner, last night's leftover chicken and two glasses of wine. One glass is my limit, but I deserved the second glass after today's debacle. Afterward, I dozed off.

The persistent ringing of the telephone woke me up. I stumbled in the dark toward the nearest light switch. The answering machine went on and, after a few minutes, Carlo's frantic voice filled the room. "Gilda…Gilda are you there? Please be there. Gilda pick up. You need to hear—"

I picked up the phone. "Carlo, it's me. What's wrong?" My heart pounded as I waited for the dreaded words.

"Is Sofia there? Has Sofia or someone…anyone been with you today?"

"Sofia and I were together this afternoon." Disturbing thoughts invaded my mind, making my mouth go dry.

"What time did she leave?"

"Oh, I don't know. I got back here around two. She went to help with tomorrow's tea at the church. I imagine she's still taking care of some last-minute details." I swallowed hard. "Has something terrible happened?"

"We discovered two dead bodies behind the Lodge."

I gasped. "Don't tell me they killed both Anna May and Jenny Marie?"

"You got one right. Anna May." An awkward silence followed.

My throat constricted, and I could only croak. "Who else?"

"Natalia Gorsky."

My mind went into overdrive. I had so many questions to ask but knew that Carlo would be unable to answer them.

"I'll give the superintendent of your building a call in the morning." He sighed loudly into the phone. "I'll have to go through all of today's video surveillance tapes."

"There aren't any. The system is down."

His voice became muffled as he said something indistinguishable, probably to someone in the room with him. Another sigh. "I should have you come down now, but it is late, and I will give you a break. First thing tomorrow morning, I want you and Sofia to come downtown."

"Carlo, you don't think I—"

"It's not what I think that matters," he said. "There are just too many coincidences, and you seem to be involved in some way with each murder. Three of the women are related, and the other is not. I don't know what to think anymore."

"Blondes, they're all blondes," I mumbled to myself. "This is a season for killing blondes."

"You're starting to worry me. Where's Sofia? I thought she was staying with you."

"I told you already. She's helping out with tomorrow's tea. I don't know if she'll have any time to—"

"She will have to make the time. I want both of you here tomorrow morning at nine o'clock with or without your lawyers." Carlo slammed down the receiver.

Where would I find a lawyer at this hour on a Saturday night? The only lawyer I knew was Henry Keenan, and he wouldn't want anything to do with me. I had to find Sofia. She would know what to do. I picked up the phone and dialed a familiar number. "Aunt Amelia, it's me, Gilda. Is Sofia there?"

"She left right before supper. Why are you calling here so late? Is something wrong? Are you sick?" She dropped the phone, and I could hear her calling. "Paolo…Paolo wake up. There's trouble. We need to get Assunta and go over to Gilda's." She spoke to me. "Don't worry, Gilda. We'll be there soon."

I shut my eyes and banged my head against the wall. What was I thinking? The last thing I wanted to do was alarm my mother or my aunt, and I had succeeded in doing both. And to top it all, I still couldn't locate Sofia. They would be here in less than half an hour. As I started to tidy the living room area, the key turned in the lock and Sofia entered the condo.

"What a long day! I'm exhausted and ready for bed." Sofia took off her jacket and started to unbutton her blouse as she headed for the guest bedroom.

"I don't think you'll be going to bed for a while. My mother and your parents will be arriving soon."

"At this hour?" Sofia laughed and shook her head. "They're in bed, and even if they are up, my father never drives anywhere after dark. It would have to be some kind of emergency."

"They think there is an emergency here."

"Why would they think that?"

I managed a rueful smile. "I called and asked your mother if she knew where you were."

Her eyes narrowed to furious slits. "We had an agreement when I moved in, and I didn't think you would be reporting to my mother." She glanced at her watch. "It's barely past nine o'clock, for chrissakes! What kind of curfew do you expect me to keep?"

"Carlo called and told me about the new murders, and he wanted to know where you were. I tried to reassure him—"

"Back up. What murders and why is Carlo so concerned about me?"

"Brace yourself. Both Anna May and Natalia were found dead near the spa. He wants both of us there first thing tomorrow morning with our lawyers. I panicked and dialed the first number I could think of."

Sofia buttoned up her blouse and headed toward

the kitchen. She opened one of the cupboards and pulled out a package of cake mix. She then proceeded to assemble the required bowls and mixer.

"Sofia, what on earth are you doing? They'll be here any minute now, and you're baking!"

Sofia faced me squarely. "Listen and listen carefully. I've had a very long day, and I don't have the time or energy to put up with any of their drama. So, this is our story. You fell asleep after supper. I will say I didn't want to wake you, so I decided to run to the grocery store and pick up a box of cake mix. I wanted something sweet, and we all know you don't keep any desserts around. I got delayed by…by that woman with dementia. What's her name? The one with the tabby cat."

"Mrs. Harrison?" I shook my head. "It sounds far-fetched, Sofia. I don't know if we should involve someone else. What if they start asking her questions?"

"Not if I actually bake the cake. As for involving Mrs. Harrison, how much do you think she remembers from day to day?" Sofia started to beat the cake batter vigorously. "If you want to be helpful, why don't you set the table and make some herbal tea for our mothers. When I finish here, I'll make an espresso for my father."

I was amazed at how calm and collected Sofia could be, especially when dealing with our parents. "I don't know how you do this. You're a natural at compartmentalizing."

Sofia nodded impatiently. "Yeah, yeah I know. When they get here, let me do all the talking."

Within a short time, the fragrant aroma of bananas and coconut mingled with the strong espresso coffee brewing on the stove. I continued to watch Sofia. She was acting normally, almost abnormally normal. She hadn't said one word about the murders, and I wondered where she had gone after leaving her parents' house. There was no point interrogating her now. I would find out the answers to all these questions soon enough. "Sofia, we need lawyers."

"I will take care of all that later. We need to focus on calming our parents. It will—"

The loud knocking at the door interrupted our conversation.

"Gilda! Sofia! Are you in there?" Uncle Paolo shouted. I could hear my mother's and aunt's voices in the background. I imagine everyone else on the floor heard them, as well.

I had forgotten about the system being down. I wondered how they got in.

Sofia rushed to the door and let them in. My mother headed toward me and hugged me close. Aunt Amelia hugged Sofia as Uncle Paolo stood awkwardly to one side. He smiled as he breathed in the strong espresso flavour. "It can't be all bad. After a good cup of coffee and a big piece of whatever dessert Sofia made, everything will be fine."

Sofia smiled and nodded in agreement. "You're absolutely right, Papa. That's what started all of this confusion." She shook her finger playfully at me. "This one has been sleeping all afternoon. After I left your place, I came back here and waited patiently for her to wake up. I played some music and moved a few pieces of furniture. Nothing would wake her."

My mother piped in. "Gilda is the heaviest sleeper around. Remember that tornado that touched down in the city years ago. She slept right through it."

"I got bored and decided to bake," Sofia said. "I couldn't find enough ingredients to make any of my favorite desserts, so I decided to run to the store and pick up a cake mix. On the way back, I ended up talking to that poor, confused woman with the cat."

Aunt Amelia nodded. "She never finishes her stories and she keeps repeating everything."

"I ended up accompanying her back to her condo and helping her with her keys." Sofia shook her head. "She shouldn't be living on her own. I have a good mind to phone one of her children, and let them know about her wanderings. I'm sure I spent at least thirty minutes dealing with all of that." She pointed in my direction. "Meanwhile, this one wakes up and finds herself in the dark, totally alone. So, she panics and starts phoning everyone we know."

My mother gasped. "Gilda, who else did you call?"

I had to think quickly. I didn't want to bring anyone else into this mess. "Well, well, I…I called Sofia's place and the church, but no one answered."

"And you didn't leave any messages," Sofia added. She got up and went toward the guest bedroom.

Aunt Amelia nodded in approval. "It's okay to bother us, but I'm glad you didn't call anyone else. We don't need outsiders knowing our business." She changed the subject. "That coffee smells so good, and I'd love a piece of that cake, even if it is from a mix."

"I'll have some coffee as well," my mother said.

I pointed to the teapot. "I made some herbal tea. Wouldn't that help you sleep better?"

My mother smiled. "Who can sleep now? We may as well treat ourselves." The three of them headed for the table and sat down. Aunt Amelia served the coffee and my mother cut five generous pieces of cake.

Sofia came back and signaled to me with her eyes. I followed her into the kitchen and had to strain to hear her. "I just called Roberto Ongaro. He agreed to represent us tomorrow morning."

"How did you manage that?"

She shot me a sly, sideways glance. "I called him from the other room. I had already spoken to him earlier this week about you."

"You went to see a lawyer, and you didn't even tell me."

"Sssh. They'll hear you. If you must know, he's handling my situation with Andrew. When all of this is over, I'll fill you in on those details."

Chapter 16

Sunday, October 30, 2011

"Gilda, wake up. We're meeting with Carlo in an hour, and we can't be late."

I opened my eyes and stared up at a fully-clothed Sofia. "Wow! You look stunning." The combination of a light pink wool suit and black blouse complemented Sofia's pale skin and dark hair. The sheer, dark hose and black patent stilettos completed the picture. And something else was different. Sofia wore a pair of stylish, dark-rimmed glasses. "I didn't know you wore glasses."

"I only wear my glasses after a long, tiring day. And I can truthfully say that I was totally depleted last evening."

"Well, you don't look it now." I glanced over at the clock and sprang out of bed. "I can't believe I slept this long. Why didn't you wake me up earlier?"

"I tried, but you kept going back to sleep. Now, hurry up. Roberto wants to touch base with us before we talk to Carlo."

I showered and grabbed a black pant suit from the closet. I decided on a cream-colored turtleneck and medium-heeled black shoes. I applied the minimum of makeup and then inspected myself critically in the mirror. Definitely a schoolmarm-ish look, but at this point I didn't really care.

Sofia raised her eyebrows when I went into the kitchen. "Good morning, Sister Gilda."

I made a face at her and quickly drank a cup of coffee. I knew I should eat something, but I didn't think I could keep anything down. I grabbed my purse and followed Sofia to her car. In less than ten minutes, we arrived at a parking lot near the police station and found Roberto waiting for us in a large black Mercedes. Sofia pulled up next to him, and he motioned for us to get into his car. Sofia got in the front seat and gave Roberto a quick peck on the cheek. I realized why Sofia had dressed up this morning. She was putting the moves on Roberto. Or maybe they were already an item. Of all the men in Sudbury, Sofia had to pick the one who most resembled her husband in looks and temperament.

Roberto flashed me a quick smile. "It's been a long time, Gilda. It's too bad we had to meet under these circumstances." He paused and adjusted his tie. "When we go in, do not volunteer any information. Answer Carlo's questions directly, and be as brief as possible. I will sit in on each session, and I won't hesitate to interrupt or make any suggestions. Are you okay with that?"

Sofia jumped in. "You're the lawyer. Why shouldn't we be okay with that?"

I wasn't thrilled with Roberto, but it was too late to protest.

Roberto turned his attention back to Sofia and lowered his voice. "Let's go over those times again. When did you drop Gilda off at her condo?"

"Around two o'clock yesterday afternoon."

"Where did you go afterward?"

"I went over to St. Anthony's Church to help set up for the Autumn Tea."

"How long did you stay there?"

"I left around four-thirty and went over to my parents' house."

"When did you leave your parents' house?"

"About ten after six."

"When did you arrive at Gilda's?"

"About ten minutes later."

"Was Gilda home?"

"Yes, she slept soundly in her recliner. I decided not to wake her. I went into my room and read for a while."

"When did you step out again?"

"A few minutes after eight o'clock?"

"Why did you leave the condo?"

"I craved something sweet. Gilda doesn't keep any desserts or even chocolate in the condo, so I decided to go out and buy something sweet."

"Where did you go?"

"Food Basics."

"When did you get back?"

"Sometime after nine. Gilda was awake."

"It took a whole hour to go to Food Basics and back? What took you so long?"

"I was in and out of Food Basics quickly. But I was delayed when I got back to the condo building. One of the other residents, Mrs. Harrison, wandered around on the first floor. I decided to help her."

"Does Mrs. Harrison have a problem?"

"Yes, she has dementia. She shouldn't be living on her own. The next time I see her daughter, I will mention this incident to her."

"How long were you with Mrs. Harrison?"

"At least thirty minutes. She couldn't remember her floor, so I had to check on the board in the foyer. When we got to her condo, she couldn't find her keys. She wouldn't let me touch her purse, so I waited until she found her keys. When we got inside, she started crying. I sat with her until she stopped crying. I felt guilty leaving, but I didn't know what else I could do for her."

"What's her apartment number?"

"Seven-oh-eight."

"Well done, Sofia." Roberto patted her knee affectionately. "You're ready for Fantin."

I couldn't believe what I had just heard. Sofia had concocted all these lies, and she was ready to tell them to Carlo. I wanted to protest, but I couldn't. Sofia and I both knew, and now Roberto Ongaro knew, that if she didn't lie, there could be problems. Both of us needed that alibi. I also knew that I couldn't face Carlo after all of this. "I guess it's my turn now."

Roberto flashed a confident smile. "That won't be necessary, Gilda. You were in your condo reading and fell asleep. Just stick to that story."

He got out of the car and opened the door for Sofia and me. I followed Sofia and Roberto into the station. Sofia kept touching Roberto's arm and giggling—yes, she actually giggled at his comments. I hadn't seen that side of Sofia since high school. My stomach grumbled, and I regretted not having any solid food for breakfast.

Carlo stood near the front desk, chatting with one of the other officers. He frowned when he saw us. "Hello, everyone. Thank you for being so prompt." He spoke directly to Roberto. "I'll start with Sofia, and then I'll question Gilda. Her lawyer will have arrived by then."

Roberto interjected, "I'm representing both of these lovely ladies." He took Sofia's arm and headed toward Carlo's office.

Carlo approached and whispered in my ear. "I can't believe you've agreed to this. Gilda…Gilda, for a smart woman, you…" He threw up his hands and walked away, not giving me a chance to respond.

My eyes welled up with tears. I donned my sunglasses, went over to the main desk, and spoke to the officer on duty, "I'm just stepping out for half an hour or so. If Carlo needs me before then—" I took out my cell phone.

The officer nodded. "Take your time. I have a feeling that Carlo will be a while, and if he does finish earlier, he can wait. Go and have a good strong cup of coffee."

I walked out of the station and headed for the Gonga Grill just down the street. I knew I would be able to eat and get out of there quickly. There were a handful of patrons in the restaurant. I went all out and had poached eggs, bacon, and home fries along with two strong cups of coffee. I arrived at the station just in time to see Carlo disappear into his office. Sofia and Roberto approached, all smiles. I forced myself to smile. "I guess it's my turn now. Is Carlo ready to see me?"

Roberto patted my shoulder. "He doesn't need to see you at all. Sofia and I took care of everything, and you are free to enjoy the rest of this lovely day."

"How is that possible? Two women are dead—"

"Carlo accepted my alibi." Sofia finished my

sentence while focusing on Roberto. “I promised my parents I would go to the eleven o’clock mass with them, and I’m tied up with the Autumn Tea all afternoon and into the evening.”

“I’ll give you a call later in the week when the documents are ready for your signature,” Roberto said. “Now, I will be on my way. Nice seeing you again Gilda. I’m glad I could help. Call me if you need any more legal advice.”

I didn’t speak until Sofia was on the road. “I can’t believe that Carlo just dismissed me. If you had heard him last night, you would have been convinced he was ready to throw me in jail.”

“Relax, Gilda. You’re not going to jail. I provided you with an alibi for last night. All those times that Roberto and I rehearsed worked.” Sofia glanced over at me. “Aren’t you pleased? You’ve said very little since we left the station.”

“I guess I’m just so shocked and overwhelmed. I can’t believe it’s over. Are you sure—”

“Roberto will take care of any problem if one should arise. Just give him a call.” She giggled again. “Isn’t he wonderful?”

There was so much I wanted to say, but I didn’t want to upset Sofia. Especially after all the lies she had told on my behalf. “Is it wise to get involved with someone else so soon?”

“I don’t know how much you have heard.” When I didn’t answer right away, Sofia continued. “My marriage hasn’t been working for a very long time. Andrew and I stayed together for the sake of the boys. We didn’t want to put Peter and Paul through an ugly divorce or sell the house or split the money. All that changed when you won the lottery. Your million-dollar gift to me and your generous backing of the boys made it very easy for Andrew to leave. He quit his job and flew to Italy where he met a lovely thirty-year-old who caters to his every whim. At least, that's what I've heard from my in-laws. No one is taking Andrew's side, but he doesn't care. He is free at last, and he doesn't have to support me."

"Do your parents…does my mother know?" I couldn't believe she had kept all of this under wraps.

"I think my in-laws and parents still communicate, so they probably know all the details. But you know what my mother is like. If it's not happening here, and none of her Sudbury friends know, then it doesn't matter. As for your mother…I don't know how much they have told her."

"She did mention some of this a few days ago. But I don't think she knows the whole story. When will your divorce be finalized?"

"Sometime this week or next." Sofia laughed bitterly, and her eyes narrowed. "Andrew found an Italian lawyer who moves at lightning speed. He sends everything by fax or next-day express. Andrew can't wait to be free of me. He doesn't even want any share of that million you gave me."

That didn't sound like the money-hungry Andrew I knew. The Italian woman must have bewitched him. "I wish you had told me sooner. I can't believe you're going through a divorce, organizing the tea, and taking care of me and my problems."

Sofia's laugh was a hollow one. "My social mask is firmly in place."

"You shouldn't have to feel that way, and you must

promise to share your problems with me. I can help you."

"Gilda, please. My problems can't be solved with money. My husband left me, and my sons are thousands of miles away." She raised her hand in protest when she saw that I was about to speak. "I know that Peter and Paul had their hearts set on American universities, but I secretly hoped they wouldn't get in."

"You couldn't hold onto those boys much longer. Even if they had stayed in Sudbury a few extra years, eventually they would have moved on."

"I would have been okay with just a few extra years. Especially now that Andrew has left me." Sofia's lips trembled, and her eyes welled with tears. She sniffed and then managed a smile. "I did manage to snag a lawyer. Almost as good as a doctor. I haven't told my parents about Roberto yet. I'm waiting until the divorce is final."

Did Sofia really think her fling with Roberto would turn into a long-term relationship? Roberto was a well-known womanizer and heavy drinker who frequented the bars in search of younger, female companions. He would comfort his older female clients, but he married women under thirty. He had three ex-wives and, surprisingly enough, no children to show for his fifty-plus years. I couldn't imagine him changing for Sofia. I managed to plaster a fake smile for her benefit. "I won't say anything until you are ready to come out with him."

"You would think he was gay or something." Sofia laughed as she powdered her nose and fixed her eye makeup.

"Or something," I mumbled. I glanced at my watch and exclaimed, "It's almost eleven o'clock. Weren't you planning to go to mass with your parents?" I usually went as well, but I didn't feel up to it today.

Sofia waved her hand. "Oh, I can be a little late. Everyone will think I'm doing something for the tea."

"Are you still planning to go through with all of that?" I couldn't imagine spending an entire afternoon smiling and making small talk after telling all those lies to Carlo. Sofia must have nerves of steel.

"Don't worry about me. The Autumn Tea is just the diversion I need."

Chapter 17

I watched Sofia pull away and head toward the church. With her social mask firmly in place, no one would think anything amiss. I then realized I would have to put in an appearance at the tea. I wouldn't hear the end of it from my mother and Sofia if I didn't attend. I owed Sofia, and now I also owed Roberto Ongaro. That still rankled.

I entered the building and headed toward the elevator. I noticed an older woman sitting in the lobby. Mrs. Harrison. A large tabby cat purred at her feet, and a small suitcase sat on the floor next to her chair. "Good morning, Mrs. Harrison. Are you going somewhere?" I pointed to the suitcase.

"Am I supposed to go somewhere?" She frowned at me. "Who are you?"

"I'm Gilda Greco. I live on the fifth floor. My cousin Sofia and I usually see you in the elevator."

"Gilda…Sofia…I don't know any of these people." She started to tremble. "And I don't know where I'm supposed to go."

A younger woman appeared. "Please stop confusing my aunt with all these names."

"I'm so sorry. I didn't mean to confuse her. I just wondered where she was going."

"That's none of your business, but if you must know, she's not going anywhere. We've just come back from North Bay. She spent a week there with me and my family. I dropped her off at the front door and then went to park my car in the visitors' lot. I wanted to save her a few steps." She smiled at Mrs. Harrison. "Aunt Rita, let's go upstairs and have a nice cup of tea."

They took the first elevator up, and I waited patiently for the next one as my mind started spinning. Sofia had used Mrs. Harrison as part of her alibi, and she hadn't even been in the building. What if Carlo called today and decided to question her while her niece was still visiting? And then my mind filled with all the other questions I should have asked, but didn't. Where had Sofia gone last night? I doubted very much that she sat quietly while I slept. And as for buying the cake mix, I wondered if it had been in the cupboard all along. I hadn't bought it, but Sofia could have picked it up during one of her shopping expeditions. The whole day loomed before me. I knew that I couldn't just sit around and do nothing. I changed into my sweats and went downstairs for a short workout. Afterward, I swam several laps.

As soon as I entered the condo, the phone rang. I groaned. Could Carlo be calling? When I checked call display, I saw Jenny Marie's number. "Good morning…I mean afternoon, Jenny Marie. I'm so sorry to hear about Anna May's death. We didn't always see eye-to-eye, but I never wanted to see her end up like this." My pulse quickened. "I don't know what you've heard."

"Relax, Gilda. I never suspected you for a minute. Not in Anna May's or any of the other deaths. I just got back from the police station."

I thought of Sofia and her lies. Carlo must have

caught her in one of them. I was so engrossed in my negative thoughts that I barely listened and caught the tail end of Jenny Marie's conversation.

"...and she'll be here for the rest of the week."

"I'm so sorry, Jenny Marie. I didn't get much sleep last night. I only caught that last part about somebody being here for the rest of the week."

"Anna May left her cell phone behind when she went out last night. I checked her messages this morning and discovered a number of calls from certain men. You remember Ray Centis, Anna May's ex? Well, he and some of his pals have been in regular contact with Anna May. I don't know the full extent of their involvement, but Carlo feels it bears investigating." She sighed deeply. "They found blonde hairs in Anna May's right hand and in Natalia's left hand. I hate to say this, but I think my sister might have been involved with the other two deaths. And my daughter agrees. She's driving up from Toronto, and she'll be here later this afternoon."

I felt badly for Jenny Marie. In addition to losing two sisters and her cousin, she also had to deal with the fact that Anna May was a murderer or an accessory to the fact. My thoughts turned toward Ray Centis. I had little use for Ray and his crowd, and I had no plans to get involved with any of them. They were always getting into trouble and stirring things up. I had considered attending Anna May's memorial service, but I didn't want to run into Ray or any of his cronies. "What about you, Jenny Marie? Aren't you afraid of them? What if they've been killing off your family—?"

Jenny Marie interrupted, "There's no proof of that. I always liked Ray, and I thought that he was misunderstood by everyone. As for the others, they're harmless."

"I still remember all those dead animals we kept finding in our garden." I shuddered. "And every summer, a few garages and sheds were set ablaze. One of them…I can't remember which one even tried to burn down the school. You need to be very careful. If they're after blondes and Godfreys, you could be the next victim."

Jenny Marie laughed. "I didn't think anything could make me laugh today. Where on earth did you get that idea?"

"The evidence speaks for itself. No brunettes or redheads."

"You've been reading too many murder mysteries," Jenny Marie said. "Don't worry about me being alone. My daughter will be here in a couple of hours. I hope you can meet her before she leaves."

"How about coming over this Thursday or Friday evening?"

"Thanks, Gilda. We'll come Thursday evening around seven. See you then."

"Bye, and thanks for calling." I hung up the phone and glanced at the clock. Two fourteen. My mood had picked up. I would go to the tea and touch base with Sofia. While I still didn't feel comfortable with her lies, Carlo knew I wasn't involved.

I caught a glimpse of myself in the hall mirror and groaned. I took a quick shower and restyled my hair. I took extra care with my makeup. I added more blush than normal and experimented with different shades of mauve eye shadow. I wore my black pinstripe pants with a light mauve cashmere sweater and my purple leather jacket.

I arrived at the church shortly after three o'clock. I paid the admission fee and went downstairs to the hall, packed solid with women. I stopped to chat with a couple of my mother's neighbors and got caught up on the latest gossip. No one brought up any of the murders.

My eyes traveled around the hall. Sofia had outdone herself. Pumpkin, green, and cream streamers were strategically arranged throughout the room, and each table had a unique cornucopia as its centerpiece. The sponge cakes were arranged in colorful hat boxes on a side table, again repeating the pumpkin, green, and cream color scheme. How did Sofia come up with these spectacular and ingenious ideas?

Sofia was surrounded by a group of ladies who gushed and made the appropriate noises. I waited until they left and then approached. "The hall looks great, and everyone is singing your praises. You must be thrilled."

"Thanks, Gilda." She then gave me an appraising once-over. "I didn't think you would show up this afternoon. I even prepared our mothers for your possible absence."

"Why don't you just relax and let things happen."

"I've had more than enough experience with things just happening in the last year," Sofia said.

I winced. "I had forgotten about Andrew."

"We are not going down that road again." I heard a sharp edge to her voice. And then she flashed a smile that didn't quite reach her eyes. "I'm curious. This morning you could have passed for an aging nun. And now you're back in the land of the living. What gives?"

I gave her a brief rundown of the conversation I

had with Jenny Marie. Sofia's smile faded and gave way to a frown. "I don't know why you need to continue your involvement with the Godfreys. Let it go, Gilda. You're scot free. You heard it first from Roberto and me, and now you've heard it from Jenny Marie. What more proof do you need?"

"I know that Carlo doesn't think I had anything to do with the murders, but I still want to know why someone would go to all the trouble of helping Anna May frame me for the murders."

Sofia shrugged. "It could just be a coincidence, random murders."

"All blondes, all killed after meeting with me. What are the chances of that happening?"

"I don't know. You're the mathematician. You figure it out."

"Very funny." I made a face and then continued. "I am looking forward to seeing Jenny Marie and Grace. I want to hear more about those men who called Anna May."

"I hope you're not planning to investigate any of them or follow them around or—"

I shuddered. "Sofia, please. Think of the members of that crowd. Ray Centis, Mike Grant, Jamie Douglas. I didn't like them when they were bad boys. Why on earth would I have anything to do with them now?"

Sofia yawned. "They've all settled down to boring middle-age lifestyles with wives and children."

"If that's the case, why were they calling Anna May?"

Sofia threw up her hands in defeat. "I don't know and have no interest in finding out. You won't be too upset if I don't join you and Jenny Marie when she comes over?"

I had no intention of inviting Sofia to join us. "No, not at all. I'm hoping that we could all get back to our own lives. You don't have to stay with me anymore."

Sophia smiled widely. "I have been itching to get back to my place and redo my bedroom. I'm pitching everything and buying a new bed, furniture, linens, the works.

"Isn't that a bit extreme?" Sofia redecorated every other year, and she had spent a large chunk of her million on home decor.

"I want to purge Andrew out of every corner of my home and start fresh with Roberto." Just mentioning Roberto's name brought an instant smile to her face, and her eyes sparkled with anticipation.

I hesitated, taking a deep breath. "I know you don't want to hear this, but I think that Roberto is another Andrew. Are you sure you want to continue your relationship with him?"

Sofia's mouth tightened. "Gilda, I love you dearly, but please stay out of my personal life. I don't know, and I don't care if Roberto isn't Mr. Right. All I know is that he is Mr. Right Now, and that's what I need."

I was taken aback by her very firm, no-nonsense tone. It was the same tone I would have used to discipline unruly students in my classroom. "I'm sorry. I just don't want you to get hurt again."

"I know all about Roberto's affairs and relationships with younger women," Sofia said. "I'm not planning to marry him or anyone else for that matter. I've played the long-suffering, dutiful wife for a very long time, and it's my turn now."

I started to turn away, and then I remembered what

had transpired a few hours earlier. "I ran into Mrs. Harrison this morning. She just came back from North Bay. She spent a week there with her niece."

Sofia frowned. "And your point is?"

"You told our parents and Carlo that you helped her last night."

Her eyes flashed with anger. "Don't worry about Mrs. Harrison. I doubt very much that Carlo will be contacting her, and if he does, I will say that I confused her with someone else."

I persisted. "But the rest of your story. I don't know if it will hold up."

Sofia rolled her eyes in annoyance. "If you must know, I spent the evening with Roberto."

"Did he ask you to lie for him?"

"He left everything up to me, and I didn't feel ready to expose my affair to Carlo Fantin or anyone else for that matter. No one asked Roberto about his whereabouts, so he didn't have to lie." She added, "If I had told the truth, you wouldn't have an alibi."

The queasiness came back. Before I could reply, my mother and Aunt Amelia joined us.

Chapter 18

Monday, October 31, 2011

Was it good or back luck to be opening my office on Halloween? When I had made the decision last week, I hadn't checked the calendar. I just knew I needed to establish some kind of routine as soon as possible. I also knew, deep down, that if I postponed the opening, it might never happen.

I went inside and was greeted by Sofia and Belinda sitting together at the reception desk. Belinda listened attentively as Sofia explained the telephone system. I was surprised to see Sofia after our conversation yesterday afternoon, but then I remembered her offer to train Belinda. In spite of our differences, Sofia would not shirk her responsibilities or go back on her word.

I went into my office and started going through the emails from the previous weeks. I would be spending most of the morning dealing with these messages. But after twelve days of murders, confrontations and accusations, I welcomed normal, everyday stuff. One thing still saddened me. After yesterday's encounter with Carlo, I didn't think he would be calling me anytime soon.

I worked steadily and managed to get through all the messages and the accumulated paperwork by eleven. I got up and stretched. I peeked outside. Still quiet in the outer office. Hopefully, it would pick up soon. I sighed as I thought of the aborted open house. It might be a good idea to plan something toward the end of November, a pre-Christmas type of event. I would discuss it with Sofia. And then I remembered. Sofia had made it clear she was no longer interested in working at ReCareering.

There was a knock at my door followed by Sofia's entrance. "Just wanted to let you know that I got Belinda up to speed with most of the reception work. She's caught on, and I don't think there's any point both of us hanging around. It's pretty quiet out there. I'm going to go back to your condo and move my stuff out." She placed a set of keys on my desk. "You might want to give these to Belinda."

While I hated to see her leave, part of me was relieved. Our value systems were so different. She was expedient, too expedient for my taste. And I'm certain that my wishy-washiness grated on her nerves. I should hug her, but I couldn't. "Thanks. Thanks for everything."

She nodded and left.

Later in the afternoon, Maria and Rosa dropped by with a fresh zucchini cake. They wished me luck, and Maria took out her digital camera. Maria liked to fuss over her grand-daughter, and I couldn't help smiling as I heard her talking about the pictures she would be sending to relatives in Vancouver, Edmonton, Winnipeg, Montreal and, of course, Italy.

"It's too bad Sofia isn't here," Maria said. "It would have been nice to get her in a few pictures."

Rosa rolled her eyes. "I guess she has other fish to fry. Big fish to fry."

"Aunt Rosa!" Belinda reddened and tried to avoid my glance.

Maria frowned at her sister. "Rosa! Watch your mouth."

Rosa shrugged. "What's the big deal? All of Sudbury—with the exception of her parents and Assunta—know what Sofia Greco DiMatteo is up to." She nodded in my direction. "Don't tell me you're still in the dark."

I knew they were referring to Sofia's relationship with Roberto, but I was shocked to hear about her lack of discretion. Where on earth were they meeting? I managed a tight smile and said nothing.

Rosa shook her head. "Does she really think that no one is watching when that black Mercedes shows up in her driveway? Half of Moonglo is Italian. Who is she fooling?"

How foolish of her to even think she could get away with having an affair at her place. The next time I saw Sofia, I would alert her to the gossip.

"I wonder what she's going to do when her husband returns from Italy," Rosa asked. "I can't see Andrew putting up with it, and Roberto Ongaro won't stop pursuing her. You know what he's like when—"

"Shhh!" Maria said. "They're coming."

My mother, Aunt Amelia and Uncle Paolo were at the door, and they didn't look too happy. My mother came over and hugged me. "We just came from D & A Meats. Everyone's talking. And it's probably the same at Giacomo's and Tarini's. You and Sofia shouldn't keep things from us.

"We're always the last to know," Aunt Amelia moaned.

Could they have found out about Sofia's affair? Maria and Rosa exchanged glances but said nothing. Belinda listened attentively.

"I called Detective Fantin and left a message on his machine," Uncle Paolo said. "When he calls back, I'll make sure that he knows you and Sofia were with us Saturday night."

I breathed a sigh of relief. "You're talking about the murders."

"What murders?" Maria asked. "What's going on?"

"Thank goodness, we're not the only ones who didn't know," Aunt Amelia explained. "The other sister, Anna May was killed, and a Russian woman, I don't know her."

"Natalia Gorsky," I volunteered. "She's the owner of the Lodge out in Minnow Lake.

Maria's eyes widened as she glanced in my direction. "Do they think you did it?"

Before I could say anything, Belinda decided to join the fray. "No, they have evidence against Anna May. She had the Russian woman's hairs in her hand."

Maria made the sign of the cross. "Let's hope that's the end of it."

Belinda opened her mouth to speak. She had probably heard talk of an accomplice. I caught her eye and shook my head. But before I could change the subject, Aunt Amelia had already moved on. "Where's Sofia?"

"She had some errands to run, so she decided to leave Belinda in charge." I didn't know if Sofia had mentioned she was leaving my place and quitting her job, and I had no intention of sharing the news with Aunt Amelia. "Maria, why don't you take more pictures? Get my mother, Aunt Amelia, and Uncle Paolo in a few of them."

While everyone positioned themselves, a young couple walked in. I welcomed the reprieve and went over to introduce myself. We chatted about the upcoming free workshops during the month of November. They signed up for two of them and took my card and several brochures. As we were talking, I noticed my mother, aunt, and uncle leaving. They waved in my direction.

Belinda had an amused expression on her face. "It's like *Days of our Lives* around here. So many plots and secrets. What were you afraid I would say when you gave me that evil eye?"

I smiled at this young woman who reminded me of my former students. "I didn't want to upset my mother and aunt with any speculation. But I'm curious. What were you going to say?"

"Last night, everyone buzzed about the murders. Someone mentioned that Anna May Godfrey probably got an old boyfriend involved. Is it true she went out with fourteen different guys during high school?"

I figured that Belinda had inherited the gossip gene from her grandmother, and I didn't want any of my statements tossed about at bars, coffee houses and wherever else Belinda hung out. "Anna May was very popular in high school. I didn't keep a running total of all her boyfriends."

"Well, it seems a lot of women did. Especially those who married her exes."

The wives of the bad boys must be talking. I would have to share this information with Jenny Marie when she visited on Thursday.

Belinda winked at me. “Don’t worry. I will be discreet. Sofia told me all about confidentiality. What goes on in the office, stays in the office.”

“You got it, Belinda.” I went back into my office and started to work on the PowerPoint presentation for the first workshop. The phone rang consistently throughout the afternoon until about four o’clock. I went into the outer office and chatted with an enthusiastic Belinda. She informed me that she had booked consultations with fifteen potential clients. I would be busy for the rest of the week.

At five-thirty, I decided to call it a day. Minutes after Belinda left, I heard the door open, and a familiar voice call out. “Gilda, are you still here?”

My heart started pounding, and I could feel my stomach fluttering. Jean Taylor. I took several deep breaths—yoga breaths ironically enough—and came out of the office. A tall, well-built man stood next to Jean. They held river rock lucky bamboo plants in their hands. This must be the famous Michael Taylor. He was older, probably even older than me, and reminded me of a younger, leaner Nick Nolte.

I forced a smile and waved them toward my office. “Come on in.” I held out my hand to Michael. “I’m Gilda Greco.”

He shook my hand. “Michael Taylor. Pleased to meet you.”

They sat across from me. Jean spoke first: “I’ve come to apologize for my behavior last week. I haven’t been myself since all these murders started. The Godfreys were my only family when I was growing up. After Aunt Elizabeth died, I must have grieved a whole year. One thing I’m glad about. She didn’t live to see two of her daughters and a niece die such brutal deaths. And Natalia was like a daughter to her." She shuddered. "I can't bear to think of how much they suffered."

Michael squeezed her hand. "It's been hard on me as well. I've always loved Carrie Ann, in spite of everything that happened in the past. We married too young and didn't really know what we wanted in life. I had just seen her that afternoon before she died and—" His voice trailed.

Jean put down the plant and hugged him.

I wondered what they had talked about, but it wasn't my business. Did Carlo know? I sighed. I could email him the information, but I didn't feel comfortable doing that. And I didn't want to risk another Jean attack. I smiled at both of them. "I accept your apology, Jean. These last twelve days have been hard on everyone, even those of us not directly connected to the Godfreys." I studied Jean. Her eyes were clear. The calm, supportive yogini had returned. Angry Jean was well hidden.

Jean pointed to the plants. "I brought one for your office. And one for Sofia. We dropped another one off at Karen's office before we came here." She added, "It's important to clear the air and replace all the negative feelings with positive ones."

They were smaller than the original plant she had given me, but I didn't feel comfortable having Jean's plant in my private office. "I'll place my plant in the outer office. That way all my clients can experience the positive energy." Jean smiled and nodded in approval. I continued, "Sofia doesn't work here anymore. I'll make sure she gets the plant."

Jean's eyes widened in surprise. "Is she sick?"

"The events of the last twelve days also affected her. She's not really a career girl, and I think she's glad to get back to her usual routine."

Michael cleared his throat. "We don't mind dropping it off at her place."

"I need to talk to Sofia," Jean said. "I won't feel right until I've put this incident behind me. Could you give me her number?"

I scribbled her number on a memo and handed it to Jean. I didn't want to call Sofia so soon. We both needed our space.

Michael's eyes traveled around the room. "She did a great job of decorating this office. I wonder if she'd be interested in redecorating my studio."

"It's time for a change. Out with the old and in with the new." Jean liked to sprinkle her conversations with old adages and clichés.

As I watched both of them, I realized that they hadn't come to see me. They came to see Sofia. And what I found more interesting was that Michael waited until Carrie Ann and Anna May were both dead before deciding to redecorate. If the Godfreys were family, why couldn't Jean approach Three Sisters Decorating and ask Carrie Ann for advice?

Michael glanced at his watch. "We could call Sofia now and drop by tonight or tomorrow." He took out his cell phone.

Jean frowned. "I've got back-to-back yoga classes tonight. We'll be tied up with Anna May's memorial service tomorrow, and Natalia's funeral is on Wednesday. I'll give Sofia a call later tonight and set something up for Thursday or Friday." She favored me with one of her stunning smiles. "Great seeing you again, Gilda. And I hope to see you at Wednesday night yoga. Let's move forward and put all of this unpleasantness behind us."

Michael and Jean Taylor had recovered from the four deaths and were more than ready to start a new adventure, one that did not include the family that had once rescued Jean from an unhappy childhood.

Chapter 19

Thursday, November 3, 2011

The next three days were jam-packed with appointments. In addition to the fifteen Belinda had scheduled, I also met with eight walk-ins. While most of them were searching for a free, friendly ear, five booked more sessions.

When I conceived the idea of ReCareering, my intention had been to help other boomers transition into second careers or retirement. Interestingly enough, all twenty-three visitors were under the age of forty. I was surprised to hear so many young people hated their jobs and craved a change after five or six years of employment.

One young man wanted to toss his MBA and start over as a paramedic. When I pressed him to explain his reasons for this sudden change of direction, he faltered. And then mumbled about CSI and other such programs on television. I also spoke with a seventeen-year-old girl who talked about taking a gap year and wanted advice on what to do. After texting her mother, she booked five sessions.

The other three who booked additional sessions were unemployed women in their thirties. Two had college diplomas, and one was a high school dropout. I took notes and listened as these clients talked wistfully about their lost jobs and unrealized dreams.

Thursday morning, I remembered that Jenny Marie and Grace would be coming over that evening. I asked Belinda not to book any appointments after four o'clock. I wanted to go home early, have a quick supper and relax before my guests arrived.

The two women arrived shortly after seven. I took them on a tour of my condo and the building. Jenny Marie was very happy and relaxed. Each time she glanced at Grace, her features would soften, and her smile would widen. She adored her only child and hung on every word she said. I was also impressed by Grace. She was even more stunning than Melly Grace and Carrie Ann, the two beauties of the Godfrey clan. Her blonde hair fell in waves, and her large, cornflower-blue eyes appeared animated and interested in her surroundings. Dressed in head-to-toe black, she was pencil-slim and stunning.

During a lull in the conversation, I realized I had been staring at Grace "You remind me so much of Carrie Ann. It's like time has gone back thirty years, and we are high school again."

Jenny Marie nodded in agreement. "It's uncanny how much she resembles both Carrie Ann and Melly Grace."

Grace hugged her mother. "I look a lot like you, too. Apples do not fall far from the tree."

Jenny Marie may have had problems with her husband and Anna May, but she had raised an extraordinary daughter.

At the end of the tour, we sat down in the living room. I poured the tea as we talked about condo buildings, the Toronto real estate market, and Grace's career as an interior designer.

Grace put down her cup and steered the conversation in another direction. "This has been lovely. But we need to talk about the murders."

"It's so nice chatting about normal things again. Do we have to talk about the murders?" A shadow crossed Jenny Marie's face.

"We need to find the murderer," Grace said, as her jaw hardened. "I won't leave you alone in that house knowing that you could be the next victim."

Jenny Marie laughed nervously. "Grace also thinks the accomplice is after Godfreys and blondes. It's a strange coincidence. I wonder if anyone else has noticed it." No one said anything, so she continued. "Grace is determined to find out more out about Anna May's affairs. I don't know what more she can find out. Carlo has already touched base with our suppliers and all those men who called Anna May. It's embarrassing to have to admit that—"

"Was she skimming money from the business?" I asked.

Jenny Marie's eyebrows shot up. "Have you spoken to Carlo?"

"No, it's second-hand, no, third-hand information that I heard from Sofia," I explained. "She heard Anna May tampered with the supplier accounts."

Jenny Marie nodded. "Anna May started taking money about six months ago. Carrie Ann and I suspected something, but we didn't learn the details until just before Carrie Ann's death." She sighed. "You need to hear the whole story."

Her eyes filled with tears, and she paused to collect her thoughts. "Last year, Anna May started visiting casinos on a regular basis. She developed a gambling problem and accumulated close to fifty thousand dollars in debt. Then, she applied for and maxed out a number of credit cards and sold off all her jewellery. At first, Carrie Ann and I gave her small loans of money, but later we decided that we were enabling her, and we stopped. When that source of money dried up, she started to skim the accounts, and she contacted some of her old boyfriends. You remember them, Gilda?"

"Did she contact all of them?" Anna May must have devoted considerable time and effort to getting all those phone numbers.

"You know how pushy she can be," Jenny Marie said. "She Googled all their names and emailed them. Five of them gave her money."

"Who gave her money?" I asked.

Jenny Marie handed me a sheet with a list of names: Ray Centis, Mike Grant, Jamie Douglas, Paul Nardi, and Marco Ventura. "It figures those guys would give her money. They were always in some kind of trouble."

Jenny Marie shook her head. "These men have all settled down with wives and children. They have respectable jobs and do volunteer coaching for their kids' teams. They may have been wild in their younger days, but their present lives are very stable ones. They were horrified when Carlo called them into the station for questioning, but they all had alibis for the night of Anna May's murder. Carlo checked them out, and some of the wives had to learn about their husbands' involvement with Anna May. I don't know how much of this is public knowledge, but I am hoping that reputations and marriages won't be affected by all of this."

"Don't worry. I will breathe none of this to anyone. But there are a few leaks at the police station, and word may get out soon." I hoped that Jenny Marie or Grace would relay that information to Carlo.

Grace shrugged her shoulders. "None of them are being held for the murders. They'll just have to deal with a bit of unpleasant gossip. Carrie Ann must have suspected a more sinister plot." She turned to me. "You saw her just before she died. How did she appear to you?"

"She was so mellow that day," I said. "We talked about travel, careers, and reminisced about our high school days. She was at a crossroads in her life and ready to make a decision of some kind. I wonder if she was planning to base her decision on Jim Nelson's report."

Grace leaned forward. "Hmm. Why would you say that?"

"She kept glancing at her watch and murmuring that she needed to get to an office before six o'clock. She didn't have a portfolio or briefcase with her, so I knew she wasn't seeing a client. I thought she might be seeing a doctor, but I guess she wanted to get her hands on that report." I spoke directly to Jenny Marie. "Did you know Jim Nelson was investigating Anna May?"

"Carrie Ann didn't confide in me at all," Jenny Marie said. "We had a very busy summer, and Anna May seemed to disappear for days at a time. Carrie Ann and I decided to confront Anna May, but we wanted to wait until later in the fall when we weren't as frazzled."

Grace nodded in agreement. "Carrie Ann wanted ammunition before confronting Anna May. I think she might have shared some of this with Melly Grace."

"Melly Grace came up here and started talking about auditing the books and investigating suppliers and clients," Jenny Marie said. "She reprimanded Anna May a number of times on her gambling and drinking." She managed a smile. "You remember that night at the restaurant, Gilda?"

"How could I forget that tongue lashing I received from Melly Grace?" I shuddered as I recalled the events of that memorable evening.

Grace frowned. "Did she think you had anything to do with Carrie Ann's murder?"

Jenny Marie shook her head. "She resented the fact that a certain detective might be interested in Gilda."

"I get the picture," Grace said. "You were moving in on one of Melly Grace's men from the past. And I think I know which detective we're talking about. He's pretty hot!"

"Grace!" Jenny Marie's eyes widened. "He's old enough to be your father."

"Relax, I'm not putting the moves on him. So, Carlo and Melly Grace were once a hot item. How long did that last?" Grace asked.

"That relationship lasted a couple of months," Jenny Marie said. "But you know Melly Grace. She did love to maintain appearances and still be the object of everyone's attention and admiration."

Grace sighed. "It sounds like Melly Grace created quite a stir the day of Carrie Ann's funeral. I wish I had been there."

"It's better you weren't." Jenny Marie shook her head. "Anna May spun more and more out of control. You did not have to witness that." She turned to me. "It all started the day we came to visit you and Sofia. Had I known that she would fly into one of her rages, I would never have suggested it."

"It was your idea to visit?" All along, I assumed that Anna May planned to visit and pin the murder on me.

Jenny Marie's eyes filled with tears. "I wanted to spend some time with the last person who saw Carrie Ann alive. I wanted to hear her last words, thoughts—" Her voice trailed off, and she cried softly for several minutes.

Grace hugged her mother and offered her some tissue. "You can't blame yourself. Anna May is…was a grown woman and responsible for her own actions. She didn't have to lash out at Gilda and Sofia and murder two other women."

Jenny Marie blew her nose. "She couldn't deal with anyone else's success. As soon as we got into the elevator, she started ranting and raving. And when she saw you and Sofia living so well, she lost it. I don't think she thought of you as a possible suspect until then."

On its own, envy is a powerful emotion. Combine it with raging hormones, alcohol and drugs, and it can become toxic. It wasn't too long ago that I dealt with these same issues, but with a much younger population. I could recall at least two or three meetings per year where I met with Students Services to discuss students with impulse control problems. Autism, Asperger's, fetal alcohol syndrome, Tourette's. Each year the list grew longer. I thought back to Anna May's flushed cheeks and angry tirades. "Did she mix drugs and alcohol?"

"She had a pharmacy in her purse," Grace said. "Painkillers, antidepressants, sleeping pills, allergy medication. We found empty wine bottles in the trunk of her car and the back of her closet."

"She hasn't been the same since our mother died." Jenny Marie sighed. "Carrie Ann and I should have staged an intervention."

"Grandma died five years ago," Grace said. "That's a long time to be mourning and behaving badly."

"A lot happened to her in those last five years," Jenny Marie said. "She had that bad car accident, went through menopause, gained fifty pounds, and started gambling."

A stubborn, judgmental look appeared on Grace's face. "You had your share of stuff during that time. I don't see you drinking, gambling, and begging for money."

"I am not too proud of the way I have handled my own stuff." Jenny winced. "Getting older is not always a smooth passage, though I must admit Gilda seems to have found the fountain of youth."

I felt myself blushing "I've been lucky, I guess."

"It must be awesome to have all that money," Grace said.

"It has given me more choices. And it has also given my family and friends more opportunities."

"Gilda has paid off mortgages and major debts for a number of people, some even total strangers," Jenny Marie explained. "She has changed a lot of lives."

"That's the best part of it, seeing people who are struggling under mountains of debt suddenly coming up and breathing normally. I would have paid off all of Anna May's debts." Despite our differences, I would have helped Anna May.

"After all that happened, you would still have done that?" Grace asked.

I could empathize with Anna May. Before winning the lottery, I experienced one lean year where I had to count the pennies. "If I knew about all of this a few weeks ago, I would have paid off all her debts, anonymously, of course."

"But you wouldn't have helped her. Within a month, she would have gambled everything away again. She needed professional help that none of us could give her." Jenny Marie's eyes filled with tears.

"Her back was up against the wall," I said. "Two things I have learned since I won the lottery: money talks and lack of money screams. Anna May was screaming for help, attention, love. Money doesn't solve every problem, but life can be made more comfortable, and I am happy to be in a position to help anyone who needs it."

Grace chuckled "I wouldn't advertise that, Gilda. You might have a lot of takers and be left with nothing."

"Not to worry. The money is well-invested, and I sign all my checks. When I decide to give money away, it's always after careful deliberation." I wondered about the state of Jenny Marie's finances. Did she need an infusion of money in her account?

Grace stood. "We should get going. I want to finish going through Anna May's closet tonight. I won't have time tomorrow. We have that early appointment tomorrow morning with Ronald Carruthers over at the Bank of Montreal."

"Ten o'clock is not that early." Jenny Marie shook

her head. “I can’t believe you still sleep in each morning. In my day—”

“You were up with the chickens and walked five miles to school,” Grace said.

We laughed, and my eyes met Grace’s as they left. We were on the same wavelength. I would send off an email tonight, and call Ronald first thing tomorrow morning. He had already helped with several of my other bank transfers.

Chapter 20

Friday, November 4, 2011

Ronald Carruthers called a few minutes after nine. He didn't share any details of the Three Sisters Decorating account, but listened as I tossed out different amounts of money. I intended to cover any outstanding debts and provide a small cushion of comfort for Jenny Marie. I had learned, the hard way, not to overwhelm friends and family members with extravagant amounts of money. I still cringe when I think of the fifty thousand dollars I gave a young relative who proceeded to spend all of it within three months. And when I refused to give more, her entire family stopped speaking to me.

Ronald and I decided on a transfer of three hundred thousand dollars. This would be enough to pay off all accounts payable and Anna May's gambling debts, and leave Jenny Marie with a severance. She would need the extra money after she closed down the business. Ronald assured me that he would be discreet and not mention my name to Jenny Marie. After last night's conversation, she might suspect my involvement, but knowing Ronald, he would offer a complex but convincing explanation about "found" money.

As soon as I hung up the phone, Belinda buzzed to let me know my first client of the morning had arrived.

After the second appointment, I glanced at my schedule and realized I didn't have any appointments scheduled until two o'clock. I could phone and ask Adele out to lunch. She liked spur-of-the-moment invitations. We could pop over to Culpeppers.

Before I could punch in Adele's number, Belinda buzzed and informed me that Grace Robinson had arrived. The name sounded vaguely familiar. As I tried to recall where I had met her, Jenny Marie's Grace entered the room. I rose to greet her, and before I could speak, she hugged me close. "Thank you. Thank you. Thank you." When she let go of me, I saw tears in her eyes.

We both sat down, and she continued to gaze at me adoringly. For several moments, neither of us said anything. "Does your mother know?"

"Ronald rambled on and on about special circumstances and insurance on some accounts. He even brought up one of Grandpa's investments from way back. I didn't understand a word he said, and Mom frowned and shook her head several times. She thinks Grandma's spirit had something to do with it."

I smiled as I thought of the kind, generous woman who had worked tirelessly on fund raisers and taken in foster children and other strays. "Good, let her think that."

"But I know, and someday I'll tell Mom."

"Nothing wrong with believing in angels," I said.

"I'm glad we have a chance to chat without Mom around," Grace said. "If we don't do something, the murderer will go scot free. The police don't have any leads, and they're willing to accept all those alibis at face value."

Last night, I had gone through all the possibilities but still had trouble coming up with a suspect. One large piece of the puzzle still troubled me. "I've considered all possible suspects but keep coming up with the same question: Why would anyone help Anna May kill three women? She didn't have money to give them. What could they possibly gain by going along with her?"

Grace shrugged. "Knowing Anna May, she manipulated or bullied some man into helping her. And when he had enough, he killed her."

While I didn't like the bad boys, I didn't think any of them capable of murder. "Do you think one of Anna May's ex-boyfriends killed her?"

"Maybe or maybe someone we've been overlooking." She leaned closer. "I'm hoping you and I can work together to catch the killer."

Nothing would give me more satisfaction than catching the person who helped Anna May frame me for those deaths. While I hadn't shared that concern with anyone, it still rankled that someone would go to such lengths to set me up. While Anna May was the instigator, the accomplice did agree to cooperate. "I don't see how I can help. And I don't know what you can do. Aren't you leaving for Toronto soon?"

"I'm leaving after lunch today." She took out a black notebook. "This is Anna May's diary. I found it last night while cleaning out her closet and chest of drawers. I'm going to read through it and try to make some sense of the last two months of entries."

I gasped. "You need to turn that over to that police. It's evidence!"

"Not in its present form." She handed over the

diary.

As I flipped through the pages, I saw what she meant. There were squiggles, doodles and scattered initials and jumbled words. "She must have been drunk or stoned when she wrote in this diary. I don't mean to sound negative, but I don't think you'll find any clues here."

"Oh yes, I will. I know some of that code she used."

"What code?"

Grace explained. "When they were all teenagers, Melly Grace came up with a code their parents wouldn't understand. One summer at French River, they spent time practicing it on those cool, rainy days. Whenever they sent letters to each other, they would use the code to talk about their boyfriends and other personal stuff. Melly Grace and Carrie Ann stopped using it when they left home, but Anna May continued journaling all her life. There are more diaries in Mom's basement, but I'm not interested in Anna May's distant past."

"Why don't you ask Jenny Marie to decipher it?"

"Mom doesn't know about the code," Grace said. "She was the youngest and the tattler of the family. Anna May and the others didn't trust her with it."

"How did you find out about it?"

"After I graduated from Ryerson, I spent three months with Melly Grace in Tennessee. One day, I found an old diary of hers, and she explained the code to me. A corresponded to Z, E to Y, and there was a twist with the consonants. I don't remember all of it, but I know it'll come back to me. I'm good with puzzles."

I hated to think that Grace would waste her time on such a fruitless endeavor. “That would be helpful with some of the words that Anna May used, but I don’t know how you can make sense of the squiggles.”

“That’s Pitman shorthand. Anna May and Mom studied that in school.”

“You know Pitman shorthand?” I hadn’t heard of anyone taking shorthand in years.

“Well…no…but, I can get a book and figure it out.”

“Okay, so you figure out. What then?”

Grace winked. “I prepare a transcript and show it to your boyfriend.”

“He’s not my boyfriend. We’ve never gone out.”

“You’ve got to be kidding!” Grace pointed to the phone. “Call him up and invite him over to dinner. Dazzle him with manicotti, fettuccine Alfredo, or one of your other signature dishes.”

The confidence of youth! I didn’t have it back then, and I often wondered if I had it now. As for signature dishes…I didn’t want to go down that road. “What do you think I should be doing here in Sudbury while you are decoding in Toronto?”

“Keep your ears and eyes open. Find out where some of those men hang out and—”

“Stop right there! I have no intention of getting involved with Ray Centis and any of that crowd. I didn’t hang out with them during high school, and it would look very suspicious if I started to do so now.” And if one of them did turn out to be the accomplice, I would be in danger. “Your mother said they all had alibis.”

“Their wives provided those alibis. I’m willing to

bet one or two of them lied." She frowned. "But I can see your point. If you've never socialized with them, it doesn't make too much sense to start doing that now."

"They're not the only suspects," I muttered.

"You know something. Tell me."

"This may sound farfetched to you. These people are close to your mother's family, and I don't want to point any fingers—"

"Spill it."

"Jean and Michael Taylor."

Her eyes widened, and she paled. She said nothing for several minutes, and then she spoke more softly. "I can't see her directly involved in any way. She's too fragile. But she could be covering for him."

"You know something about him. Do you want to share it with me?" I watched as different emotions appeared on her beautiful face. Shock. Anger. Fear. The confident young woman started to unravel.

"Only Melly Grace and Carrie Ann knew about this," Grace said. "You must promise not to tell anyone else, especially not my mother."

I nodded and watched as she swallowed hard and forced back tears. "When I was about three years old, Michael Taylor tried to molest me. He and Carrie Ann were babysitting me while my parents were out one evening." Her lower lip puckered, and tears pooled in her eyes.

I reached over and squeezed her hand.

"Carrie Ann came into the room just as he unzipped his pants while standing next to my bed. She made him stop and didn't let me out of her sight for the rest of the night. The next morning, she phoned Melly Grace for advice, and they both decided not to tell my parents."

"Carrie Ann left him the following week." Tears streamed down her face.

I went over and hugged her. While I had heard variations of this story during my teaching career, it still shocked me. For several minutes, we sat there locked in a tight embrace. Her thin body shook as she sobbed. I didn't want to share a troubling thought with Grace. Michael could have molested her on other occasions before Carrie Ann confronted him. When she stopped crying and sat up straighter, I continued the conversation. "When did they tell you?"

"Melly Grace visited the summer of my twelfth birthday. She and Carrie Ann told me the whole story then. They believed I had a right to know." Her jaw tightened. "Michael and Jean were getting married that fall."

"Did you have any further contact with him?"

"After Carrie Ann divorced him, my parents cut off ties with him. Grandma continued to support him, through his depression and suicide attempts."

"Why didn't Carrie Ann tell her parents about Michael?"

"That would have scandalized Grandma and Grandpa. You remember how straight-laced they were." She shuddered. "God only knows what they would think about the four deaths and Anna May's behavior."

"Did you ever confront him?"

Grace smiled triumphantly. "Years later, after Carrie Ann agreed to mend fences for Jean's sake, I told him what I knew, and what I was prepared to do if he ever tried anything again."

"Did you get any counseling?"

"Carrie Ann arranged for some sessions with a social worker. I went a couple of times and then stopped. I didn't remember the incident, and Michael was not part of my life."

"You were fortunate to have those strong women on your side, but I think Carrie Ann should have told your parents and reported him."

Her eyes widened. "I wonder if Anna May found out about it. She had a habit of sneaking around and eavesdropping on conversations. If she had something, anything on Michael, she would have used it to get what she wanted."

This was becoming too uncomfortable for her, so I decided to let it go for now. "When Jean and Michael dropped by the other day, he mentioned seeing Carrie Ann earlier in the afternoon."

"Does Carlo know?" Grace asked.

I doubt that would have come up in any phone conversation. When he called the Taylor household, Carlo would not have thought to ask about Michael's whereabouts. His primary concern was Jean's visit to my office. I started to share this information and then stopped. Now that I knew about Michael's disgusting behavior, I felt the need to protect Grace from the Taylors. "I'm not certain what Carlo knows. He did call Jean several times, so he might have suspected something."

"Hmm. The plot thickens. How do you feel about snooping on them?"

Part of me wanted nothing to do with Michael Taylor. I didn't think I could even look at him without wanting to throw up.

But deep down, I knew Grace was right. If we

didn't get involved, the police would never find the killer. And then I had an idea. "What if I hire Jim Nelson to keep an eye on Michael and those men who gave Anna May money?"

"That sounds great." Grace clapped her hands. "Does he have enough resources to follow six men?"

I remembered that small, cramped office and wondered if he had any other partners. "I'll ask how many he can handle. I still remember the names on that list. I know that Ray Centis would be at the top of my list of suspects. I'll rank them and then decide which ones are priority one."

"This is starting to sound exciting," Grace's eyes lit up. "I wish I could blog about our investigation. It has the makings of a novel and maybe even a feature film."

"Don't you dare! We don't need any attention directed our way. I feel uncomfortable keeping this from your mom. She should know what's going on."

"No! You'll only upset her. She's not as strong as Carrie Ann and Melly Grace. And she still hasn't recovered from Anna May's bullying. That woman made her life hell since they started living together."

I thought of my own need to protect my mother. It seemed to be a trait many of us shared, one that had crossed over into the next generation of women.

"I want to get to Toronto before rush hour." She rose and headed toward the door. "Give me a call if you find out anything at all about those men. I'll let you know when I finish decoding Anna May's diary."

I walked with her to the front door.

Before she left, she hugged me again. While I had never regretted my decision not to have children, today I wondered what it would be like to have a daughter, especially one as beautiful, intelligent and kind-hearted as Grace Godfrey Robinson.

Chapter 21

I went back into my office and called Nickel City Security. I got the answering machine and left a message asking Jim if I could drop over later in the afternoon. I decided not to call Adele. All I could think about was the investigation Grace and I had decided to launch. Instead, I heated up a Michelina dinner and worked through lunch.

My first client of the afternoon arrived. Janice Evans, a retired boomer. I perked up. This was the distraction I needed to tide me over until the end of the day.

Unlike the younger clients, Janice volunteered very little information. I had to pry it out of her. It took over half an hour to find out the details of her life. The fifty-nine-year-old retired nurse was already bored after one year of retirement. She and her husband had taken a Mediterranean cruise last summer, and Janice had spent the month of September visiting a friend in Provence. The rest of the time, she puttered around her house and garden.

"I need more structure and variety, and I don't know how to get it," she said as she clenched and unclenched her hands. "It seems all I do is clean the house, make meals, do laundry, and visit my mother." She sighed. "There aren't any grandchildren yet."

"What had you hoped to do during retirement?" I

wondered about her expectations and wanted to know just how realistic they were.

"Oh, I don't know." She sighed and looked out the small window. "Thought I would be traveling more, at least three or four times a year. Maybe taking a few cooking courses. Improve my French. Volunteer." She managed a tight smile. "I know I'll be busier when the grandchildren come."

"The grandchildren aren't here yet. And I would be very careful about making that kind of commitment. You don't want another full-time job for the next five years." I thought of the many retirees who were now *parenting* the next generation of children. Some of them relished their new role while others were exhausted and counting the days until the children went to school full time.

"My husband has made it clear he doesn't want a full-time babysitting job." She made a face. "I think that's why he isn't planning to retire for a while."

A touchy subject I did not wish to address. I was not a marriage counselor and, given my own track record with relationships, had no intention of helping others in that arena. I decided to focus on her retirement goals. "Are you planning any other trips?"

"We're going to Mexico in January, and I have an open invitation to visit Marie in Provence—" Her voice faltered. "The days are much too long."

"What about the volunteering?"

"I'm pretty active in my church, and I've been helping with some local fundraising events, but I don't find any of that stimulating. Too many meetings and committee work. And lots and lots of politics."

I paused as I checked my notes. "Check into

cooking or language courses at Cambrian College. Ask your friend in Provence to check out Cordon Bleu courses in France."

While Janice smiled and nodded at the right places, I knew that she wouldn't rush home and start implementing any of these suggestions. Could she be depressed? New retirees are disappointed when life on golden pond turns out to be as exciting as watching grass grow.

I decided to try another approach. "Do you swim, golf, ski…?"

"I'm not that athletic. I thought of joining a gym, but I didn't like any of the ones I visited. They remind me too much of high school Phys Ed which I hated with a passion."

"You could do yoga. It's very relaxing and much easier on the joints. I go to Jean Taylor's studio regularly." At least I did until recently. Regardless of my feelings toward Jean, I had no qualms recommending her to any of my clients.

"I could do that."

"Are you getting out each day? You could incorporate a twenty-minute walk into your schedule."

"I try to consolidate all my trips into three days a week," she said. "It saves on gas."

I shook my head. "Get out each day. You need to interact with people."

Janice forced a smile. "I should go. I promised my mother I would drive her to her doctor's appointment."

I handed her several brochures. "Give us a call if you want to schedule more appointments." As I watched her leave, I wondered if she would return.

A puzzled Belinda came into my office after the

last client left. "A woman called from Nickel City Security. She said that Jim would be available any time after four-thirty. Are you upgrading the alarm system?"

She must have assumed Jim Nelson handled that type of security. Just as well. I didn't want to arouse any of her suspicions, which could feed the gossip mills of two separate generations.

"It doesn't hurt to research other options." I pointed toward the back alley. "We could use more lights and security back there." I glanced at my watch. "It's almost four. Why don't we call it a day? I can pick up any calls that come in now."

Belinda left within minutes. I tidied up, checked my email messages and left shortly afterward. I considered walking over, but still felt apprehensive about the back alley. It wouldn't hurt to beef up the security and the lighting.

I drove over to the other plaza and parked my car at a distance. This time, a receptionist greeted me when I entered the office. The young woman had a hard look about her—blue-black hair asymmetrically cut with pale skin, heavily made-up eyes and piercings. She wore a black turtleneck which probably covered up multiple tattoos and more piercings. But her smile was authentic and lit up her face.

"Good afternoon," she said. "How can I help you?" Her pleasant voice belied her appearance.

"I'm Gilda Greco. I'm here to see Jim."

"You've got a four-thirty with him." She nodded toward the closed door. "He's on the phone right now. You can take a seat over there." She pointed toward two chairs.

The office had undergone a major transformation

since the last time I had visited. There were no loose files, odors or remnants of food. And there was a fresh coat of paint on the walls along with four Monet prints. I smiled at the young woman as I read her name plate—Mel Nelson.

She flashed me another beautiful smile. “He’s my dad.”

I gestured toward the walls. “And did you do all of this?” I watched her nod enthusiastically. “You’ve done a lovely job.”

Mel beamed. Before she could make any further comments, the door opened. Jim frowned and motioned for me to follow. As soon as I sat down, he started speaking. “What can I do for you this afternoon, Miss Greco? Doing more research for your boyfriend?”

I winced at the mention of Carlo. Jim appeared hostile toward me and didn’t sound too thrilled about Carlo. I wondered if Carlo or one of the constables had taken him to task when they visited last week. “I want you to follow these men. Let me know what they’re up to.” I handed the list to him.

He gave the list a quick glance and then threw it down on his desk. “Lady, you’re barking up the wrong tree. These guys had nothing to do with the murders.” He paused. “I’m assuming you’re still on that kick.”

“Yes, I’m still on that kick. And what makes you so sure that these men are innocent?”

“For starters, five of them are my buds.” He picked up the list and pointed to the five men who had given Anna May money. “I don’t investigate my friends.”

I wondered if we had been at school together. I didn’t recall his name or his face, but over three decades had passed, and he had not aged well.

He smiled, but seemed distracted. “I was at Sudbury Secondary when you were there, but our paths didn’t cross.”

I didn’t want to go down Memory Lane with Jim, so I decided to focus on the task at hand. “What about Michael Taylor?”

“The photographer?” He raised a brow at me. “Are you serious?”

I pushed the list toward him. “Four women are dead, and nothing is being done about it. I think a professional was involved, and that’s why I want to hire you.”

“You think that Michael Taylor is a professional?”

“He may not have committed the crimes, but I think he knows who did.” Or Jean knows. That would be one explanation for her bizarre behavior. “That’s why I want him followed. I believe he will lead us to the murderer.”

“Sounds farfetched to me, but it’s your money and if that’s how you want to spend it.” He paused. “Now if I had your money, I wouldn’t be wasting it on a police investigation.”

“What would you be spending it on?” The career counselor in me wondered what he would be doing if he didn’t have to work.

“I’d close up this business and get out of Sudbury. Start all over somewhere warm, somewhere where that little girl of mine could get a fresh start.” Jim’s face softened. “She’s had too many hard breaks for one lifetime. She deserves a better deal.”

I wondered about Mel’s past, but didn’t want to pry. In spite of appearances, Mel Nelson was still the apple of her father’s eye.

He scowled at me. "Did your boyfriend ask for your help? Is that what this is all about?"

"Carlo Fantin is not my boyfriend, and he did not ask me to get involved with the investigation. It's a personal choice I have made, and I need your help. Now do you want to do it or not?" I had switched to my teacher voice.

Jim sat up straighter. "Let's get something straight from the beginning. I don't want police constables at my door. I'll report to you and only you once a week until you decide to terminate the investigation. As for my rates—"

"Bill me at the end of the investigation." I had no intention of bickering about money. "When can you start?"

"How about tomorrow?"

I nodded in agreement. We shook hands, and I left the office.

Exhausted, I forced myself to stay awake until after supper. My first full week in almost two years. Thankfully, I hadn't made any plans for the evening.

Chapter 22

Sunday, November 6, 2011

Adele and I drove to Sudbury's first holistic fair. Teresa, Laura's daughter, was one of the organizers and very keen to help the practitioners in the city. All the booths had been allocated a few months before I decided to open ReCareering. Teresa had promised me a booth if one of the participants canceled, but that had not happened. For the time being, I was content to visit and observe.

Teresa and her committee had selected an excellent location. The Howard Johnson was one of the older hotels in the city, located within walking distance of downtown and near Highway 69. And more important, there was lots of free parking. When Adele and I arrived, we found the large hall bustling with activity. Laura and Teresa waved to us from across the room. We made our way there, nodding to a number of friends and acquaintances along the way.

Teresa jumped up and rushed toward me, arms outstretched, and gave me a tight hug. "I'm so glad you could come." She gestured toward the crowd. "Isn't this a great turnout?"

"You've got a full house here," I replied.

"We'll hold the fair over two, maybe three days next year. And maybe we'll book a hall at the university," Teresa said.

Laura touched her lightly on the shoulder. "Calm down. Focus on today. Stay present."

We laughed. Teresa is a Reiki master who specializes in soul intuitive readings and mind clearing. Usually, she's the one telling everyone else to calm down.

"Let's pick our workshops," Adele said.

I studied the day's program and indicated my choices: *Balancing Your Energy Field*, *Blossoming Heart Healing,* and *The Forgiving Heart*. Adele picked *All About Reflexology* and *Getting Clear*. Laura would be spending most of the day manning Teresa's booth. We decided to go for lunch at twelve thirty.

Adele and I spent some time visiting all the booths. I recognized many of modalities represented: personal health coaches, nutritional counselors, acupuncturists, emotional freedom practitioners, Reiki masters, reflexologists, and shamanic healers.

I spent some time with the young woman who did akashic records readings. These were new to me, and I listened as she explained, "Akashic records are the record of everything that has ever happened as well as the possibilities for the future. During the reading, you can ask questions about your life, relationships, work…whatever you want and I will reveal the answers. That is, if you give me permission to access your akashic records." She handed me her card. "If you want, we could do a twenty-minute reading here."

I fingered her card. "I'm attending a couple of workshops this morning. I'll drop by later in the afternoon."

As we walked away, Adele whispered, "You're not

serious about that?"

"I'm curious." While I didn't usually go for New Age readings, I was intrigued by the thought of someone accessing records in my brain.

My heart beat faster as we approached the largest booth in the room. Dressed in royal-blue-and-black matching outfits and flashing perfect smiles, Jean and Michael Taylor stood behind a beautifully designed booth. Blue balloons and streamers showcased the yoga clothing, accessories and books from Jean's studio. Jean came out from behind the booth and hugged both Adele and me. Michael smiled and nodded in approval.

I longed to change direction, but I forced a smile as Jean shook a finger at me. "I haven't seen you at yoga for a while. I hope you're still not upset with me. You need to relax, and let things go. And you need to get out of that office. Remember, you need balance in your life."

I had been too busy to think about yoga, but I knew I could never go back to Jean's classes. It wouldn't be the same. "Things should settle down in a week or two." I changed the subject. "Your booth is amazing."

"We have Sofia to thank for that," Michael said. "When she heard about this fair, she volunteered to organize our booth. She arrived at the crack of dawn and spent over two hours putting the booth together. She left about thirty minutes ago."

Why would Sofia go out of her way to help Jean? I had many questions I longed to ask my cousin, but I had to tread carefully. And I had to watch what I said about Roberto. She had always been very sensitive to criticism and would bristle at the slightest negative comment.

"Sofia did a fabulous job." I glanced at my watch.

Adele picked up on the cue. "The workshop on *The Forgiving Heart* is starting in a few minutes."

As we made our way to the smaller hall, Adele whispered, "You're not that comfortable with them. Is it him?"

Before I could reply, one of Adele's friends approached and hugged her. We spent the next two hours listening to practitioners talk about forgiving hearts and being open to change. While I took notes, I realized most of the information was not new to me. But the physical act of taking notes distracted me from troublesome thoughts about Sofia, Jean, and Michael.

We met with Laura in the main lobby. Adele volunteered to drive. Within minutes, we arrived at Culpeppers. We managed to get a booth at the far end of the restaurant, away from the entrance. We sat down and studied the menus. Adele and I decided on large green salads with grilled chicken while Laura selected the club sandwich and fries. She had been working all morning and decided to treat herself to a substantial lunch.

After the waitress had taken our orders, Laura spoke, "I'm so glad we decided to eat out. I needed a break from all that positive energy and body heat. We're packed in like sardines, and you can barely hear yourself think."

"Teresa and the other organizers must be pleased," I said.

"Everyone's ecstatic. Kudos to that lovely daughter of yours." Michael Taylor appeared at our table. He smiled at Laura and patted her on the shoulder. He then included all of us in the conversation. "And how wonderful to run into the three of you here. May I join you?"

I watched as Laura's face paled and Adele raised her eyebrows. None of us liked this man, but good manners prevailed, and we all nodded in agreement. Adele spoke on our behalf, "Of course."

He sat down next to Laura directly across from me. "Isn't this cozy? I haven't been here in years, and on a whim, I found myself driving in this direction. And to top it all, I get to spend time with three lovely ladies."

The waitress reappeared and offered him a menu. He shook his head. "Not necessary. I'll have a veggie burger with a large green salad. Hold the buns and salad dressing."

He leaned back and smiled. "Jean likes to talk about her Wednesday night class. It's her favorite one. She feels so light and happy afterward."

"She's a great instructor," Adele said. "Everyone likes her and flocks to her classes. We all missed her last week."

While Michael continued to smile, his forehead creased with a frown. I would have liked to pursue that conversation, but he skillfully changed the subject and started talking about the different yoga poses. He described his favorite ones and made a point of using the Sanskrit names. Thankfully, we did not have to wait too long for our orders. Michael nodded in approval at his own plate and the salads that Adele and I had selected. He shook his head when he saw the fries and club sandwich that Laura had chosen.

"Calories and cholesterol. You need to watch it, Laura."

While Laura blushed, he continued, "There's no

point doing yoga and participating in all those other activities your lovely daughter offers and then poisoning your system afterward." He winked at her. "I still remember that cute little figure you had once upon a time. How old were you then…twenty-five…thirty?"

How dare he criticize Laura's choices and then make such an inappropriate comment about her figure? And in that familiar tone. To my dismay, I noticed that Laura lowered her eyes and said nothing. She ate quickly. avoiding everyone's glance. I wanted to say something but couldn't think of anything. And then I remembered Anna May making the same comment when she and Jenny Marie visited me. I wondered if Michael had ever directed that comment toward Anna May.

Adele didn't miss a beat. "Nothing wrong with the occasional treat. It's all about balance, one of your wife's favorite topics."

As I tried to come up with my own zinger, our waitress appeared and asked if we were enjoying the meal. The moment passed, and we all focused on our food. I could sense him watching us and smiling that smug superior smile he must have perfected over the years. There were a few exchanges between Adele and Michael about the weather and the fair, but Laura and I remained quiet for the rest of the meal. He got up first and left.

"What a jerk!" Adele said. "I can't believe he threw that in your face, Laura."

"It's all right." Laura grimaced. "When I was young and foolish, I was young and foolish. I don't know who said that, but it fits this occasion."

"George W. Bush said it when reporters inquired

about his drinking and partying days." I wanted to hear about Laura's involvement with Michael, but didn't want to embarrass her any further.

We finished our meals, and when we asked the waitress for our bills, she informed us that the handsome gentleman had taken care of it.

"Now, we owe him," Laura muttered.

No one spoke during our drive back to the hotel. After Laura had gone back to her daughter's booth, I suggested that Adele and I walk outside for a while.

"You had already left town by the time Laura and Joe separated," Adele said as soon as we were out of earshot. "She hadn't met Matthew yet, and Carrie Ann had just dumped Michael. He was in bad shape, but that didn't stop him from putting the moves on other women. He and Laura went out for several months. She stopped seeing him when she found out about his many one-night stands. I guess he's been waiting all these years to pay her back." Adele sighed and continued, "I'm willing to bet he's messed up a lot of other women. Jean's a saint to put up with him."

I considered Jean a far cry from sainthood but didn't want to alert Adele's suspicions. "Let's go back in. The workshop on reflexology should be starting soon."

We spent the rest of the afternoon listening to the other workshops. As we were leaving, I heard a slightly accented voice behind me. "Miss Greco, did you want me to do your reading now?"

I turned and came face to face with the akashic records practitioner. While I didn't look forward to another encounter with Michael in the larger auditorium, I wanted to hear what the younger woman had to say.

Adele jumped in. "Go ahead. I'll run over to the Independent Store for groceries and pick you up on my way back." She spoke directly to the practitioner. "How long will it take?"

"I can do a mini reading in twenty minutes." Her eyes lit up. "If you want, we can do it in the restaurant. It's pretty quiet in there, and I don't think the waitresses will mind."

Adele nodded and left. I followed the younger woman into the restaurant. As she chatted about the fair, I tried to recall her name…Lisa, Liz…One of the L names. "I'm sorry, but I've forgotten your name."

"Lizette Mensour." She pointed to a table in the far corner. "Is that table okay, Miss Greco?"

"It's fine, and please call me Gilda."

Lizette got down to business. "I know you agreed before, but I just want to double check. Do I have your permission to access your akashic records?"

"Yes, of course." I couldn't help smiling at the intense expression on her face. She couldn't be a day over thirty, but she took her work seriously.

"Good. Since we have a short time together, I will address one question…any question you may have about relationships, goals, money—"

I wondered how much Lizette knew about me. After I won the lottery, my pictures and story were splattered all over the local newspapers. And my name and business had been mentioned in conjunction with the four murders. I wouldn't be too surprised if she had Googled me. That's what I would have done.

While it would have been interesting to ask Lizette if she could name Anna May's accomplice, I decided to focus on relationships instead. “I’m wondering about some of the people in my life and their motives.”

“Do you feel threatened by someone?” Lizette leaned forward and took my right hand.

“More uneasy than threatened.”

She closed her eyes and was silent for a minute or so. She spoke slowly, “You are surrounded by many people. Most of them are loyal to you and wish you well, but I sense that there are several who are more interested in promoting their own agendas.”

General advice that could apply to almost anyone. I was disappointed with Lizette’s answer and hoped she would elaborate.

“I know it’s not what you want to hear, but I can’t give you too many specifics until you provide me with more details.”

“What kind of details?” I didn’t feel comfortable sharing the names of possible suspects with her. Especially Jean and Michael Taylor. The Sudbury holistic community was a small one, and I wouldn’t be too surprised if they met and networked on a regular basis.

“Names would be good,” Lizette said. “Or even descriptions.”

I knew there weren’t too many Ken and Barbie holistic couples in Sudbury. “I’m not comfortable doing that. Is there anything else that you see?”

Lizette frowned. “I don’t think you are in any real danger. That is, I don’t think anyone is trying to harm you. But you should be careful. Don’t confide in too many people.”

More general, useless information. I should cut my losses here—it was only twenty dollars—and start walking toward the Independent Store.

"Why don't you describe that special man you would like to have in your life?" Lizette winked knowingly at me.

Could Lizette see through me, or did she assume any woman who didn't wear a wedding ring was searching for a man? I decided to play along. "He's tall and lean and has salt-and-pepper hair." I purposely left out the blue eyes.

Lizette's features softened, and her eyes fluttered. She smiled confidently. "Yes, I can see him. He's on the periphery of your life right now. It's what you both want, but that will change soon."

"How soon?" My heart skipped a beat.

Lizette shrugged. "That will depend upon you. You have to make the first move."

More irritating advice. I couldn't believe I had allowed myself to be suckered in. I reached for my wallet and pulled out a twenty-dollar bill.

Lizette smiled as she pocketed the money. "You are disappointed. You expected me to give you answers that you need to discover on your own."

We shook hands and parted company.

Chapter 23

Monday, November 7, 2011

I was booked solid Monday morning and had little time to think of anything else but the clients who sat in front of me. All Millenials this morning. While I wanted the challenge of working with boomers, I had to admit it was easier dealing with younger clients who reminded me of my former students. Many of them were still living at home and trying to find jobs in their chosen careers. Those who had been fortunate enough to find entry-level jobs were desperately unhappy and wanted to change career direction.

While talking with these frustrated young people, I tried to focus on what was working in their lives. Too many of them wanted to start a new career based on a recent article they had read or a friend's recommendation. While a handful of them were prepared to embark on a lengthy career exploration process, I suspect the majority wanted a sympathetic ear and would not be booking any more sessions.

When lunch time arrived, I heated up a Michelina dinner and ate while reading my emails. I was surprised and irritated when Belinda buzzed me. I had made it clear that I needed at least thirty minutes for an uninterrupted lunch.

"I'm sorry to disturb you, Gilda," she whispered,

and I had to strain to hear her. “But there’s a man here who insists on seeing you. He’s returned three times this morning. I told him you’re having lunch and booked solid all afternoon, but he won’t budge. He says he only needs ten minutes of your time.”

He must be on the verge of a breakdown and ready to quit his job. Angry young men have little patience and often fly off the handle. All they need is a time-out before making a decision. “All right, Belinda. Wait five minutes and then send him in.” I finished up my meal, tidied up my desk and freshened up my makeup. Starting tomorrow, I would force myself to leave the office during lunch time. If not, I could see myself going straight through the day with very few breaks. That had happened too often during my teaching years.

Within minutes, a smiling Michael Taylor entered my office. I resisted the urge to scream and throw something at him. How dare he bully Belinda and force his way into my office! I didn’t bother plastering on a smile. “Good afternoon, Michael. Belinda tells me you’ve come by several times today. Are you having a career emergency of some kind?”

He laughed and shook his finger at me. “Very funny, Gilda. Sofia and Jean are decorating my studio and have kicked me out for the day. I thought I’d drop by and chat.” He added, “You’re doing well for what…your second week of business. Enjoy it while you can. It’ll trickle down as we get closer to Christmas. Not too many people interested in looking for a new job around that time. Now, my business picks up for the holiday. Let me know if you need any shots for your newsletter and cards. I’m sure we could work out some kind of deal.” He winked at me.

The man's level of self-absorption defied all bounds. Every conversation would revert to him. I thought back to yesterday's lunch. He had monopolized the entire conversation, and we had let him. And then he had wounded Laura with that malicious comment. A narcissist through and through, classic textbook case.

"Thank you for that kind offer," I said as I glanced at my watch and moved several files. "I'll touch base with Belinda, and let you know what we decide."

His smile wavered. "You don't like me, do you?"

I clenched my jaw, fighting back a surge of anger. "Now why would you say that?"

"You look so uncomfortable and ill at ease whenever we meet. At first, I thought it was because of Jean's shocking behavior in your office." He shook his head. "But then I noticed how little you said yesterday at lunch, and today…today you can't even manage a smile." He spread his hands wide. "Have I said or done anything to offend you, Gilda?"

Was he that obtuse or was he playing me? I thought back to my dealings with narcissistic colleagues—thankfully there hadn't been too many—and recalled always being on edge whenever they crossed my path. And afterward, feeling emotionally drained and out of sorts. I decided to divert him and talk about the murders. "It's been a very stressful time for me with the four murders."

"You've been cleared of all suspicion, and there haven't been any more murders. You need to move on, Gilda." He waved his hand around the office. "And you've got to get out of this office. It's not healthy to work through lunch and take no breaks. Go back to Jean's yoga class. Spend some time at a spa. Have more fun." He lowered his voice. "I could help with that."

I stood. "My next client will be arriving any minute now. You need to go."

He held up his hands. "I know. I know. Your receptionist made it very clear that you were booked solid all day. That young woman is too intense, a lot like you. You both need to lighten up." He rose and headed toward the door. "Give me a call about the photo shoot."

As soon as he left, I took several deep breaths and got up and paced around the office. I wanted to go outside for a long walk, but I didn't have the time. My next client would be arriving soon.

The rest of the afternoon flew by as I focused on the fresh faces of my new clients. That's what I enjoyed the most about this new career. Each day, I would be dealing with a different set of people and their career concerns. Within seconds of my last client leaving, Belinda buzzed me. "Gilda, you have another persistent caller."

"Now who is it?" I groaned.

"Jim Nelson, the guy from Nickel City Security, has been calling all afternoon. What is it with these guys? Don't they have jobs and lives?"

I couldn't help laughing. "I guess not. Jim must be calling with an estimate." I decided to let Belinda continue thinking that Jim was beefing up security in the alleyway.

"Business must be slow at his place," she said. "But at least he's not coming in here and putting the moves on me."

My pulse raced a little faster. "What happened with Michael Taylor?"

"Oh, you know. The usual stuff that goes on with a guy who thinks he's God's gift to all women. His shtick is old, just like him."

"What did he say?" I chose not to remind Belinda that Michael and I were about the same age.

"He talked about taking pictures of me for a modeling portfolio."

"A modeling portfolio!" I couldn't help exclaiming and then caught myself. "I'm sorry, Belinda. You're a lovely girl and have a nice figure."

Belinda sighed. "But I'm only five-two, and I'm not a size zero. He told me I had a petite advantage, and he'd help me get rid of those last twenty pounds."

"You don't need to lose any weight, Belinda. You're beautiful just the way you are." I couldn't help adding, "I wish Maria or Rosa had been here when he said that."

"He'd be dead meat." Belinda started giggling.

Good! Belinda had not taken any of Michael's comments seriously. He had put down Jean, Laura and God knows how many other women. I wondered if he had ever belittled Carrie Ann.

After I finished speaking with Belinda, I called Jim.

"Well, it's about time." Jim sounded more worried than annoyed. "I've been calling all afternoon."

"Sorry, it's been busy. I've had clients all day. Michael Taylor paid me a visit."

"Yeah, I noticed. He was there three times today. That's why I'm calling. The object of our attention and not our affection has been busy for the past two days. And he's been gracing your company as well."

"Not really gracing it, but tell me what you have

discovered."

"Yesterday, Mel was on his tail and—"

"You had your daughter follow him?" Despite her tough girl exterior, I believed that Mel bruised easily. I hoped she wasn't considering a career in her father's field.

"I wasn't about to spend my day at a holistic fair," Jim said testily. "She volunteered and then followed him to Culpeppers. She was sitting at the next booth."

"I don't remember seeing her, and I would recognize—"

"Yeah, I know. She was in disguise yesterday."

I wondered what disguise could cover all those piercings but decided to focus on Michael. "What did she find out?"

"First of all, she discovered he's a perv. He put the moves on every woman under the age of thirty, including her. I guess he likes them young," Jim said. "He wasn't too nice to your friend. Mel couldn't believe how mean he was, and she was upset that you didn't let him have it. You kinda fell a few notches in her estimation."

"It wasn't my finest hour." There was no point sugar-coating what had happened.

"Last night, he went over to your cousin Sofia's place. That sleaze ball of a lawyer was there. You know who I'm talking about?"

"Yes, I know all about Roberto Ongaro." I could hear the resignation in my own voice as I spoke. I hated to be reminded of that Sunday morning when Roberto waved his sleazy magic wand and ended all hopes of a relationship with Carlo.

"Your cousin keeps interesting company," Jim

said. "And this morning she was there bright and early at Michael's studio."

"With Jean," I added.

"Jean didn't show up until later in the morning. That's when Michael left the studio and started pestering you. I take it he saw you."

"Yes, we had a short visit at lunch. Where did he go afterward?" I forced myself not to think about a possible relationship between Sofia and Michael.

"This is where it gets interesting. After he left your office, he drove out to the cemetery and visited three grave sites. He spent a lot of time at the first site. I found out later it was Carrie Ann's. He also dropped by Mrs. Godfrey's and Anna May's sites. Didn't stay there too long."

Was he feeling guilty? Confessing his crimes? And then I remembered about Natalia. "Did he visit Natalia Gorsky's site?"

"Nope. He just visited those three, and then he went back to the studio. He's still there with Jean. Sofia left about thirty minutes ago." He added, "I thought you might be interested in some other information I've dug up about Taylor. There have been two cases of harassment, both handled by Ongaro."

I felt a knot of fear form in my belly. "When did this happen?"

"Nineteen ninety-two. Both cases within the same year. Two sets of parents filed charges after their teenage daughters complained about inappropriate touching. While taking pictures for their modeling portfolios, he got carried away."

"What happened?"

"After Ongaro got involved, the parents dropped

the charges. I don't know, but I have a sneaking suspicion large sums of money were involved."

That would have been about the time that Carrie Ann left him. I wondered who had put up the money. Outside of Jean and Mrs. Godfrey, it didn't sound like too many people were there for him. And I couldn't imagine either woman having enough money to bail him out. Could Roberto have helped him?

Jim sighed. "I don't trust this guy. Give Fantin a call, and tell him about your suspicions. You could be in danger."

"Whoever the murderer is, he's after Godfreys and blondes. I'm more worried about Jenny Marie." I paused. I wasn't ready to break Grace's confidences.

"Believe me, murderers are not that discriminating. They will kill whoever gets in their way."

"Once I have solid proof, I will give Carlo a call. Not before."

"It's your call, Gilda. But don't say I didn't warn you." He hung up.

Michael and Jean were somehow involved in the murder. I could feel it. What was starting to trouble me was Sofia's connection to the couple. Why was she spending so much time with these people? I longed to call her, but didn't want to argue or create more of a rift. She had made it very clear she wanted Roberto in her life and, from what Jim had just revealed, was also willing to entertain the members of his posse.

Chapter 24

Tuesday, November 8, 2011

I didn't have a minute to myself until close to noon. When I stepped out of my office, I found Sofia sitting in the foyer.

She came over and hugged me. "Hello, stranger."

She had glammed up since the Autumn Tea. She was wearing more eye makeup than usual. Her hair was several shades lighter and had been straightened into a pageboy style. She bore an uncanny resemblance to a younger, thinner Anna May.

"It's great to see you. I've been meaning to call, but it's been busy around here. How have you been?"

"Simply wonderful." She gestured toward Belinda. "I took a peek at your appointment book. Business is taking off. You must be pleased."

"Yes, yes, I am." That is, happy enough while investigating four murders and dealing with Michael Taylor.

"I'm planning a dinner party for this Friday night. My divorce has come through. Roberto and I are officially coming out as a couple." She spoke breathlessly. "We're hoping you can come."

While I didn't like Roberto, I had to admit I was curious about their relationship. And I was certain he would behave with Sofia's parents and my mother around. “Sure. What time do you want me to come over?”

“We’ll have hors d’oeuvres around seven and eat later, around eight o’clock.”

“Isn’t that kind of late?” It would be past midnight before we finished eating. Knowing our parents, they would complain of indigestion the next day and blame Sofia for their ailments.

Sofia smiled. “It’s not just about our parents.”

“Who else is coming?”

“There’ll be twenty-six of us.”

“I thought this would be a family affair.” I wasn’t in the mood for one of her grand parties overflowing with too much food and liquor. One positive emerged: I wouldn’t be subjected to Andrew’s mean drunk antics.

“Oh, Gilda, please!” Sofia hugged me. “This is my coming out party and Roberto does not do small, intimate gatherings. He likes big parties—the bigger the better.”

“It’s a good thing you like entertaining. Who else is coming?”

Sofia started counting on her fingers. “My parents, your mother, you, Carlo—”

“You’re inviting Carlo?”

“I have invited Carlo, and he has accepted.” Sofia continued, “Elsa and Martino will be there—”

My eyes popped. “You invited Andrew’s sister? I’m surprised you didn’t invite his parents.”

“I did invite them, but they couldn’t make it.” She started counting on her fingers again. “Jean and Michael Taylor—”

“I thought you didn’t care for Jean?”

“I don’t.” Sofia made a face. “But Roberto and

Michael go back a long way. They were roommates at Western, and Michael was best man at Roberto's first wedding." Her features tightened, and I sensed that she did not enjoy spending time with the Taylors.

She continued with her list. "Claire and Paul Nardi, Susan and Mike Grant, Dina and Jamie Douglas, Ray Centis, Jenny Marie and Grace—"

"You invited all those bad boys and their wives. When was the last time you saw these people socially?"

"At Anna May's memorial service."

"You went to the service?"

"I have nothing to hide, and neither do you. The sooner we get back to normal the better. Anna May and I didn't always see eye-to-eye, but I felt the need to have some kind of closure. And I bear no ill will toward Jenny Marie." Her lips curved into a smile. "She didn't say too much at the funeral home, but when I ran into her at the mall she couldn't stop talking about your condo. I gather that Grace took notes."

"I wouldn't be surprised if Grace incorporates some of your ideas into one of her future designs." My voice softened as I thought of Grace.

"I'm flattered by Grace's interest, and I'd love to chat with her about interior design, but I doubt we'll have much time to do that on Friday night."

I did a quick mental count. "That's seventeen. Who are the other nine?"

"Maria, Rosa and some of my neighbors are coming as well. I don't think you know these people, but they like a good time, and they'll liven up the place. And one couple has a visiting nephew from Australia, about Grace's age."

Planning a dinner party for twenty-six would

overwhelm me. At this stage of my life, I would hire a caterer or go to a nearby restaurant. But Sofia would be energized by the whole affair.

Sofia winked. “Don’t worry. I won’t ask you to bring anything. I’ve got it all under control.”

“I have no doubt it will be a success.” I paused. “How was the service?”

“Hardly anyone was there. Father Cleary refused to speak on Anna May’s behalf so Henry Keenan took his place and talked about Anna May’s early years. You would think she had died at age twenty. Later, I saw him deep in conversation with Carlo.”

“Wonder what that was all about?”

“Both men had grim expressions on their faces.”

“Interesting. Anything else happen?”

Sofia frowned. “I hope you’re not poking around on your own.”

“No, I haven’t the time.”

“Good! It’s time we all put this unpleasantness behind us. It’s over.”

“Not really. There’s a murderer out there who had some hand in killing four women. What’s to stop this person from striking again?”

“It’s been over two weeks, and no one else has died.” Sofia used her discussion-ending voice, the one she had perfected with the CWL members.

“Let’s hope it stays that way.” I decided to change the subject. No point alerting her suspicions. “I guess you must have been impressed by the bad boys.”

Sofia frowned. “Those men are so tame and domesticated. Their wives seem to have all of them on a tight leash.”

“I can’t imagine that.”

"It seemed all of them were trying to placate their wives in some way. Is it possible they all had major arguments before arriving?"

I started to explain and then thought better of it. Jenny Marie did not want the details of Anna May's unsavory past out there. If Sofia hadn't heard about the men's involvement with Anna May, I had no intention of enlightening her. "Well, you never know about middle-aged men." I glanced critically at Sofia's face. "Still going to Curves?"

"Roberto and I are sharing his personal trainer. Adrian comes every morning and we work out for ninety minutes."

"You must be up at the crack of dawn."

"Five o'clock." Sofia grimaced. "Roberto gets up at that hour every day, even on the weekends."

"Oh, Sofia, how can you stand that?"

"I must say I do get more done each day."

While burning the candle at both ends and getting less than six hours of sleep each night. What some women will do to maintain a relationship!

Sofia had already shifted gears and changed the topic. She described her new black, cocktail dress at length and then asked me pointedly, "What are you planning to wear? I'm tired of seeing you in black pant suits."

"Worked well for Hillary Clinton."

She rolled her eyes. "Everyone is dressing up, so I thought I would give you the heads up on that. Why don't you wear that red cocktail dress you picked up in Hawaii? I'm willing to bet you've never worn it."

"I haven't had the occasion, and I find it a bit showy."

"Wear it with a pair of strappy stilettos." Sofia winked at me. "There will be a couple of eligible men there, so you never know."

"Two single men? I know Carlo is one of them."

"And Ray Centis, Anna May's ex."

I groaned. "You expect me to put the moves on Ray Centis?"

"Give the man a chance. Who knows, you might even make a certain detective jealous."

"I don't think I can expect much from that quarter. He hasn't called or spoken to me since that Sunday."

"That will change on Friday, trust me." Sofia glanced at her watch. "I promised Roberto I would meet him for lunch at his mother's."

"You are making progress."

"His mother entertains all his friends." I could sense her weariness and frustration. "He crashes there between his relationships and marriages. She keeps the upstairs apartment free for him."

I couldn't believe a man pushing sixty still lived with Mama. She probably waited on him hand and foot. I shook my head. "Are you sure that's what you want?"

"As I said before, he's Mr. Right Now. *Que sera, sera*. I won't be too bent out of shape if and when he moves on."

Or was she planning to move on? I had always thought of Sofia as a one-man woman, Andrew's woman, but she had already broken out of that mold. "It sounds like you already have a Plan B in place."

"Why do you think I am inviting Ray Centis on Friday?"

"And here I thought you were serious about him connecting with me. I'm curious. What's Ray up to these days?"

"After he divorced Anna May, he got into plumbing and opened up his own business. He had a few long-term relationships, but he never married again."

"Anna May must have done quite the number on him."

"She didn't have time to do too much damage. They were married for less than a year. Remember that disaster of a marriage." She gasped. "I'm sorry, Gilda. I forgot about your—"

"My disaster." I finished the sentence for her. Since the conversation with my mother, I found myself reacting less and less to that one-year wrinkle. "I wonder what happened with Anna May and Ray."

"The scuttlebutt was that Anna May was an insufferable bitch and impossible to live with. She mysteriously disappeared for a year afterward."

"Where did she go?"

"Probably spent time with Melly Grace or some other unfortunate relative." Sofia smiled triumphantly. "And she's permanently out of our hair now."

"Out of everyone's hair. I can't say I liked her, but I never wished this kind of death on her."

"She brought in on herself," Sofia said. "No one will ever know what happened, but I don't think she will be missed by anyone. Jenny Marie's looking a lot happier, and I think she's lost a bit of weight."

"I'm glad to hear Jenny Marie is doing well. Let's hope that we can all have some peace and tranquility in our lives."

Sofia barely heard me as she waved goodbye and ran out to her car.

Chapter 25

Friday, November 11, 2011

Three uneventful days followed. No more encounters with Michael or telephone calls from Jim. I decided not to call Carlo. While I trusted Jim's judgment when it came to criminal behaviour, he might have overreacted to Michael. Jim wouldn't be too thrilled with any older man who put the moves on his daughter.

I found myself looking forward to Friday evening's dinner party and hoped to touch base with Grace afterward. I wondered how much progress she had made with Anna May's diary.

I left work early on Friday and took extra care with my appearance. I put on the red lace dress and was pleased with the final effect. It felt looser than before. I must have lost five or six pounds since the spring. I drove over to Sofia's and arrived to find most of the guests already there.

A challenging mix of guests, but Sofia pulled it off. She had attended to every detail, and the final result was a spectacular one. She had accommodated all the guests at two dinner tables in the large eat-in kitchen and adjoining dining room and two card tables in the family room. She produced dish after dish of delicious food. Although, she could cook almost anything, Sofia had stuck to Italian basics and pleased everyone. There had been much behind-the-scenes preparation, and I am certain our mothers had helped, but it was Sofia's master plan.

A well-sated and proud Roberto praised the gnocchi, the osso buco, and the tiramisu. Sofia received appreciative glances from all the men at the table, and the ladies nodded in approval. I caught a few wary glances and raised eyebrows among the wives of the bad boys. I had to stop thinking about them like that. Sofia and Jenny Marie were right. These men had matured, and their childish pranks needed to be both forgiven and forgotten. I was favorably impressed by many of them, especially Ray Centis. He was a good listener and offered me sound advice about growing my business.

Carlo nodded politely in my direction but steered clear of any prolonged conversation. He spent most of the evening talking with Uncle Paolo and the other men, with the exception of Roberto. It was almost impossible to have a conversation with Sofia or Roberto. They moved about as a unit, and Roberto would often touch her hair or squeeze her arm.

Grace surprised me the most. She did spend most of dinner talking with Scott, the Australian nephew, but afterward she weaved in and out of all the groups. I recognized and appreciated a master networker in action. I thought of all the books and articles I had read on the topic. I had even conducted several of those workshops. And here was a young woman, not yet thirty, who could give me lessons in that department.

I found myself on the periphery of the room and stood alone contentedly watching everyone else in action.

"Mingle!" Sofia said. "You can't just stand around and not talk to anyone."

"Not that you've noticed, but I have mingled. You've been busy with Roberto."

"Is it that obvious?"

"The two of you are attached at the hip. I don't think he will stray too far from you."

Her face brightened. "You think there is hope for us as a couple?"

"Yes, I honestly do." I waved my hand up and down. "After all, you're the complete package: the best of mama's cooking, a great social hostess, and beautiful to boot." Sofia's black cocktail dress fit snugly over her toned and slender body, and her eyes shone with excitement. The old Sofia had returned. All those years she had been married to Andrew, she had been on guard and with good reason. Andrew was a critical, demanding husband, and his obnoxious behavior was exacerbated by his excessive drinking.

"Thank you, Gilda. That's one of the nicest compliments you have ever paid me."

"You look so relaxed. Like a large burden has been lifted from your shoulders and your life."

"Andrew is out of my life forever." Sofia flashed a radiant smile, one I couldn't recall ever seeing before.

"I had my doubts about Roberto, but he is behaving very well this evening."

"He likes to party, but he knows his limits. He doesn't get drunk, and he has never, ever criticized me in any way." Sofia was about to add something and then changed her mind.

"But—"

"What do you mean?" Sofia gave me her full attention.

"There is a but. I feel one coming."

She narrowed her eyes in doubt. "He has started to talk about one of the women he is representing."

"Maybe he's just sharing with you."

"That's what I thought at first. But this lady is different. She is younger than his usual clientele, blonde and beautiful."

"So that explains the lighter hair."

"I had to go back again to get the color right." Sofia laughed as she touched her hair.

"I didn't care for it the other day, but it looks great now." I added, "You shouldn't worry so much. After all, you have a Plan B, and I am certain that Ray would be more than interested."

"If I didn't know you any better, Gilda Greco, I would say you were interested in Ray yourself." She squeezed my hand. "Or maybe you're trying to make a certain detective jealous."

"Not to worry. I have no designs on Ray. But I agree with both you and Jenny Marie. He has changed and for the better. Did you know that he is considering getting into local politics?"

Sofia leaned closer. "Local politics…interesting."

"You'd make a great mayor's wife."

"Listen to us. We sound like teenagers at our first dance." She nudged me with her elbow. "What about Carlo? Did he say anything to you tonight."

"Other than hello and how are you, nothing."

Sofia frowned. "I even put him next to you at dinner."

"He spent most of the night talking to your father

about the good old days and Italy. I'm glad that Ray was sitting next to me."

Sofia surveyed the room with a critical air. "An eclectic group, but it did work."

"Our mothers had a good time as well."

Sofia's eyes flickered with annoyance. "They spent most of the evening in the kitchen, attending to details that had already been attended to."

"They did sit and socialize with Elsa and Martino." I would never have invited an ex-sister-in-law to a party celebrating a new relationship. But it seemed the relationship between Sofia and Elsa had survived Andrew's defection.

"She's been a good friend," Sofia said. "She doesn't begrudge me my relationship with Roberto."

"Whatever makes you happy is fine with all of us. That's all we want for you. You've done so much for everyone, and now it's your turn to be happy."

"Yes, it's my turn to be happy."

"And you make me very happy, pretty lady." Roberto's arm circled around Sofia, and he spun her around expertly.

I slipped away and headed toward the opposite end of the room. Carlo and I approached the dessert bar at the same time. I felt awkward but knew I had to say something. "Isn't this a beautiful spread?"

"It's been a while since I've had such an elaborate meal. Your cousin sets a fine table." He sounded relaxed.

"She's our Martha Stewart."

"I'm sorry I haven't had a chance to chat with you this evening." He lowered his voice. "There's so much I would like to tell you, but it's not the right time or place."

"About the murders?" My heart skipped a beat.

"That and a few personal issues," he said. "I haven't forgotten about our date. It's just that I'm swamped with work right now, and I'm under a lot of pressure to bring some kind of closure to the murder cases."

"Are you close to that stage?"

"Getting there. We have narrowed down the field of suspects."

"Do you have the one?"

"Almost there."

"Looks like you two are plotting a coup. Lighten up and enjoy the party." Roberto approached without Sofia in tow. "It's so nice to see everyone in a normal setting." He gestured toward the room. "Sofia knows how to put on a good show. If I ever decide to run for political office, she'll be at my side all the way."

Another wannabe politician in the group, I thought.

"And what office would that be?" Carlo asked.

"Oh, I don't know. With the right woman at my side, I would consider running provincially or federally. What do you think, Gilda? Would Sofia be up for it?"

"Up for what?" Sofia joined him and linked her arm through his.

"Helping Roberto become premier or prime minister." I was surprised to hear myself give Roberto such lofty ambitions. Must be the wine talking.

"Hey, slow down. I just said I would consider running as MPP or MP. I don't know about going for the whole enchilada. But thanks for the vote of confidence, Gilda. I'll be sure to call on you as campaign manager." Roberto winked at me and then pulled Carlo aside. “Excuse us, ladies. I have a few matters to discuss with my favorite detective.”

Sofia frowned. “I wonder what that’s all about.”

I imagine Roberto had his own theories about the murders and wanted to share them with Carlo. I squeezed Sofia’s arm. “Don’t worry about the blonde bimbette. After tonight, I don’t think he’ll be talking about her too much longer.”

Before Sofia could respond, her parents approached and announced they were leaving. My mother and several other couples were also starting to make motions to leave. Sofia left me to say goodbye to her guests.

“Blonde bimbette! I hope you weren’t talking about me?” I turned and saw Grace standing behind me.

“Someone else who has nothing at all to do with us,” I said as I hugged her close. “And never will.”

“Another blonde on the chopping block?”

I shivered. “How can you even suggest such a thing? If you must know, we were talking about one of Roberto’s clients. She is young, blonde and vulnerable.”

“He’s probably hit on her,” Grace said matter-of-factly. “He doesn’t waste too much time.”

“Grace, what are you saying? Did he…?” I couldn’t believe Roberto would even consider approaching another woman right under Sofia’s nose.

“Yes, in a very subtle way, but I put him off.”

It sounded like Roberto had not changed his stripes. I couldn’t believe how disappointed I felt. I had been prepared to give Roberto the benefit of the doubt, but now I wondered if I should be warning Sofia instead. Not that she would even listen. “I thought he and Sofia might have a chance together."

"That's a possibility, but it doesn't preclude him cheating on her. He likes harems."

My eyes traveled around the room. "I hope he hasn't hit on anyone else in the room. Most of these ladies are friends of Sofia. It would be so awkward if anything happened."

"Not to worry," Grace said. "He likes them young and blonde. As for these women being friends, I don't think they're all that close to your cousin."

I put thoughts of Sofia out of my mind and focused on the lovely, young woman standing next to me. "You seem to have circulated very well. Where did you learn to work a room?"

"I spent a few months with Melly Grace after I graduated, and I learned a lot from that woman. I used to joke that I received a ninety-day MBA from her."

"She was so good at making herself comfortable and flourishing in all situations. I see you have that gift as well."

"I had an ulterior motive tonight," Grace whispered. "I wanted to learn as much as possible about the murders."

"You discussed the murders with these people?" If Sofia learned about Grace's networking, she would be furious.

"Not directly. I'm much more subtle than that. But I was able to uncover some interesting tidbits about Anna May."

"Such as…?"

"With the exception of your mother and Scott, everyone else has had some kind of negative experience with Anna May in the last six months." Grace leaned closer and whispered in my ear. “I can feel the presence of the murderer in this room.”

I gasped, and my hand flew to my mouth.

“I’ll drop by your office tomorrow morning. In the meantime, smile and try to look as if nothing had happened. If you must, think of everyone in this room in their underwear or naked.” She winked at me and then headed toward the dessert bar.

I was still trying to collect myself when the Taylors approached. Michael’s face was flushed, his jaw clenched.

Jean spoke, her voice warm with sympathy and concern. “What’s wrong, Gilda?”

“Did Grace say something to upset you?” Michael asked. “That young woman has a habit of stirring up trouble. Someone needs to sit her down and have a long chat about appropriate behavior.” He muttered, “I can’t believe she’s still talking about those murders.”

So much for Grace’s subtlety. I hoped that no one else had caught on to her real motives. Michael looked like he wanted to throttle Grace.

Jean put her hand on his arm. “Relax, hon. You know how intense Grace can be. I imagine she’s still mourning her two aunts and cousin. I know she was really close to Carrie Ann and Melly Grace. And Anna May—”

“Anna May tried everyone’s patience, even her mother’s,” Michael said. “I have always wondered how someone as kind and considerate as Elizabeth could produce such a selfish, egotistical child. While I hated to see her die, it’s a blessing she did not live to see her eldest daughter involved in three murders.”

Jean’s eyes welled with tears. Elizabeth Godfrey

was the only mother figure she had ever known. It must be very hard for Jean to recall her death.

Michael continued, oblivious to his wife's discomfort. "Elizabeth bailed her out so many times. Full of beans, she used to say. After her divorce and breakdown, she blamed poor Ray." He nodded in my direction. "You're a counselor, Gilda. Would you diagnose her as…as what…a narcissist?"

Takes one to know one, I thought. My eyes traveled to the half-full glass of wine in his hand. I wondered how many glasses he had consumed. I didn't want to dwell on Anna May's pathology, so I decided to deflect the situation. "I don't like to think about that whole unpleasant episode. It's behind me now, and I hope to move forward."

I was rewarded with a grateful smile from Jean. "I'm so glad to hear that, Gilda. You must come back to Wednesday night yoga. It's not the same without you. There's an empty space between Adele and Laura that needs to be filled." She repeated, "You must come back."

I found myself nodding in agreement. "I'll try to make it this week." In spite of everything that had happened, I still missed that feeling of calm after her sessions.

Chapter 26

Saturday, November 12, 2011

I arrived at the ReCareering office bright and early the following morning. I had planned to get a lot of paperwork out of the way, but I couldn't concentrate. Grace had calmly and matter-of-factly stated that she felt the murderer's presence at the party, and I had believed her. After a lifetime of ignoring my own mother's premonitions and dreams, I had accepted the younger woman's intuitive feelings as fact. While tossing and turning all night, I had gone through Sofia's entire guest list. A few days ago, I would have accused one of the bad boys, but I wasn't so sure anymore. I believed that Michael Taylor was capable of murder, and he might have held a grudge toward Carrie Ann and Melly Grace, but what would motivate him to help Anna May kill Natalia?

As for Aunt Amelia and Uncle Paolo, it was ludicrous to consider the two of them as suspects. But I was curious about their encounter with Anna May. Strange that Sofia never mentioned it.

Loud knocking on the picture window interrupted my thoughts. I looked up and smiled at Grace. Dressed in jeans, a sweatshirt, and a baseball cap, she was still drop-dead gorgeous. The combination of porcelain skin framed by a cascade of ash blonde curls needed no further embellishment. I let her in, and Grace followed me into the smaller counseling office. She then turned and walked back toward the front window and looked out into the parking lot. Satisfied, she returned to the office and closed the door behind her.

"Is something wrong?" I asked.

"I think someone might be following me."

"Does Carlo know?" I reached for the telephone.

"I have no real proof, so there's no point alarming the police. I can feel someone watching and waiting for me to make some kind of move." She shivered. "The murderer is still out there."

"And you think we were graced with his presence last night?"

"I'm certain of it."

"How can you be so sure?"

"I have strong visceral reactions to both extreme positive and negative events and people. I've only felt this way twice in the last few weeks: at the memorial service and at Sofia's party." She added, "The diary supports my feelings."

I wondered what she had found and motioned for her to continue.

"I've come up with my own version of events, but it would never stand up in court. We need more proof." She clenched and unclenched her hands.

I sensed that Grace wasn't ready to share the diary with me. I decided to focus on her intuitive feelings. "All we have to do is figure out who attended both events. That should cut back on the number of suspects."

She pulled out a sheet of folded paper from her backpack. "We're down to seventeen possibilities."

"Seventeen of last night's guests were at the memorial service? Sofia told me fewer than twenty people were there."

"Sofia came later in the afternoon," Grace explained. "We had a steady flow of visitors. Most people didn't stay too long."

I didn't expect to see so many of Sofia's neighbors on the list. "You mentioned that almost everyone had some kind of negative experience with Anna May. I'm curious about my aunt and uncle. What kind of business would they have had with Anna May?"

"Exactly that," she said. "In June, they hired Carrie Ann to help with their window treatments. The wrong set of blinds were delivered and, when they complained, Anna May took the call and became loud and abusive. Your aunt started crying, and your uncle yelled and demanded a refund. Carrie Ann got on the telephone and managed to calm everyone."

"I wonder why they didn't just ask Sofia for her advice and help."

"Your aunt mentioned something about Sofia being too busy with your condo and left it at that."

"Well, it's a moot point. They aren't on your list, and I never considered any of them suspects. Let's check out some of these other people."

"The bad boys, as you like to call them, all had alibis conveniently supplied by their wives, with the exception of Ray Centis, of course."

"Do you think Ray might have been involved?"

"I don't know much about him, but he is a decent sort, and I think he would steer clear of Anna May after that disastrous marriage." She paused and added, "He participated in a fund-raising event all day Saturday and didn't get home until dark. Well after both Natalia and Anna May were killed."

"He's off the hook. But from your tone, it doesn't sound like the other four couples are. Any gut feelings about one of them?"

"The men have admitted to giving Anna May money, and I don't think it went any further. Some of those wives are a bit possessive of their husbands, and they don't like other women moving in on their territory." Grace added, "Last night, they made catty comments about Sofia, especially after that outstanding meal. Did she get any outside help with that?"

"My mother and aunt helped, but Sofia is the mastermind when it comes to anything domestic." I waved my hand toward the rest of the office. "She even helped design and decorate my offices."

Grace nodded approvingly as her eyes traveled around the room. "She could have given Three Sisters Decorating some real competition." Grace circled the names of two ladies on the list. "Let's move on to some of the other suspects. Sofia's next door neighbor, Leah Dottori spoke in very angry tones about Anna May. Both Leah and Anna May go to Curves. They were very close and supported each other's progress. Then Anna May became jealous of Leah and started making inappropriate comments about her husband and children."

"Anna May went to Curves?" I mumbled, "Sofia never mentioned it."

Grace raised her eyebrows. "Sofia goes to Curves? I wouldn't bother with a gym if I had invested all that money in exercise equipment. That room must have cost her a pretty penny."

"Sofia has an exercise room?" While I never listened too closely when Sofia discussed her decorating projects, I would have recalled any mention of an exercise room. "When did she put that in?"

"I don't know, but now that I think about it, everything did look brand new." Her eyes widened. "Don't you go there?"

"She comes over here, or we end up meeting at our parents' homes. I don't know what will happen now that Roberto is in the picture." I added, "Or not. It sounds like Roberto is still on the trail for hot blondes."

"He better not look my way again." Grace shuddered. "He's too slick and too old for my taste."

I pointed to Roberto's name on the list. "Did he attend the memorial service with Sofia?"

"My mother and I were surprised to see them as a couple last night, so they must have come separately. She came alone and didn't stay too long. I remember my mother introducing her as your cousin, and then she disappeared right after the service."

"They hadn't come out as a couple yet," I explained. "Her divorce wasn't finalized until last week, so they could have been in the room at the same time."

"I wondered why she threw that gala event last night."

"What was Roberto's beef with Anna May?" I couldn't visualize any kind of relationship between those two.

"While grocery shopping with her son, Mrs. Ongaro lost control of her cart and hit Anna May's stationary car. No major damage, but there were a few scratches. I don't know how Anna May even noticed.

Her car was at least ten years old and not well-maintained. Anna May started to yell and threatened to call the police and insurance company." Grace shook her head. "Mrs. Ongaro became very upset and burst into tears. Roberto wrote Anna May a check. A generous one."

"What a spoiled brat! Did Anna May have any friends left at the end of her life?"

"Other than my mother, I don't think so."

"Your poor mother is a saint."

"She went through a very difficult period after my father left," Grace said. "But she's starting to pick up now. Before I left last week, I cleaned out all the junk food from the cupboards. She's walking each morning with one of the neighbours, and she's thinking about joining a gym." Grace put her hands on mine. "You've made it so much easier for her to continue."

"I'm glad. Do you think she'll stay in Sudbury?"

"I'm trying to convince her to move to southern Ontario. She detests Toronto, but she could live in Kitchener or Barrie. We have relatives in both cities." She took a deep breath and continued, "My mother is the main reason I'm here today. I want closure on the murders. I want to find the murderer and bring that person to justice. And I need your help to do it."

"I'd love to help, but I don't think I can. We haven't had much success whittling down this list of suspects. Do you think those two wives were involved?"

"I've narrowed it down to a couple of people," Grace said. "But I am not ready to share that information with you. It could be dangerous, and I don't want to upset you."

"Then why are you here?"

"Because I want to ambush the suspects in the alleyway behind your office."

"And then what?"

"I want a confrontation and a confession."

"Does your mother know about any of this?"

"I haven't shared any of my premonitions with her. It would upset her, and she's made too much progress to have a setback now. I won't mess with that."

"But you'll mess with a murderer. You could be the next victim. You're a blonde, and you have Godfrey blood. That's a dangerous combination these days."

"I'm not afraid."

"We need to get the police involved." I picked up the phone. "Let's call Carlo."

"How do you think he'll react when I talk about my intuitive feelings?"

"You convinced me."

"But you are open to the possibility. You've had a lifetime of listening to your mother's prophetic dreams."

"How did you know about her dreams?"

"She told me about the dream she had the night before Carrie Ann died."

I remembered my mother mentioning a dream, but I had pooh-poohed her concerns. She hadn't brought it up again until last night. I turned my attention back to Grace.

"You may downplay them, but in your heart of hearts, I think you believe in them. And you want closure. Until this matter is resolved, you and my mother won't have any peace of mind."

"Melly Grace taught you well," I said. "If you ever

get tired of the creative life and want more money, consider a legal career."

"Maybe someday. Right now, I love what I'm doing." She persisted. "So will you help me? I don't expect you to become directly involved. For you, the risk is a minimal one."

"I will need to know all the details, and Carlo Fantin must be told about the plan. We won't talk about prophetic dreams. We'll mention gut feelings. Most men can identify with that. Those are my two conditions."

Grace groaned. "Oh, all right. I know you want an excuse, any excuse to call him."

"Grace!"

"It's okay. You're allowed to have the hots for him. I totally approve, and I want to ambush the murderer."

Chapter 27

It was the first time I saw Carlo in jeans and a sweatshirt. His pants were clean but well-worn and the dark blue Roots sweatshirt looked like a recent purchase. He arrived at the back door of the office in less than fifteen minutes after I placed the call.

"Are you trying to set a new record for responding to voicemail?" Grace asked as she winked at me.

"While dropping off some forms, I happened to hear Gilda's voice on the machine." A hint of a smile crossed his face as he turned to me. "It seems every telephone conversation with you has some kind of drama attached to it, but I must say today's message took the prize. And to make it even more mysterious, you insisted I use the back entrance."

"Grace thinks someone has been watching and following her," I explained

"How long has this been going on?" Carlo turned to Grace.

"I noticed it the day of the memorial service and this morning." Grace said.

Carlo's eyes met mine. "I take it you have news of some kind."

"I don't have all the details, but Grace has a plan to ambush the murderer." I wanted Grace to take over the conversation.

"I thought you had uncovered a new piece of

evidence. What's this about ambushing the murderer? Do you know how dangerous that is?" He maintained eye contact with me.

"Slow down, Detective, and chill a bit." Grace smiled confidently. "I have very strong gut feelings about the murderer. I have narrowed it down to two suspects, both of whom were at last night's party."

She had Carlo's full attention. "Strong gut feelings. Hmm. How often do you get these feelings?"

"I felt this way when my grandma died and when my father took up with the office bimbo."

"Who do you suspect?" Carlo folded his arms, his expression newly tense.

"I'm not ready to say." Grace nodded toward me. "It would be too dangerous."

"If you don't plan to share this information, why did you even bother calling me?" His jaw tightened and his lips formed a thin line of anger.

"I told her I wouldn't get involved unless you knew about this," I said. "I'm still holding you to that promise, Grace."

Carlo cast a steely glance in my direction. "What kind of plan have you hatched?"

I nodded toward Grace. "I'm waiting for Grace to be more forthcoming."

"Oh, all right. I'll tell him but only him." She leaned closer and whispered in his ear.

Carlo paled and closed his eyes.

"You agree with her, don't you?" I started to tremble and had to lean on my desk.

"Yes, yes I do." He maintained eye contact with Grace. "How did you come up with that?"

"After Anna May died, I spent an entire week

helping my mother clean out her office and bedroom. I found a diary which Anna May kept. It's written in a secret code and shorthand which I have been able to decipher. I had to fill in some of the missing spaces—"

"You found Anna May's diary, and you didn't think to turn it in?" Carlo raised his voice. "Young lady, you can't just take evidence away. You could be charged—"

"It wasn't at the crime scene," Grace spoke defiantly. "The diary was in one of Anna May's chest drawers. And if you had found it first, you wouldn't have been able to do much with it."

"You should have let me be the judge of that," Carlo answered testily.

Grace unzipped her backpack and pulled out the diary. She handed it over to Carlo.

As he flipped through the pages, his eyes narrowed. He threw the diary on the desk. "This is a mess. She must have been drunk or high on something."

"I figured out the code," Grace said.

"What code? There's no rhyme or reason to any of these scribbles." Carlo's eyes flickered with anger and impatience as he glanced toward the door.

It's Melly Grace's code," Grace explained. "She shared it with me when I visited several years ago. I remembered most of it, and I figured out the shorthand from an old Pitman textbook."

Carlo's features softened at the mention of Melly Grace's name. He gave Grace his full attention.

Grace pulled out a folder and handed it to him. "I typed up a transcript of the diary for you, and I included a sheet with the code."

Carlo skimmed through the document, nodding as he read. “I’m impressed, Ms. Robinson. So, what’s your plan?”

Grace flashed him one of her stunning smiles. “You’re in. Great!”

“I am willing to listen. That’s all. I cannot condone anything that would endanger either your life or Gilda’s.” Carlo leaned back in his chair. “So, let’s hear it.”

Grace took out two envelopes with carefully folded sheets of paper. “I plan to send each of the suspects the following note.” She handed one copy to me and another to Carlo.

The computer-generated note was brief and to the point:

I have found Anna May’s diary, and I think you may be interested in reading some of the October entries. Meet me on Wednesday at 6:00 p.m in the alleyway behind the ReCareering office.

Grace Robinson

I shivered, and Carlo raised his eyebrows. No one said anything for several minutes.

Grace became impatient. “I thought it would be very appropriate to meet where all of this started. I also picked the same time and day of the week as the first murder.”

“It’s intriguing,” Carlo said. “What makes you think either one of them will bite?”

“How do you plan to send these notes?” While I couldn’t imagine involving anyone else in this scheme, I didn’t want Grace delivering the notes.

“One of my friends is a florist, and she often handles special deliveries,” Grace explained.

"I hate to sound like a broken record, but I need to ask the question again," Carlo said. "What makes you so sure they will show up?"

Grace shrugged. "Curiosity and guilt are great motivators. I won't be alone in that alleyway."

"All right, so they show up." Carlo spread his hands. "What then?"

"I'll share several entries," Grace said. "There will be some kind of reaction, and then I'll force a confession."

"Just like that!" Carlo snapped his fingers. "Grace, it may not happen that way? Are you prepared for angry words…or worse?"

"That's where Gilda comes in. I plan to wire myself, and she will be able to listen in on the conversation. If things get heated, she can call you."

"Where is Gilda supposed to be while all of this is happening?" Carlo asked.

Grace waved her hand around the office. "She could hide out in here."

"Too dangerous!" Carlo shouted. "I won't allow it."

"I have to agree with Carlo," I said. "This is too far-fetched. I don't even know the names of these people, and I'm worried."

"What do you know about wires?" Carlo asked.

"Melly Grace showed me how it's done. When I visited her, I watched as she wired herself before meeting with one of her clients. She gave me a wiring kit, and I have tested it several times. I used it last night at the party."

"You were wired last night?" I thought back and remembered how demure Grace had looked in a high-collared and long-sleeved blouse with black dress pants.

"I fooled all of you, didn't I?"

Carlo stroked his chin while maintaining eye contact with Grace. "I'm still uneasy about all of this, but my gut feeling is telling me that you might be able to pull this off if you do exactly what I tell you."

"I'm listening." Grace gave him her full attention.

"I'll wire you myself and give you a test run tomorrow. On Thursday, I'll get one of the officers to drive Gilda and me to the alleyway in an unmarked van. He'll be dressed in undercover clothes, and after dropping us off, he'll walk toward the plaza. Anyone watching won't think anything of it. There's at least one vehicle parked illegally in that alleyway each day." He turned to face me. "Gilda and I will be stationed in that van while you confront the murderer. We'll be able to listen to the conversation, and act immediately if there is a problem. I'll be armed, and I'll make sure that there are several police cars nearby."

"Sounds like a plan." Grace clapped in excitement. "Let's do it!"

"Grace, this is serious," Carlo said, eyeing her with concern. "You know what these people are capable of."

"It's the only way, Carlo." Her lovely face grew tight with concern. "I can't expose my mother to any more of this senseless violence."

His dark brows drew together in a suspicious frown. "Why do you think Jenny Marie is in danger?"

"Because the murderer doesn't know how much she knows."

"What does she know?" Carlo asked.

Grace shook her head. "She's vague and changes the subject every time I bring it up."

“I’m still not convinced this will work, but I am willing to give it a try.” My heart beat wildly, and I doubted that I would be able to sleep until Thursday.

“Fine.” Carlo nodded in Grace’s direction. “Come to the station tomorrow. It’s Sunday, and it’ll be quiet. I want to see how well you handle the wire, and we’ll go over some of the other details.” He turned to me. “I imagine you’ll be working on Thursday. Leave around five-fifteen and drive over to the Canadian Tire Plaza. I’ll be waiting there in a dark blue van at the far end, near the bank. Make sure your receptionist and anyone else working here leaves early. And don’t tell anyone else about this plan.”

My eyes welled with tears. “My family and friends think I have moved on.”

“But you’re still inwardly obsessing,” Carlo spoke softly.

“I can’t get those four women out of my mind,” I said. “Those murders were senseless and did not have to happen. We owe it to their memory to bring the murderer to justice.”

“And we will do that on Thursday.” Grace clapped her hands. “I can feel it.”

Chapter 28

After Carlo and Grace left, I couldn't focus on my paperwork and didn't know how I would get through the next five days. I had to keep busy and be out and about as much as possible.

My thoughts were rudely interrupted by incessant banging at the front window. I glanced at my watch. Not even ten o'clock. Who would be clamoring for career advice at this hour on a Saturday morning? As I approached the front office, I caught glimpses of four worried and tired faces at the window. Aunt Amelia, Uncle Paolo, Rosa Geraldi and Maria Rossi peered into the office while continuing to bang at the window.

I laughed as I let them in. "Is someone in desperate need of career advice?"

Aunt Amelia made the sign of the cross as she entered. "We were across the street at the grocery store, and we saw the dead woman coming out of the alleyway."

"The first dead one," Maria said. "The pretty one from Sudbury."

"I'd know Carrie Ann anywhere," Rosa spoke confidently. "I used to alter her clothes."

"I saw her too." Uncle Paolo nodded toward the back door. "We should call Detective Fantin right away. Have him check out that back alley."

I held back a smile. Imagine calling Carlo and

asking him to investigate Carrie Ann's reappearance. That would be an even more memorable telephone message than the one I had left this morning. "That was Grace Robinson, her niece, Jenny Marie's daughter," I explained to Aunt Amelia. "She was at Sofia's party last night. Remember the pretty young woman who talked to you and Uncle Paolo?"

Aunt Amelia groaned. "There were so many strange people there last night, I couldn't keep track. I had such a headache, and I worried there wouldn't be enough gnocchi for everyone."

"I don't know why you worry so much about food," Uncle Paolo said. "Sofia is the best cook around."

"I could have sworn that was Carrie Ann," Rosa said. "It's remarkable how much the niece resembles her. Even more than she resembles her own mother."

"I'm so glad we cleared that up," Maria said. "We were so worried that you might have another murder on your hands."

"Don't even think it!" Aunt Amelia made another sign of the cross and mumbled a Hail Mary. Her eyes traveled around the room. "Remember how beautiful this office looked before…?"

Maria sighed. "Those delicious stuffed figs and amaretto cookies. It's too bad more people didn't get to see it."

"What a disaster!" Uncle Paolo said. "All that food and drink ordered. We had to give most of it away."

I did not want to continue this trip down Bad Memory Lane. "We'll have another one."

"It wouldn't be the same." Aunt Amelia frowned in disapproval. "And it's too soon after the murders."

"I agree with Amelia," Maria said. "It would be bad for business and could work against you."

"We could do a Christmas open house." If all went well with Grace's plan, the murders would be solved in less than a week's time. "Maybe plan a party with Santa or the Befana for needy children. We could order from the Sicilian bakery again and have a totally different decorating scheme. Let's have it on a Saturday or Sunday." I spoke directly to Maria. "Do you think Belinda could handle the extra work?"

"Of course she can," Maria said. "She loves to plan parties. And I would help."

"We'll all help." Aunt Amelia sighed. "But don't expect too much help from Sofia. She's got her hands full dealing with Roberto."

"I don't understand that daughter of yours," Maria said. "She got rid of one loser, and then she found herself an even bigger loser."

"Why does she do this to herself?" Rosa asked.

"The money is making her very attractive to Mr. Ongaro," Uncle Paolo said. "He usually goes for the young ones who can't cook, and who let his mother take over all the time."

"That woman never smiles." Aunt Amelia shivered. "She refused to attend last night's party." She noted the shocked expressions on our faces and continued, "*La signora* needed more time to recover from her dental appointment of two days ago."

"You don't know what she had done," I said. "Some of those procedures can leave you with bleeding and sensitive gums for a few days."

Aunt Amelia put up one finger. "She had one small filling, that's all. She just didn't want to give Sofia any satisfaction last night. She's a bitter old woman who wants Roberto all for herself."

"Is Sofia planning to marry this man?" Maria asked.

"Roberto held on to her pretty tight last night," Uncle Paolo said. "He talked to everyone about getting into politics and having Sofia help with his campaign."

"She's good at that kind of thing," Rosa said.

"It's too much for her." Aunt Amelia's eyes darkened. "I can tell she's tired all the time. Why does she need to worry about pleasing someone like him anyway?"

I didn't want to get into a discussion about the merits of Mr. Right Now. But I did agree that Sofia was burning herself out.

Before leaving, Maria and Rosa promised to help with the Christmas open house. As they went out the door, they started to talk about some of the desserts they would bake. My relatives waited until they were out of earshot.

"We're worried about Sofia," Aunt Amelia said. "You need to talk to her about Roberto."

"He's another Andrew," Uncle Paolo said. "I saw it last night."

"He praised her all night," I said. "Andrew never did that."

"He did at the beginning of their marriage," Aunt Amelia said. "Remember how he used to brag about her cooking and compare it to his mother's? You know how competitive Sofia can be. She has to be the best, and she knocked herself out to please him."

"I'm worried about the money." Paolo lowered his voice. "He has three ex-wives, and I heard he had to borrow money from his mother after paying off the last one."

"Last night, I heard him talking about boats and cottages with some of the other guests."

Aunt Amelia's eyes welled with tears. "He'll go through her money in no time."

"What does Sofia say about all of this?" I knew how she had reacted to my comments. I wondered if she spoke that abruptly with her parents.

"She refuses to listen to any criticism of him." Paolo shook his head in defeat.

I decided to enlighten them about Sofia's plans. "She's flattered by his attention. It's normal to feel that way after a divorce. It's just a fling."

"Why would she ruin her reputation for someone like that?" Tears pooled in the corners of Uncle Paolo's eyes.

Aunt Amelia managed a weak smile. "I know it doesn't sound very good, but I'm glad she doesn't plan to marry Roberto." She turned to her husband. "We'll just go along with anything they do, and try not to get too upset."

"You…not get upset," Uncle Paolo eyes widened. "Amelia, you've been having migraines since you found out about Roberto."

"I don't want that man as a son-in-law," Aunt Amelia said. "Last night, I thought about our wonderful grandsons and all the holidays. I couldn't bear to see Roberto and his mother at Sofia's house on all those festive occasions. But if it's just a fling, I can deal with it." She spoke directly to me. "How long do these flings last?" Aunt Amelia had assumed that I was an expert in this area.

"Not too long. They fizzle out in a few months, maybe a year." I thought back to my own forgettable flings, but I wasn't about to share that information with my relatives.

"If it's just a couple of holidays with Roberto and his mother, I can bear it." Aunt Amelia breathed a sigh of relief. "We'll make sure there's a crowd, like last night."

Uncle Paolo made a face. "I thought last night was too much for you."

"Do I have to repeat myself?" Aunt Amelia raised her voice. "It's only temporary. Once she gets him out of her system, we won't have to deal with him again. And if Sofia invites a lot of people, there are distractions. I won't have to talk to his mother all night. That is, if she ever decides to come."

"We need to get home and put the groceries away." Uncle Paolo nodded toward the back door. "Do you want me to check the alleyway before I leave?"

I remembered that Carlo had also used the back entrance. He might still be around surveying the area and planning for Wednesday. I couldn't afford to take any chances and further alert my relatives. "It's over. Past history. No more murders."

"The dead woman didn't come back," Aunt Amelia said. "There's no point looking for any more trouble."

Chapter 29

Wednesday, November 16, 2011

I meticulously planned each day and made sure I had no time to think about Wednesday. I surprised—maybe even shocked my mother—when I decided to spend Sunday cooking and baking with her. Adele and Laura must have wondered why I planned outings for three consecutive week nights.

On Wednesday, I faced a day jam-packed with appointments, and I even forgot to eat lunch. I sent Belinda home early and finished up some paperwork. At five-thirty, I drove to the Canadian Tire plaza.

By ten to six, I found myself safely and comfortably seated in the back of an unmarked police van with Carlo Fantin as my sole companion. The van was spotless, and well-equipped with a large rectangular cooler filled with a variety of cold drinks, fruit, buns, cheese, and cold cuts. We were parked about three hundred feet from the back entrance to my office. Carlo had set up his laptop on a few boxes. One of the other officers had set up a security camera at a high angle, just outside the office. In addition to hearing the conversation, we would also be able to see everything going on. Everything was in place as we awaited Grace's arrival.

Carlo smiled at me. "Technically, this could

qualify as our first date. We are alone in the back of a van, and we are eating. What do you think, Gilda?"

"It's not what I had in mind when you suggested dinner, but I must say this food looks delicious." I made myself a sandwich and started eating.

Carlo pointed to the laptop. "Grace has arrived." We watched as she unfolded a director's chair and sat down.

I squinted and tried to make sense of what Grace was wearing. While I couldn't distinguish color with the black-and-white footage, it looked like she had selected head-to-toe white, ivory or light tan clothing. She carried a large tote bag and had a printed scarf around her neck. I had seen a similar outfit before, but not on Grace. I gasped. "She's dressed like Carrie Ann on the day of her murder. Is that wise?"

"She wants to recreate the murder scene. She feels it will trigger some kind of action on the murderer's part."

"She could pass for Carrie Ann or even Melly Grace." I watched as Grace read a magazine. "She's so calm and collected. How does she do it?"

"Different people. Different temperaments," Carlo said. "I don't even think there's a genetic link of any kind. The three Godfrey sisters are living proof of that. Anna May always flew off the handle about something, Jenny Marie is the quiet one, and Carrie Ann…well, Carrie Ann has…had all the grace and poise."

"Melly Grace had it, too."

Carlo shook his head. "Melly Grace put up a good front, but she could be very loud and confrontational when things didn't go her way."

"Is that why you broke up?" I asked.

"It was more complicated than that." Carlo explained, "Mr. Godfrey didn't believe in long distance romances. He approved of me, but he wanted me to move to Tennessee and get my police training there."

"What did your parents say?"

"It didn't get that far. I made it very clear I wasn't ready to settle down, and I didn't want to leave Canada."

"Melly Grace could have come up here."

"Melly Grace didn't want to live in a cold climate, and she didn't want a long engagement. She loved the heat and wanted me to accommodate her."

"And so it ended."

"Yes," he sighed. "And I didn't see her again until Carrie Ann's memorial service."

"I wonder if she expected you to go back to her."

"Trust me, that woman did not pine away because I wouldn't relocate to Tennessee. She was fire and ice and got a bit nasty when things don't go her way. Not too many men would stand for her mood swings. At least, not the men that Melly Grace wanted in her life." Carlo added, "It wouldn't have worked out, anyway. We were so different, and our families would have never meshed together."

"I wonder—"

"A car has just pulled up next to Grace. I need to focus."

The large black car came to a stop. My heart started beating at an alarmingly fast rate. I was suddenly afraid and desperate for any means of escape.

"You can't leave now," Carlo said. "You'll see and hear a few things you would rather not see and hear. But we've reached the point of no return in this investigation. I need to focus on Grace." His firm and emphatic tone made it clear he did not have the time or patience to deal with any drama.

Roberto Ongaro got out of the car and went over to shake Grace's hand. "Grace, how wonderful to see you again. But under these circumstances, it is not so pleasant for either one of us. We could have met in a restaurant or café, but I decided to humor you. I have never been able to resist the demands of beautiful young women." He sighed. "That is my one and only weakness, and it has cost me dearly."

"Only one weakness, Roberto," Grace said. "Have you corrected all your other faults?"

"Pretty lady, you are wounding me severely." Roberto made a motion with an imaginary saber piercing his heart.

"Oh, please spare us all." I faced Carlo. "I want a copy of the DVD and audio for Sofia. She will need to see and hear this."

A shadow crossed his face, but he made no comment.

Roberto spoke again. "Now, what's all of this nonsense about a diary? Poor, poor demented Anna May. Even in death she manages to torment us all." A pause and static from the tape. "…Jenny Marie has a full plate of problems and I don't think she needs the added aggravation…madness. Give me the diary. I will dispose of it immediately." More static. "…it has disturbed you."

Carlo frowned as he fiddled with the laptop. "This should do it," he mumbled.

"Do you know what's in it?" Grace asked.

Roberto shook his head. "How could I possibly

know what went on in that demented woman's mind?"

"How do you know she was demented?"

"Gilda and Sofia were constantly harassed by Anna May. Neither one of them could go anywhere without being subjected to one of her angry tirades." He continued in a more serious tone. "Please give me the diary. It's the only way to have some kind of closure here."

"I don't have the diary with me."

"You lured us here, and there's no diary," Roberto shouted. "What kind of game are you playing?"

"Us?" Grace asked. "Is there someone else in the car with you?"

Roberto went over to the back seat of the car and spoke to someone. I couldn't make out what he said, and neither could Carlo. Grace also strained to hear. The door of the car opened, and Sofia stepped out.

I felt a sudden rush of nausea.

"Take deep breaths." Carlo patted my hand reassuringly, but his eyes stayed glued to the laptop.

Grace held out her hand to Sofia. "I'm glad you could join us, Sofia."

Sofia ignored the outstretched hand. "Where's the diary? I want to read that woman's lies."

"What makes you so certain she has lied?" Grace spoke clearly, enunciating every word. "You haven't seen it yet."

"This is ridiculous," Roberto said. "If you don't have the diary with you, there's no point continuing this conversation. Sofia and I will leave, and that will be the end of it."

"You mean you don't want to read any of the entries?" Grace rummaged in her tote and took out two folders. "I took the liberty of photocopying several entries. Take as long as you want to read them, and then we can discuss them."

Carlo handed me a folder. "Grace left me a copy of the folder. She wrote it up herself in her best forgery of Anna May's handwriting. She wanted you to read it at the same time as Roberto and Sofia."

My hands shook as I started to read the entries.

Wednesday, October 19th

She's gone. My dear Carrie Ann is gone, and it was all so unnecessary. Why did she have to go and get others involved? That slimy detective and Gilda Greco, of all people. Why did she have to investigate me? I'm her sister, not some criminal or other low life. And God only knows what she told Gilda. It's bad enough she's a rich bitch. She'll be a rich, condescending bitch if Carrie Ann told her about my problems.

I didn't mean to push Carrie Ann, but I couldn't stand it when she told me she wanted to dissolve the company and get out. I wanted to knock some sense into her. I didn't want her to die. She hit that Dumpster at the strangest angle, and if that wasn't bad enough, Roberto Ongaro and Sofia DiMatteo suddenly appear out of nowhere. And now I'm in bed with those two.

Roberto asked me how I wanted to play it. If I were dealing with him alone it wouldn't be so bad. But I also have to worry about Sofia. They agreed to help me arrange the body in the Dumpster. It seemed the best solution. It won't be emptied until Friday, and by then the body will have started to decompose. Sofia tells me they are expecting over two hundred people at tomorrow's open house. There will be too many suspects so the police will drop the investigation. I'm not drinking anymore. I will make this up to you, Mom. I'm so sorry.

Thursday, October 20th

What a disaster! And it's all Sofia's fault. She was supposed to make sure no one went near that Dumpster until after the open house. She let her own parents discover the body. How stupid can you get? Now, she's going to pay for her mistake.

Jenny Marie insisted on visiting Gilda at her condo. She needed some kind of closure and thought Gilda could give it to her. I wish we hadn't gone. I wish I hadn't laid eyes on Gilda Greco. When I saw her living high off the hog, I struggled to keep from screaming or hitting her. That was supposed to be my life, not Gilda Greco's. I scared Gilda, and I shook up Sofia. Good! Those women haven't seen or heard the end of this. Someone's got to pay for Carrie Ann's death, and it may as well be Gilda. If she hadn't started with all that career changing nonsense, Carrie Ann would be alive today.

If Sofia decides to talk, she'll implicate herself. I'm sure Roberto explained all that to her. He's involved, but I'm not worried about him. We go back a long way, and I don't think he wants any of that early dirt coming back to haunt him. We're picking up Melly Grace in a couple of hours. I can't believe she got a flight that quickly. I have to watch it with her. She's sharp and doesn't miss a thing.

Monday, October 24th

It's getting worse and I can't stop drinking. It all started at the restaurant. Carrie Ann must have tipped off Melly Grace about the accounts. How that woman loves lording it over me and everyone else. I got a reprieve when she looked Gilda's way, but I know Melly Grace. She's like a dog with a bone. She won't stop until she gets what she wants. I need to stop her before she does too much damage. I could lose everything if something isn't done. I'm calling Roberto.

Tuesday, October 25th

It had to be done. I can't believe how easy it was to get Melly Grace out to Olympia. She believed me when I told her the owner of the restaurant was blackmailing me. And Roberto came through for me. He may be sleazy, but he's on the ball. Which is more than I can say for Sofia. She just stood there and watched us kill Melly Grace. She kept saying that she didn't want to get involved. Well, lady, wake up and smell the coffee, you are involved, and you've been aiding and abetting us. I'll get you and that rich bitch of a cousin.

Friday, October 28th

That rich bitch must have slept with Carlo or paid him off. Can you believe it? He drove out to the island to get her an alibi. And now she's scot free. Free as a bird to enjoy all that beautiful money and never have a day's worry again.

Sofia has stopped coming to Curves, so I'm not getting the daily updates, and Roberto hasn't answered any of my calls. But I'm not through with them yet. Especially Sofia. I want a piece of that pie, that big pie that has fallen out of the sky and landed on Gilda Greco's table. It's my turn to be happy. I deserve it.

Saturday, October 29th

Mom, it would have broken your heart to see that heartless bitch of a Natalia turn on me. Your Russian daughter has forgotten where she came from, and how much we all did for her. She's going to pay for it. I will not be made the laughingstock of Sudbury. How dare she humiliate me like that and lump me in with that rich bitch and the lackey? They're all going to pay for it. I'm calling Roberto.

Sofia burst into loud, racking sobs. I tried to ignore her and focused instead on Roberto.

He also ignored Sofia and spoke to Grace. "You've upset Sofia with this pack of lies."

"They're not lies," Grace said. "These entries were written in Anna May's own hand. I have the original documents."

"They are the rants of an emotionally unstable woman, and I don't think they will hold too much weight with anyone. I wouldn't show this diary to anyone else, Grace dear. You need to give it to me and not trouble your pretty head about it." He added, "Go back to your own uncomplicated life in Toronto. What is it that you do?"

"I'm an interior designer."

"I'm willing to bet your boss is working you too hard. You're young and talented, and they like to take advantage of that."

"I'm a big girl."

"Wouldn't it be wonderful if you could call your own shots and not have to take orders from anyone?"

"And how would I go about doing that, Mr. Ongaro?"

"For starters, stop calling me Mr. Ongaro. All my friends call me Roberto, and I like to think of you as a special friend. We could continue this friendship beyond Sudbury. I'm in Toronto at least twice a month. We could have the occasional dinner and discuss your future in the interior design business. We could have you set up in your own shop in no time at all." He glanced at Sofia and repeated, "In no time at all."

Sofia sniffed. "I hope you're not including me in this royal we of yours."

Roberto's tone became sharper. "Sofia, stop being so difficult and start cooperating. We have a situation here."

"No, you have a situation here," Sofia said. "I'm not involved in any of it. Anna May even said it."

I gasped and watched as Roberto threw the pages toward the Dumpster. "Lies! These are packs of lies. Sofia, I suggest you go sit in the car. You're starting to upset me, and I wish to continue my pleasant conversation with Grace."

"We're finished!" Sofia shouted. "You want to pay off this bimbo. Do it with your own money, or if you're desperate, you can always go visit your mother. I'm sure she doesn't want to see you disbarred or tried for murder."

He spoke again to Grace. "It's the menopause. I think she's on the verge of losing it completely. She blames me for everything that goes wrong in her life." He moved closer to Grace and put his hands on her shoulders. "Now, let's get back to you, dear Grace. We need to make sure that you are properly settled in Toronto. I'll make some inquiries and get back to you."

Sofia started hitting Roberto with her purse. "You bastard! You're to blame for this mess. You and Anna May."

"Shut up! You're making things worse. I told you not to come. But you insisted and promised to keep quiet and say nothing. Why can't you do that?"

"No one tells me what to do anymore. I got Andrew out of my life, and I don't need you in it anymore." She turned to Grace. "Do whatever you want with the diary. I had nothing to do with any of the murders. I didn't touch any of the bodies."

"Will you shut up once and for all?" Roberto grabbed Sofia by the hair and slapped her so hard she fell to the ground.

Carlo dialed an extension, and I heard a terse, "Move in now."

And then I succumbed to the darkness.

Chapter 30

I woke up to find myself lying fully clothed on my bed. I heard the soft whispers. "She's awake. What should we do?"

"Nothing. Let her sleep until the morning."

"She might want to change into a nightgown."

"We'll deal with everything tomorrow morning."

"Should we ask her?"

I sat up and tried to focus. There were two women in the room, but I couldn't make out their faces. "Who's here?"

One of the voices whispered, "Maria and Rosa."

"You're keeping a vigil," I said. "Isn't that something you do for people who are dying?"

"You are not dying, Gilda Greco." Rosa spoke slowly and clearly. "You are alive and well, and tomorrow you will get up and start again."

"That's right," Maria said. "You've been through a lot, and you need to get your rest."

I sat up and squinted at both of them. "But what about the both of you?"

"We can sleep tomorrow," Maria said. "One night of lost sleep will not kill either one of us. Go back to sleep, and don't worry about anything. Remember, I'm your godmother, and I'm honoring those promises I made at your christening."

"You really take your responsibilities to heart." As

I lay down, my eyes started to close, and I found myself slipping into a dark womb of comfort.

I awoke hours later to the aroma of freshly brewed coffee. “Rosa. Maria. Are you still here?”

Both women entered my bedroom. Maria beamed. “You’re starting to look like yourself again.”

“I’ll call Grace and Carlo,” Rosa said. “They want to meet with you sometime today. Are you up to it?”

“What happened?” My mind went blank as I tried to recall the events of the previous evening.

“We don’t have all the details,” Maria said. “Carlo told us they found the murderers of those four women, and you witnessed some of it. It was too much for you, and you fainted. Grace dropped you off here, and then he phoned us to come and sit with you. I guess he couldn’t get hold of Sofia. Do you remember anything else?”

It hadn’t been a dream. Roberto was one of the murderers, and Sofia was an accomplice. The news wasn’t out yet, and I wasn’t about to tell these two well-meaning but chatty women anything. I yawned. “I don’t remember much. I’ll call Carlo and see if he wants me to go downtown.”

“I’ll call him,” Maria said. “You take a shower and get dressed. Have a cup of coffee before you go, and then you can meet him for lunch.”

“That’s right,” Rosa said. “Make a date of it. You never know what will happen.”

More matchmaking! These women were unbelievable. “He’s involved in a murder investigation. I don’t think he’ll have time for lunch today.”

Maria became more adamant in her tone. “You think too much. That’s your problem. Now go and get ready."

I showered and picked out jeans with a new cranberry sweater topped by a fitted black leather blazer. I took extra care with my hair and makeup and was pleased with the final result. I grabbed my purse and headed toward the kitchen. Maria and Rosa nodded in approval and had a steaming cup of coffee ready. Rosa handed me a page torn from the kitchen notepad. "Meet them at Verdicchio's. We told Carlo you'd be there by one o'clock. You have time to drink your coffee and go."

"You have me on a very tight schedule." I smiled as I sipped my coffee. Finally, I would be getting closure on the murders. I finished drinking my coffee, hugged the two women, and drove to the restaurant.

When I arrived at the restaurant, my eyes traveled around the room and discovered Grace seated at a table apart from the other patrons. No sign of Carlo.

Grace got up and hugged me. "I'm so glad to see you. Carlo won't be here until later."

I held her close as my eyes welled with tears. "You can get me caught up before he comes." I wanted to hear every last detail, and I knew Grace could speak freely without Carlo around.

"Carlo said you fainted when Roberto slapped Sofia. So, I'll start there." She shuddered. "It was like a monster had been unleashed. He called me a number of choice names and started to describe what he planned to do. He was going to kill me first and then Sofia. As he lunged toward me, policemen emerged from every corner of the alleyway. They were all armed and pointed guns at him. Two officers grabbed and cuffed him."

I put my hand on hers. "Thank goodness he didn't harm you in any way."

She continued her story. "Sofia had a bruise near her right eye, her hair was a mess, and her clothes were covered with dirt. She started to whimper and pointed at Roberto. She said everything in the diary was true, and she was willing to give her statement. Carlo advised her to get an attorney first."

I shook my head in amazement as I recalled the diary. "While I read those entries, I actually felt Anna May's presence."

Grace shrugged. "I've known Anna May all my life. It wasn't that hard to imagine what she could have done."

"You even forged Anna May's handwriting. Why did you bother?"

"I knew that Roberto had once been involved with her. I didn't know if he had ever paid any attention to her handwriting, and I couldn't afford to take any chances. I remember Melly Grace telling me about one of her cases. A client had concocted an elaborate plan to embezzle money from her firm and then got caught on a minor technicality—the wrong checkout time. Winning is in the details. She firmly believed that."

Back to Melly Grace again. But this time I felt nothing but a twinge of regret that I never got to know a truly unforgettable woman. I no longer envied her.

Grace leaned toward me. "Are you okay? If this is too much for you, I can stop."

I shot her a grateful smile. "I'm fine. What happened next?"

"Sofia started spilling all of the beans. Carlo tried to stop her, but she wouldn't let him. I remember him shouting something about getting the paramedics. They came about ten minutes later, but Sofia had done enough damage by then." Grace shook her head. "I don't know your cousin very well, but for a while there she reminded me of Anna May. It was so sad, so pathetic to see someone that put together fall apart."

I closed my eyes and thanked God I had been spared Sofia's meltdown.

Grace spoke softly. "Anna May never meant to kill Carrie Ann. Both women were having a down-and-out fight when Sofia and Roberto saw them. And then Carrie Ann fell and hit her head at the corner of the Dumpster."

If Anna May had come clean about her fight with Carrie Ann, Melly Grace and Natalia would be alive today. And Anna May would have received the help she so desperately needed. Why did Anna May have to resort to all that subterfuge and drama? So many questions whirled through my mind. I didn't know where to start. I decided to focus on Sofia. "What were Roberto and Sofia doing there?"

"Sofia said something about dropping by to tell you to go home." Grace frowned. "I don't know what she meant by that."

"She did that every day. She wanted to make sure I got home at a reasonable hour."

Grace shook her head. "That's one good deed that cost her a lot of grief."

"What happened next?"

"Anna May refused to listen when Roberto kept repeating that Carrie Ann's death was an accident. He even offered to represent her if needed, but Anna May wouldn't listen. She became hysterical and started screaming that she didn't want any police involvement. Roberto gave in to her rants and suggested they place the body in the Dumpster, and let nature take its course. There would be over two hundred people at the open house, too many to investigate, and the police would not pursue it too closely. Anna May jumped at the idea and asked Sofia to look out for the body and make sure no one got too close until after the open house."

"It was a stroke of bad luck that my aunt and uncle found her," I said. "Sofia left her parents unattended for a few minutes."

"They hadn't banked on such an early discovery by your uncle," Grace said. "Anna May verbally attacked Sofia. Roberto also reprimanded Sofia. They made it clear they would not hesitate to implicate her if she did not cooperate with them."

"Why did they have to kill Melly Grace?"

"Melly Grace planned to conduct her own investigation, and Anna May feared she would learn about her skimming of the accounts and her under-the-table deals with some of the suppliers. Roberto protested, but Anna May warned that if she fell, she would bring Sofia and him down. Somehow, they lured Melly Grace to the restaurant."

"What on earth motivated Anna May and Roberto to kill Natalia, a complete outsider to all of this mess?"

"Anna May was furious when Natalia kicked her out of the spa. By that time, she had lost all touch with reality. When she phoned Roberto to tell him she wanted Natalia killed, he hung up on her. He thought it over and decided that he had to get rid of Anna May. He couldn't handle any more of her theatrics, and he feared she would unravel and implicate him. He phoned

Anna May back and agreed to help her kill Natalia. Roberto forced Sofia to go along with him and promised it would end that evening and that he would help with your alibi. She went along with it. But as Anna May said, she never touched any of those bodies. That's why Anna May's body lay on the ground. She wouldn't help Roberto arrange it in the Dumpster."

"She was so happy that Sunday," I said. "I remember her carrying on with Roberto. Why did she stay with him?"

"She had participated in four murders, and he had a definite hold on her. She also knew what he was capable of."

"Why didn't she come to me?" My eyes welled with tears. "I would have helped her."

Grace put her hand on mine. "She was too embarrassed and ashamed to come to you. How could she tell you she feared Roberto and Anna May and for her life?"

I struggled to process all the information. "She kept saying she had no intention of marrying Roberto. She even had a Plan B in motion." Sofia had been at her prettiest and happiest the night of the dinner party.

"I'm willing to bet she was good at compartmentalizing," Grace said. "A part of her probably thought it wasn't really happening and that somehow Roberto would disappear from her life."

All those years of telling white lies finally caught up with her. Thinking back, I recalled a number of instances where she purposely withheld information or glossed over the details. Each time, she said it was easier and less stressful for everyone concerned if the truth didn't come out. After marrying Andrew, she became even more obsessed with presenting a brave front to our parents and the rest of the world. I gasped. "We'll have to tell her parents. I don't think I can—"

"Don't worry about that." I heard Carlo's voice behind us. I looked up and met his unblinking blue eyes. He sat across from me. "Father Ianni went to see Amelia and Paolo last night and took care of everything. Sofia's sons will be arriving later this afternoon." He spoke with greater emphasis. "Don't worry for one minute about any of them."

"I don't want to see Sofia for a while." I could feel myself detaching from her. We had never been close until the last eighteen months, and I suspect my one million dollar gift to Sofia had a lot to do with her friendship. It must have been hard for her to watch as I spent and gave away money so effortlessly. The envy had always been there, but I had just chosen not to acknowledge it.

Carlo nodded in approval. "She'll be released on bail, and then the courts will decide."

"I imagine Roberto will be disbarred and tried for murder." Grace asked, "Has he said anything?"

"An old classmate from Osgoode is flying in from Vancouver, and we will be meeting later this afternoon," Carlo said. "Father Ianni also met with Mrs. Ongaro. One of her neighbors is staying with her until a niece arrives from Italy." He sighed deeply. "I hope Sofia hires a good lawyer. She'll need one."

"What about the Taylors?" I asked.

Carlo frowned. "What do they have to do with any of this?"

I watched the changing expressions on Grace's face. She avoided my glance and looked down at her hands. She needed therapy, and she needed to tell her mother the truth. She could no longer keep this secret to herself. We would have that conversation very soon.

I chose my words carefully. “I had a feeling that Michael might be involved in the murders.”

Carlo laughed. “Are you starting to have those gut feelings?” His eyes narrowed. “I’ve never liked that sleaze ball, and nothing would give me greater pleasure than nailing him, but I have no proof of any involvement.” He was probably thinking about the harassment charges that had been dropped years ago.

I spoke directly to Grace. “Was there anything in the diary that could implicate him or Jean?” Jean had visited my office that night. If she had encountered Anna May in the parking lot, Anna May would have blabbed everything to her. Jean had that effect on people.

Grace shook her head. “Anna May mentioned Jean’s name once and added a thank you next to her name. She could have been thanking her for almost anything.”

In my heart of hearts, I believed those two knew about the murders and were using that knowledge to blackmail Sofia and Roberto. Why else would Sofia set up Jean’s booth, decorate Michael’s office, and spend so much time with them? Outside of family, Sofia didn’t go out of her way to help other people. But Carlo couldn’t connect the Taylors with the murders, unless Sofia or Roberto decided to implicate them.

“Earth to Gilda!” Grace waved to get my attention.

“Sorry! It’s taking me a while to process all of this.” I turned to Carlo. “When did you start suspecting Sofia and Roberto?”

Carlo winced. "I wish I could say I suspected them right away, but I didn't. I started to suspect Roberto at Anna May's memorial service. He and Sofia arrived separately and pretended not to know each other. Roberto approached all the Godfrey relatives and praised Anna May lavishly. It just didn't feel right."

"He had his nerve," Grace said. "Mom and I couldn't believe he would even show his face."

"I'm missing something here," I said.

"Roberto broke up Anna May's marriage," Grace explained. "They had an affair which ended as soon as the ink on Anna May's divorce was dry. He then married one of his young nubile secretaries, and Anna May had a meltdown. She spent a year with some relatives in Kitchener and received heavy-duty counseling. When she returned to Sudbury, she picked up the pieces of her life and never mentioned Roberto's name again."

I swallowed hard. "When did you start suspecting Sofia?"

"After the memorial service, a few things started clicking," he replied. "I remembered all those times Sofia had rattled off on Sunday. They were too precise, and everything flowed too perfectly. I had both of them followed after the memorial service. She spent a lot of money on him that week—several new suits and all that exercise equipment. The night of the dinner party, Roberto showed me brochures of boats and cottages. The next day, Grace shared her gut feelings…and you know the rest."

I took a deep breath and asked the question that had been haunting me since I saw Sofia getting out of Roberto's car. "When did they decide to frame me?"

Carlo squeezed my hand. “Sofia stressed the fact that she went along with the framing but would provide you with an alibi if you needed one.”

“She didn’t provide me with an alibi for Melly Grace’s death,” I said.

“You didn’t give her a chance,” Carlo said. “You spent the whole day gallivanting around the countryside, and you spoke to me first that night.”

I recalled Sofia’s comment about damage control. She had a lie ready for the occasion. After spending a lifetime telling white lies to our parents and covering up unpleasant situations, she could easily pass a lie detector test.

Carlo leaned over and put his hands on top of mine. “And another thing. There aren’t any leaks in my office. Sofia made up all that nonsense about the policemen’s wives over at Curves. She fed you—”

The tears flowed freely. While I had condoned many of Sofia’s lies, I never thought I would be on the receiving end of all that deception.

“She would have come through for you,” Grace said.

“Sofia was emphatic on that point,” Carlo said. “She would never have let you take the blame for any of those murders.”

Grace added, “She said your name over and over again and begged for forgiveness.”

At any point during the past month, I could have forgiven Sofia. But now, I’m not so sure. Four women had died, and she could have prevented three of those deaths. I whispered, “I don’t know if I’m ready to do that.”

“Right now you have one decision to make and

that's what you plan to have for lunch." Grace waved a waitress over to our table.

"I haven't eaten since breakfast," Carlo said. "I'm ready for some food."

Grace glanced at her watch. "I have to run. I want to get back to Toronto before it gets too dark."

"Stay and have something to eat before you go," I said.

"Thanks, but I had a late brunch." Grace gave us pitying looks. "The two of you need to have a real date. I can't believe you had your first date in the back of that van." She put on her denim jacket and left saying in a loud, clear voice, "Melly Grace would have had a real date long before this."

Desserts from the kitchen of Franca Albo Guidoccio:

Pineapple Cheesecake

Ingredients:

2 ½ cups graham cracker crumbs
8 ounces cream cheese
385 ml sweet condensed milk
19 ounces crushed pineapple
3 ounces pineapple or lemon Jell-O
8 ounces hot water
1/3 pound butter

Procedure:

Refrigerate condensed milk overnight.
Mix graham cracker crumbs with butter.
Press the mixture into the bottom of a 9" x 13" rectangular pan.
Bake for ten minutes at 325° F.
Cool the crust.
Boil water and dissolve Jell-O. Set aside.
Combine cream cheese, crushed pineapple and Jell-O at medium speed.
Use clean mixer spoons to beat condensed milk at medium speed.
Combine all ingredients in a large bowl.
Pour the mixture into the rectangular pan.
Sprinkle non-butter graham cracker crumbs on top.
Refrigerate for 24 hours.

Servings: 12-15

Blueberry Cheesecake

Ingredients:

½ cup brown sugar
2 ½ cups graham cracker crumbs
¾ cup butter
8 ounces cream cheese (at room temperature)
32 ounces sweetened whipped cream
1 cup sugar
1 tablespoon vanilla
3 tablespoons lemon juice
3 ½ cups frozen blueberries

Procedure:

Combine brown sugar, graham cracker crumbs, and butter.
Press into the bottom of a 9" x 13" rectangular pan.
Bake for ten minutes at 325° F.
Cool the crust.
Cream together the cream cheese, sugar, vanilla and lemon juice.
Add whipped cream and fold in blueberries using a wooden spoon.
Pour mixture into the pan.
Refrigerate for 24 hours.

Servings: 15

Blueberry Muffins

Ingredients:

½ cup vegetable oil
2 cups sugar
4 eggs
4 cups flour
2 cups milk
4 teaspoons baking powder
2 cups blueberries
Grated peel and juice of one orange

Procedure:

Preheat oven to 350° F.
Grease muffin tins with butter or margarine.
Mix oil, sugar, eggs, orange peel and juice with the electric mixer.
Gradually add milk, flour and baking powder.
Add blueberries.
Stir using a wooden spoon, not the mixer
Drop mixture into tins.
Bake for 25 to 30 minutes.

Yield: 24 muffins

Banana Muffins

Ingredients:

3 large ripe bananas
¾ cup white sugar
1 egg
1 teaspoon baking soda
1 teaspoon baking powder
½ teaspoon salt
1 ½ cup all-purpose flour
1/3 cup melted butter

Procedure:

Preheat oven to 375° F.
Grease muffin tins with butter or margarine.
Mash bananas.
Add sugar and slightly beaten egg.
Add melted butter.
Continue mixing and gradually add dry ingredients.
Drop mixture into tins.
Bake for 20 minutes.

Yield: 12 muffins

Sponge Cake

Ingredients:

6 eggs
1 ¾ cups sugar
1/3 cup warm milk
2 cups flour
2 teaspoons baking powder
1 teaspoon vanilla

Procedure:

Place oven wires near the bottom of the oven.
Preheat oven to 350° F.
Grease a tube pan.
Beat eggs.
Add sugar and continue beating.
Heat the milk and add to the mixture.
Gradually add flour and beat at high speed.
Continue beating and add baking powder and vanilla.
Pour mixture into the tube pan.
In the oven, place a pot of water beside the pan (for steam).
Bake for 50 minutes.

Servings: 15

Zucchini Cake

Ingredients:

3 cups grated zucchini
¾ cup oil
½ cup chopped walnuts
½ cup chopped raisins
1 grated orange
5 eggs
2 cups sugar
3 ½ cups flour
3 teaspoons vanilla
2 teaspoons baking powder
1 teaspoon baking soda
Sprinkle of cinnamon

Procedure:

Preheat oven to 375°F.
Grease a 9" x 13" rectangular pan and a loaf pan.
Sift flour and all dry ingredients.
In a separate bowl, combine all other ingredients using an electric mixer.
Add sifted ingredients and continue to mix well.
Pour mixture into pans.
Bake for 45 minutes.

Servings: 25-30

Ice Cream Roll

Ingredients:

5 eggs
6 ounces sugar
Neapolitan ice cream (rectangular box)
6 ounces flour
2 teaspoons baking powder
Sprinkling of icing sugar

Procedure:

Preheat oven to 325°F.
Cover the 13" x 9" baking pan with waxed paper and grease with shortening.
Beat eggs and sugar using electric mixer.
Continue mixing and gradually add flour and baking powder.
Pour the mixture into the pan and spread evenly.
Bake for 15 minutes.
Sprinkle icing sugar on a clean tea towel.
Quickly slice the ice cream from the rectangular box.
Remove the cake from the pan and turn it over.
Insert ice cream slices into the cake as you turn it.
Wrap with aluminum foil.
Place in the freezer and chill for at least 24 hours.

Servings: 12-15

Tiramisù

Ingredients:

1 package lady fingers
250 ml heavy whipping cream
250 grams cream cheese
2 cups of cold, sweetened espresso coffee
½ cup amaretto
1 semi-sweet chocolate piece, grated

Procedure:

Beat cream cheese using the electric mixer.
In a separate bowl, whip the heavy cream.
Combine the coffee and amaretto in another bowl.
Combine the cream cheese and whipped cream mixtures.
Cut the lady fingers in half, lengthwise.
Place one layer at the bottom of a 9" x 13" rectangular pan.
Sprinkle enough of the coffee/amaretto mixture to cover the lady fingers.
Spread the cheese/whipped cream mixture.
Continue layering.
The top layer must be the cheese mixture.
Cover with grated chocolate.
Refrigerate for 24 hours.

Servings: 15

A word from the author…

In high school, I dabbled in poetry but decided to wait until I had more life experiences before writing a novel. The original plan was to get a general arts degree and take a few years off to travel and write. Instead, I gave in to my practical Italian side and obtained degrees in mathematics and education.

While I experienced many satisfying moments during my teaching career, I never found the time and energy to write. In 2008, I took advantage of early retirement. Slowly, a writing practice emerged and my articles and book reviews started appearing in newspapers, magazines, and online.

www.ingramcontent.com/pod-product-compliance
Lightning Source LLC
Chambersburg PA
CBHW060526260626
47161CB00003B/777

* 9 7 8 1 5 0 9 2 0 1 7 3 0 *